# SHIRLEY DAMSGAARD

## Witch Way to Murder

**AN OPHELIA AND ABBY MYSTERY**

**AVON BOOKS**

*An Imprint of HarperCollinsPublishers*

This is a work of fiction. Names, characters, places, and incidents are products of the author's imagination or are used fictitiously and are not to be construed as real. Any resemblance to actual events, locales, organizations, or persons, living or dead, is entirely coincidental.

AVON BOOKS
*An Imprint of* HarperCollins*Publishers*
10 East 53rd Street
New York, New York 10022-5299

Copyright © 2005 by Shirley Damsgaard
ISBN-13: 978-0-06-079348-7
ISBN-10: 0-06-079348-1
www.avonmystery.com

First Avon Books paperback printing: September 2005

Avon Trademark Reg. U.S. Pat. Off. and in Other Countries, Marca Registrada, Hecho en U.S.A.
HarperCollins® is a registered trademark of HarperCollins Publishers Inc.

Printed in the U.S.A.

10  9  8  7  6  5

*The voice on the other end of the phone
still carried the soft rhythm
of the Appalachian Mountains
where she'd been raised.*

*Abby, my kind, loving, seventy-three-
year-old grandmother who I adored.
And who happened to be a witch.*

She got right to the point. "I wanted to call you before the phones went down and tell you to be careful."

I didn't ask her how she knew the phones would be dead soon. I knew the answer.

"I will be. I'm not going out again tonight," I said.

"That isn't what I meant, as you well know. This is the night of the mourning moon—a time for ending and a time for beginning. There is an evil circle that must be closed, ended, before there are any new beginnings. And it will be up to you to close it."

"Whoa, wait a second, not me. I'm not ending, beginning, or closing anything. I just want to be left alone."

"This isn't optional," she said in a no-nonsense tone. "You need to know things are *not* what they appear to be. That young man you met today represents danger. I want you to let me put salt and pepper around the house for protection."

"No. No spells. You know how I feel about that, Abby."

"At least promise me you'll wear your amulet. Oh, one more thing, be sure to sleep on the anise pillow tonight."

Then the phone went dead.

*In honor of John McConkey, 1945–2001*
*A good man, a wonderful husband,*
*and a great father. Thank you*
*for having shared your life with me.*

*Ellen Johnson*
*My cousin by blood, but my sister by spirit.*
*Without your encouragement, this book*
*never would have been written.*

# *Acknowledgments*

Writing is a journey, and I've met so many people along the way who've helped my steps down this road and who deserve my thanks:

Andy Entwistle—another writer and the first to help with the art of writing a short story.

John Tigges—my teacher and literary guru, who taught me the importance of a well-placed exclamation point, and much, much more.

The Saturday Afternoon Writing Class—Patsy, Martha, David, Dennis, and Bob. Always poised, with red pen in hand, to find the mistakes I'd missed.

Nadine Avey, former librarian and my comma catcher, for all the tips on operating a library, and for the free proofreading.

Paul Steinbach of the Iowa State Medical Examiner's Office, for the crash course he gave me in decomposition.

Carol Rayburn and the Stuart Police Department, for answering endless questions about meth labs, and the most pertinent one—"Really, how does it feel to be shot?"

Photographer Kevin McCubbin, for the time he spent to make his subject look good.

Stacey Glick of Dystel and Goderich Literary Management, for making a dream come true.

Sarah Durand and Jeremy Cesarec, my excellent editor and her equally excellent assistant, for putting up with all my questions, and for their faith in Ophelia and Abby.

My friends, who have listened to me rattle on about plot lines but like me anyway.

The Damsgaard connection—Arnie, Betty, Dot, and, especially, Maggie. You showed me the importance of persistence, which some might call old-fashioned Danish stubbornness.

And most important, my children—Eric and Cathleen, Shane and Christine, Scott, and Sara. Thank you for thinking maybe Mom's not crazy after all!

# Witch Way to Murder
## to

# Prologue

Rising panic clenched my stomach. Clammy sweat made me itch underneath my arms. The high heels of my boots beat a staccato rhythm on the empty sidewalk as I rushed to the door. Why hadn't I just gone with him?

Once inside, I scanned the hazy bar. Dim light reflected on the men standing either alone or in groups against the bar. "Dudes row," Brian had always called it. The perfect place for the men to scope out women as they entered the room, and whenever a new woman walked in their heads would turn, synchronized. At the tables around the edge of the dance floor, I saw couples, their shoulders touching and their heads tilted toward each other to hear over the loud music. Others milled around the room, looking for a place to sit down.

I searched each face, looking for his, but all I saw were the faces of the Friday night regulars. I pushed my way past them to the bar.

"Pat," I said as I gripped the edge of the bar. "Has Brian been here yet?"

From behind the counter, Pat leaned closer and

cupped his hand around his ear to hear me over the loud music and conversation. "What, Ophelia?"

"*Brian*—have you seen Brian? We were supposed to meet here, but I'm late."

"No, I haven't, but I could've missed him. We've been pretty busy. Ask Misty; she's been waiting tables all night. Maybe she's seen him."

On the other side of the dance floor, a tall girl wearing a University of Iowa sweatshirt waited tables. Misty. I bullied my way through the crowd to reach her.

"Misty," I said, grabbing her arm.

"Hey, watch it. I almost spilled this drink," she said, frowning.

"Sorry. I'm looking for Brian. Has he been here?"

"Nope, haven't seen him." Her eyes studied my face. "What's wrong? You look scared. Has something happened?"

How could I explain? I felt the tears gather in my eyes as grief seized my heart and squeezed. I'd failed—it was too late. I had to get out of there before I broke down.

I stumbled past the customers and into the street. Once in my car, I sat staring out the windshield. A fine mist gathered on the glass and collected in large drops that trickled slowly down in rivulets. The streetlight was like a spotlight on the dark puddles, turning them an oily black. Shadows crept out of the reach of the light.

Tears slid down my face, but I didn't feel them. Visions of Brian as I had last seen him at my apartment danced before my eyes—happy, smiling, excited. Had only a few hours passed? It's not fair life can shift so quickly. If I shut my eyes, would I see him dead? Would I see the blood, feel his pain, his terror? *My fault, all my fault,* bounced about in my brain. I should've been able to stop his murder. But I couldn't.

And on that dreary November night four years ago, the first stone in the wall around my heart clicked into place.

# One

I felt someone watching me as I put the returned books away. My hackles stood up and my skin tingled. I sighed and shook my head. My instincts told me it was Mr. Carroll, one of our oldest patrons, all in a twist and waiting to pounce on me about our latest book selections. He treated the library as his personal domain and me as his personal slave. He was not one of my favorites.

Sighing again and plastering a smile on my face, I turned, only it wasn't Mr. Carroll's bleary bloodshot eyes staring at me. My smile faded as I stared into the warmest pair of brown eyes I'd ever seen. I felt a shock of awareness deep in my gut, even though I'd never seen this man before.

He sure wasn't from Summerset. It was almost as if he'd taken a class, "Small Town 101: What the Natives Wear," in order to try and fit in. His blue jeans were properly faded, his leather bomber jacket had a lived-in look, and his work boots were fashionably scuffed. But he'd failed the class. His clothes may have said "small town," but everything else in his demeanor shouted "city." He had a sheen, a polish about him, that someone from Small Town, USA, lacks.

I realized I was gaping and quickly looked away. When I glanced back, he was smiling. Evidently, befuddling women, even a thirty-something librarian, was nothing new to him.

"Hi, my name is Richard Davis," he said, extending his hand. His voice was rich and husky, with a faint accent like someone from Minnesota or Wisconsin, maybe.

One of the quirks I'd developed over the past four years was an aversion to touching people, especially strangers, so rather than accept his hand, I bent to pick up an imaginary paper clip on the floor. When I stood, his hand was no longer extended.

"The girl at the desk said I needed to talk to Ophelia Jensen. Are you Ophelia?" he asked. When I nodded, his eyes widened in surprise.

"What's wrong?"

He laughed. "I'm sorry. You don't look like a librarian."

"Really? And what exactly is a librarian supposed to look like?"

"You know, older, hair in a bun, reading glasses on a chain, pencil stuck behind the ear." He smiled, eyeing my clothes. "I've never met a librarian wearing blue jeans and a T-shirt that says 'Tact is for people not witty enough to use sarcasm.' Or one with a name like Ophelia."

I looked down at my clothes. He was right. Not my normal librarian look. Mentally, I pulled my tattered dignity around me and stood straighter. "I work alone in my office on Fridays." That wasn't any of his business. Why was I explaining? "But it seems the Dewey decimal system is beyond my assistant's scope of understanding, so someone has to put these books away."

His smile never slipped. "That explains the clothes, but what about your name?"

"Do you always ask this many questions, Mr. Davis?"

He shrugged. "What can I say? I'm a curious kind of a guy. So, how did you get the name?"

"Persistent, too, aren't you?" I said, arching an eyebrow. "Okay, the truth is my mother is a retired English professor, and she always had a thing for Shakespeare. *Hamlet* happened to be her favorite. I have always felt very lucky I wasn't a boy."

"A retired professor? From what university?"

"University of Iowa."

"In Iowa City, right? Is that where you grew up?" he asked.

"Yes." I shifted and crossed my arms.

"How did you wind up in a small town like Summerset?" he asked.

Boy, did this guy ask a lot of questions.

"They needed a librarian and I needed a job." My eyes slid over to the clock hanging on the wall above the bookshelves, and then back to Mr. Davis. "Now, what can I do to help you?"

He noticed my clock-watching and smiled. "I'm sorry, I'm keeping you from your work, aren't I? I need a library card and your assistant told me to talk to you."

"I'm sorry, but you're not from around here. We don't give cards to people who don't live in Summerset or the surrounding area."

"I had hoped you would make an exception in my case. I'm a chemical salesman, I'll be here for a couple of weeks, and I'll be bored stiff without some books to read. I promise I'll bring them back." He changed the smile to a lopsided grin. Charm rolled off him in waves.

I may have spent most of my life in a small town, but I'm not stupid. I can spot a load of crap when I see one. He was lying. Where was the hat, the jacket, the pens, all with his company's name plastered on them? Without calling him a liar, I couldn't get out of this situation. I mumbled something about how arrangements could be made.

"Oh," he said, still in the charm mode. "I like to look at old newspapers. You know, read what's happening in the community. It helps me get a feel for my customers. You wouldn't have archives, would you?"

"We have our local paper, the *Summerset Courier*, on file. The archives are in the basement. We also have access to the *Des Moines Register* on our computer."

"Wow, you have a computer."

"Yes, we do." I felt offended. I get so tired of "city" people treating us like a bunch of hicks from Mayberry. "We're very progressive. We also have running water and indoor plumbing."

Out came the lopsided grin again. "I sounded condescending, didn't I? I'm sorry."

I found myself smiling back. Whatever this Mr. Davis had, he should bottle it and forget about the traveling salesman routine.

"That's okay. I tend to be too sensitive about the library. We've worked very hard to make improvements." I pointed back to the counter. "If you go to the main desk, my assistant will give you a library card and show you the archives."

"Great. It was nice meeting you, Ophelia Jensen." He paused, his gaze intent. "Thanks for your help."

This time he didn't extend his hand. He shoved his hands into the pockets of his pants. While he walked away, I wondered what it was he'd almost said. But then again, I stay out of other people's business and I really didn't *want* to know. I've enough problems without getting involved in some stranger's. Dismissing him from my mind, I returned to the absorbing job of straightening the bookshelves.

"Wow, is that guy cute or what?" Darci said when she returned from showing our bogus salesman the archives. "Did you notice how brown his eyes are?"

"Yeah, I noticed," I said, thumbing through the card file.

"He wanted to know all about Summerset." Darci propped her arms on the counter and gazed off into space with a goofy look on her face.

"What did you tell him?"

"The usual—Summerset was founded after the Civil War. The main industry then was the limestone quarries located outside of town. That a lot of the buildings are built from stone quarried there."

"Wow," I said absently. "I bet he found that information fascinating."

Darci tossed her head. "Well, he did. He was very interested. I also told him about the Korn Karnival held every fall."

"Oh, Darci, you didn't tell him about that hokey thing, did you?"

"Sure I did. And it's not hokey. It's one of the best festivals around. I love the parade, the flea market, the dunking booth. And, umm, the funnel cakes." She closed her eyes for a moment and sighed. "How can you not enjoy those, Ophelia?" she asked, opening her eyes and staring at me.

"They're fattening? The grease goes right to my hips? And I have to walk an extra two miles to get rid of it?" I answered, and slid the card file under the counter.

But Darci didn't want to talk about calories. She flattened her hands on the counter, and her small frame seemed to vibrate with excitement. "And, you want to hear the best part? *He* said it sounded like so much fun, maybe next year he'll come to the Korn Karnival."

I'm accustomed to Darci's enthusiasm. I inherited her when I took my job almost four years ago. When I'd walked into the library that first day, I thought she looked more like a cocktail waitress than an assistant librarian. In her late twenties, with big hair, big mascara-rimmed eyes, and a build like a *Playboy* model. She was typing on the computer keyboard, her long red nails clicking across the keys. A sound as annoying as chalk on a blackboard. I took one look at her and almost ran.

But over the years, I'd learned to appreciate her style. She's outgoing, bubbly, and our patrons love her. Her approach to life is very laid-back, and she doesn't even get excited about overdue books. I'm the opposite. I'm reserved. Never once in my life have I been called "bubbly." And overdue books make me crazy. My grandmother, Abby, says it's a control thing.

So we've created a balance. Darci handles the irate customers, and I handle the details in managing the library. And it works.

She continued to prattle on about Davis, but I only listened to half of her words. I knew why it had taken her so long to show Mr. Davis the archives. Darci is a born flirt. Flirting is as natural to her as breathing, and I'm sure she made the most of the opportunity. But I didn't want the details. The retelling of the thrilling exchange about the Korn Karnival was enough. The phone lines would be burning tonight, I thought. Two hundred years ago Darci would've had a successful career as the town crier.

But Darci got my full attention when she said, "So, I told him if he really wanted to know about Summerset, he should talk to your grandmother."

Oh no, bad idea. I did *not* want him anywhere near my grandmother. Our mysterious Mr. Davis asked too many questions, and that would not bode well for my grandmother.

Darci caught my glare.

"I don't know why you're so paranoid talking about Abby. That herbal remedy she told me to take for my cold worked great. You may think with all this herbal stuff she's a little off center, but I think she's radical."

Darci had no idea how off center and radical my grandmother was. Thank God. If Darci knew, everyone else would know, too. We couldn't have that; Abby had been careful over the years to protect her secrets.

"Listen, he can find out the same gossip tonight if he has a beer at Stumpy's Bar and Billiards. Or better yet, tell him to hang out at Joe's in the morning, during coffee time. Those old guys know way more than Abby." My voice sounded desperate. "Anyway, she isn't feeling too well right now. I don't want a stranger bothering her."

"She's sick? What's wrong?" Darci asked.

Wonderful, now I had to tell another lie. I'm not very good at that, never have been. Not even as a child.

"You know, just under the weather." I stumbled over my words.

"Well, I hope she feels better soon." Darci picked up another card file and began to thumb through the cards.

For once I was glad she wasn't known for being quick on the uptake. Unfortunately, it would be different if Mr. Davis asked to meet my grandmother. He wouldn't accept my phony excuses as readily. I was positive he wasn't a salesman. He had some other reason, some other agenda, but what? Until I knew the answer to that question, I needed to keep him away from Abby.

I was anxious to get home. Although it was only November, a surprise snowstorm had hit. The wind racing across the flatlands sent the flakes swirling in the air. Gusts rattled the windows of the library, and currents of cold air circled us. The ancient furnace pumped and pumped, trying to fight the chill. By late afternoon Summerset looked like a ghost town. The limestone buildings that Darci had so proudly told Mr. Davis about loomed like specters in the gathering dusk. The only traffic was the snowplow passing by with its orange lights spinning. I sent Darci home and began closing up the library when I remembered our visitor in the basement. He had spent the entire afternoon cloistered in the archives.

"Mr. Davis, we're closing now," I called from the top of the stairs. I jumped when he appeared without warning at the bottom, a briefcase in hand. Where had the briefcase come from?

"I'm sorry, I didn't realize how late it was. I got carried away reading," he said, climbing the stairs toward me. He stopped two steps down, putting us at eye level. Once again I felt that tingle.

"For a small town, you sure have had a lot of excitement around here this fall, haven't you? All the unsolved thefts of the fertilizer, the anhydrous ammonia?" He closely observed my reaction to his statement.

Not wanting to meet his gaze, I glanced to my left and said nothing.

"It sounds like there've been several," Mr. Davis continued. "The article said the thief or thieves were siphoning off the anhydrous tanks at night while the tanks were sitting in the empty fields." He pursed his lips, then said, "A dangerous chemical to be stealing, isn't it? Anhydrous freezes on contact, doesn't it?"

Hmm, a chemical salesman was asking *me* about anhydrous ammonia? Odd. The tingle became stronger.

"I suppose it does." I turned, breaking eye contact, and headed to the counter where I kept my backpack. I heard his footsteps as he followed me.

"I bet it had the gossip mill running overtime."

"Yes, it did," I said over my shoulder, and walked behind the counter.

"What was the most popular rumor?"

I turned sharply and looked at him with suspicion, my eyes narrowing. "I suppose the one about the drug ring."

"The anhydrous is used to manufacture methamphetamines, isn't it?"

The tingle was jangling, but I tamped it down and met his stare straight on.

"You work for a chemical company, don't you know?" After the words came out, I questioned the wisdom of discussing illegal drugs with a man I didn't know, and in a building that was all but deserted.

"Of course. I have a degree in chemistry. I just wondered what you thought." He gave me his disarming smile.

My nerves hummed. There were things below the surface that I couldn't see, didn't want to see. "We really need to leave. You never know how bad the roads will be during these sudden snowstorms. Getting snowed in at the library is not my idea of a good time."

From behind the counter, I shoved my things into my backpack. He stood on the other side, watching the snow pepper the windows.

"You're right, it does look bad out there. Will you make it home safely, or would you like me to follow you?"

My bag thudded to the floor. When I bent to pick it up, I felt my right eyelid begin a rapid twitch. I heard the blood pound in my ears. He was standing too close. I had to get out of there and away from him.

"N-N-No, I live nearby. I'll be okay, Mr. Davis." I slung my bag over my shoulder and headed for the door. Good sense fought with my desire to run. I looked back once to make sure he followed.

"If you're sure—and by the way, call me Rick."

"What?" I said, stealing a glance over my shoulder.

He smiled and shook his head. "Rick. My name is Rick. You seem nervous. Are you sure you don't want me to follow you?"

"No, no, I'll be fine. Storms make me jumpy, that's all." I locked the door behind me.

The snow came down in tiny icy pellets while we made our way down the library steps. He followed me too closely, and the twitch increased its rhythm. I pressed cold fingers to my eye to stop it.

"At least let me walk you to your car and make sure it starts. Like you said, you wouldn't want to be stranded here."

We were almost to my car when it happened. In my haste, I didn't see the patch of ice. When I started to slip, he reached out and grabbed my arm. I cringed while the jolt ran up my arm. My senses felt like they were frying.

I jerked my arm back and rushed to my car.

Numb fingers struggled with the door. I wrenched it open and slid in, shaking, behind the wheel. The keys rattled as I shoved the correct one in the ignition.

A tap on the window drew my attention. Rick stood there, shoulders hunched, his dark hair frosted with snow. His eyes were narrowed and his mouth set in a grim line. Totally embarrassed, I rolled the window down.

"What in the hell is wrong? Let me take you home; you're in no condition to drive," he said, looking puzzled.

My brain scrambled for another lie to explain my agitation.

"I'm all right now. I told you, storms make me nervous. I'm really not myself today. I must be coming down with something. I think, um—" I knew I was rambling. "I'd better go."

Then I drove off, leaving him standing in the street.

My little Victorian cottage sat on a street lined with maple trees. In the fall, the landscape was beautiful, with the leaves vibrant shades of red, yellow, and orange. Now it was ugly. The wind whipped through the skeletal trees, and I could hear them creaking. Icy blasts buffeted me as I plowed through the snow to my front door.

Relief eased my quaking muscles when I leaned against the inside of the door. Safe at last. I felt the calm seep into my body.

A cold, wet nose nudged my clenched hand. One brown eye, one blue, stared up at me from a face like a wolf's. Her body, like a German shepherd's, pressed close to my thigh, and her white pointed ears were cocked forward, as if she were asking a question.

"Sorry, Lady, did I worry you?" I laughed as I scratched one of my dog's ears.

Her question answered, she bounded down the hall, wheeled, and ran back toward me.

"Stop," I said, holding out my hands. "Don't jump."

Too late. Her paws couldn't gain purchase on the slick wood floor and eighty pounds of dog slid into me, knocking me down.

She laid her head in my lap and gazed at me with a forlorn look.

"Oh, it's okay. I'm not going to send you back to the pound." I cupped her long, sharp face in my hands. "You know, you're a good roommate, Lady. You don't ask questions. You don't talk nonstop. Not like some people I know. And except for the occasional mess and a few hair balls, you're pretty easy to take care of," I said, smiling.

At the tone of my voice, Lady flattened her ears and cocked her head to one side, and I knew she understood every word I said.

From a distance my cat, Queenie, disdainfully watched us—too cool to show her concern. Her green eyes stared at Lady and me, not blinking, while the tip of her black tail twitched back and forth, beckoning me to pick her up.

I stood and walked over to where she sat. Bending down, I gathered her in my arms. "So you want your share of attention, too, huh?" I said, nuzzling her fur with my chin.

Her eyes drifted shut and a purr rumbled deep in her throat. The sound eased the last of my frayed nerves.

Putting Queenie down, I went to the kitchen, where I poured a glass of wine. Drinking on an empty stomach wasn't smart, but the thought of food made my stomach churn.

After feeding the dog and cat, I built a fire in the living room. Curled up on the couch, drinking my second glass of wine, I thought about Rick Davis, feeling a thousand times the fool for the way I had acted. Normally, I'm very level-headed and practical, not prone to hysterics at all. My only consolation was that no one else had seen me. The whole thing would have made a great story for the *Courier*: LOCAL LIBRARIAN RUNS AMUCK DURING SURPRISE SNOWSTORM. Details page two.

Lost in my thoughts, feeling cozy, and finally relaxed, I picked up the phone before it rang. I usually avoid doing that. It tends to throw people off.

"Ophelia." The voice on the other end of the phone still carried the soft rhythm of Appalachian mountains, where she'd been raised.

She'd be sitting at her kitchen table now, with the soft light from the kerosene lamps warming the room and making the crystals by the window glow from within. The scent of dried herbs would be mixed with the smell of wood smoke from her cook stove. The modern conveniences sat unused. She did things the old way, the way she'd been taught in the mountains.

Abby, my kind, loving, seventy-three-year-old grandmother, whom I adored. And who happened to be a witch.

She got right to the point. "I wanted to call you before the phones went down and tell you to be careful."

I didn't ask her how she knew the phones would be dead soon. I knew the answer.

"I will be. I'm not going out again tonight," I said.

"That isn't what I meant, as you well know. This is the night of the mourning moon—a time for ending and a time for beginning. There is an evil circle that must be closed, ended, before there are any new beginnings. And it will be up to you to close it."

"Whoa—wait a second, not me. I'm not ending, beginning, or closing anything. I just want to be left alone," I said, jerking straight up on the couch.

"This isn't optional," she replied in a no-nonsense tone. "You need to know things *are not* what they appear to be. That young man you met today represents danger. The moon will be waning soon, and I want you to let me put salt and pepper around the house. It will offer some protection."

"No. No spells. You know how I feel about that, Abby." My head suddenly felt as if a tiny hammer tapped at my right temple—from the inside. With each tap, a dull ache circled my head.

"At least promise me you'll wear your amulet. The evil is growing and you must be cautious. Oh, one more thing—be sure to sleep on the anise pillow tonight." The phone went dead.

The little hammer pounded now. Looking at the silent receiver in my hand, I pictured Rick, the man with a thousand questions, meeting Abby. No, I thought, slamming the receiver down. I couldn't let that meeting happen. I had to protect Abby.

# *Two*

The next morning the hazy sunlight flowed through the open curtains in my bedroom. I don't know if it was the sun or the wet tongue stroking the side of my face that stirred my fuzzy brain to consciousness. I nestled deeper under my quilt. I am not a morning person, and woe to he, she, or it who disturbs me. But Lady didn't care. She had needs requiring immediate attention. It was either get up or clean up, so I got up.

After throwing on my old, threadbare robe, I stumbled to the door with Lady in hot pursuit. I felt well-rested. No dreams last night. Four years ago, when the nightmares first began, Abby had given me a small pillow with anise seeds tucked inside. According to folk magick, sleeping on such a pillow prevents nightmares. At that juncture of my life, I'd have done anything to stop them. They were so hideous. The pillow worked and the dreams stopped. My nights were peaceful, but my days were not. They were filled with feelings of guilt and recrimination, and there wasn't a magick pillow to fix that, even though several psychologists had tried. The consensus was that I had posttraumatic stress syndrome.

I wanted to talk about my best friend Brian's murder at the hands of a killer who was never caught, but they wanted to talk about my childhood. So after six weeks of therapy I gave up on the doctors. But I felt too fractured, too fragile, to return to my job at the University of Iowa's library; instead I came back to Summerset, where I'd spent my childhood summers with Abby and Grandpa. I would deal with my problems in my own way, in my own time.

These thoughts brought me back to what Abby had said on the phone about the evil growing. Do I believe in evil? Most certainly. Evil and I had met up close and personal. Did I want Abby to do a spell for protection? Absolutely not. I'd turned my back on Abby's beliefs years ago, but I still feared magick, feared the doorways it might open. And I'd learned the hard way that some doors were better left shut. I would cooperate with her up to a point, but more for her peace of mind than anything else. What was going to happen would happen.

As if conjured up by my mind, Abby's truck pulled into my driveway. She stepped out of the vehicle dressed in her work clothes of jeans, a cotton shirt, denim jacket, and clogs. In her arms she carried a large bag—and I knew what was in it. Lady, with her head down and tail wagging, approached her. Among other talents, Abby had a real way with animals. She had never actually said they talk to her, but she always seemed to know what they wanted. After greeting Lady, Abby walked to the door at a steady pace. Queenie, wanting her share of attention, waited for Abby by the door.

"Good morning," Abby said when she handed me the bag and picked up the cat. "Did you sleep well?"

"You have the sight, so you tell me."

"No need to get testy. Where you're concerned, I don't always see things clearly. My guess is you did because you used the pillow," she said, stroking Queenie.

"What are you planning on doing with these? As if I didn't know," I said, lifting a big black candle, a rock, and some herbs out of the bag.

"The black candle is to banish evil. The rock is hematite for protection, and the herb is angelica. If sprinkled around your house, it will ward off evil." Abby cradled the cat against her body while she spoke, and her hand continued to smooth the cat's fur. Again and again her hand moved down the cat's back.

Queenie lay in Abby's arms, her eyes half closed, her head hanging limply over Abby's elbow.

"Abby. Stop that. You're mesmerizing the cat."

Abby looked down at Queenie with a shy smile. "Oh, sorry. I wasn't paying attention."

She placed Queenie on the floor, and with a twitch of her tail, the cat stalked off. Abby sat down at the table and primly folded her hands.

I watched her while leaning against the counter. Her snow-white hair was wrapped in a thick braid around the top of her head, and little wisps of hair had escaped to frame her still lovely face. She really was a picture perfect Grandma; if it just weren't for that witch thing.

"Please, no spells," I pleaded.

"I know, but it won't hurt for you to have these. At least, burn the candle. I meant what I said last night on the phone, Ophelia. Something is seriously wrong," she said, deep lines creasing her forehead. "The order of nature is disturbed, and you are in the center of it, along with that young man from the library."

I sat down across from her.

"How did you know about him? I suppose you 'saw' him?"

"No, of course not. You know it doesn't work that way. I heard about it from Mrs. Carroll, who heard it from Mrs. Simpson, who heard it from Darci." Her lines on her forehead disappeared and her eyes sparkled.

It figured. Darci had been a busy girl last night before the phone lines went down.

"So, you know something is going to happen, but not what or when. Right?"

Abby nodded.

"How do you know he's involved? Lucky guess?" Exasperated, I glared at her. "What's the point of having the 'sight' if you don't know?"

She shrugged, and my frustration simmered.

"It might help if I could meet this young man. I might be able to tell from his aura what his role in this will be."

"Oh, no. No way." The blood drained from my face and I felt faint. "This guy is smart, and he'd be on to you in a second. This isn't Appalachia, this is Iowa. People around here don't understand folk magick. They go to doctors and hospitals, not the healer over in the next holler."

She laughed abruptly. "I've lived in this town fifty-three years and realize it isn't the same here as in the mountains where I grew up. Around here they see magick as evil. For all they know, witches stir cauldrons, ride brooms, and wear pointed hats."

"That's right," I responded. "And what do you suppose would happen if your neighbors found out you were one of those witches? Hmmm?"

"Well, burning at the stake's illegal now," Abby said, laughing again.

"That's not funny," I said sternly. "You'd either be

shunned by the entire town, or every nutcase in the state would be at your front door wanting you to cast some kind of spell or a curse for them. And you could kiss the greenhouse good-bye, too. No one would do business with you." Slinging my arm across the back of my chair, I gauged Abby's reaction. She loved her greenhouse and wouldn't do anything to jeopardize it.

"Don't be silly." Abby's chin went up and she gave me a withering stare. "No one is going to learn my secrets. I've kept them for a long time, ever since your grandfather brought me here. Meeting that young man isn't a danger to me."

Reaching across the table, I took her hands in mine. "I love you, Abby. It was your strength that pulled me through the last four years, and I don't want to see you hurt."

"This isn't just about me, is it?" she asked, squeezing my hands. "It's about Brian, what happened four years ago . . ." She paused. ". . . and your grandfather."

I looked down at our joined hands and felt the tears coming. And the familiar pain in my heart began to ache, an old wound that wouldn't heal.

"Magick couldn't have saved your grandfather, dear. Even if we'd known he had heart problems," she said in a quiet voice. "Some things are meant to be."

Releasing one of her hands, I wiped away the tears sneaking down my face and took a deep breath. "But why are they meant to be?"

"I don't know." Abby shook her head sadly. "It's just the way life is. My biggest regret is that his death caused you to lose faith in the good magick can do and to turn your back on your training." She sighed. "When she was young, your mother wanted to learn the old ways. But she never had your talent. She had to choose another path, one that led to your father and a good life as a teacher and as a mother."

"I've heard this before," I said, clearing my throat.

"I know, I know," she said, stroking the back of my hand. "And you know your mother's happy with her life, living with your father in Florida. Her path was the right one for her. But you—even as a small child I could see your gift. And I'm worried that if you don't accept the gift and follow your path, you'll never find true happiness."

"I'm sorry, Abby. I really am. But I can't follow that path. I don't believe in magick or in the old ways anymore. The magick failed Brian, and it failed Grandpa. I see it as nothing more than parlor tricks."

A look of pain crossed Abby's face. I hated hurting her, but I couldn't lie about my feelings. We sat in silence for a moment and I felt the distance caused by our differing beliefs.

"You weren't responsible for Brian's death, Ophelia," she said almost in a whisper, breaking the silence.

"Yes, I was. If the magick would've worked, or if I'd gone with Brian when he wanted me to, he would've been with me, at the bar. Not out on the street where the killer found him."

"You don't know that."

"Yes, I do. When my friend needed me most, I wasn't there. I failed, and I've lived with the guilt of that failure for four years." Another tear seeped out of the corner of my eye. I swiped it away.

"Maybe it's time you dealt with the guilt. And the grief. The grief you feel over losing not only Brian, but your grandfather, too." The love and concern in her voice seemed to span the distance between us, closing it.

"I have dealt with it," I answered.

"How? By living your life alone? Not forming an attachment to anyone?" She shook her head sadly. "That's not a good way to live."

"It's the only way I know *how* to live," I said, pulling my hand away. "What if I did allow someone other than you in my life, and I let them down, like I did Brian? I couldn't handle it, I'd be right back where I was after Brian died."

"You wouldn't. You're stronger now."

"No—I'm not. It's a big bluff. Most of the time, I'm scared," I said, staring off into space. "When I think about how I felt after Brian died, I had no control over my life, my emotions. It was such a dark place to be." I shuddered and returned my gaze to Abby's face. "I can't do it. I can't go back to that darkness."

"So you hide behind your wall and don't let anyone in?" she asked calmly.

I sniffed and wiped the rest of the tears off my face. "Pretty much. It's too painful to be involved in someone's life. I can't even bear anyone— other than you— to touch me."

Abby squeezed my hand. "You underestimate yourself, my dear. In the time ahead, I think you're going to learn exactly how strong you really are."

"We're back to the 'evil circle' stuff again, aren't we?" I asked, feeling a tightness build around my heart.

She nodded in agreement. "I may not know *exactly* what's going to happen, but I do know one thing for certain—your life is about to change, whether you want it to or not."

I thought about what she said for a minute. "Is Rick Davis involved in the change I'll experience?"

"I think so."

"Okay, all I have to do is stay away from him and my life won't change. Right?"

Abby chuckled, and the tightness in my chest eased. "Wrong. It's not as simple as that. You're not going to be able to dodge, or hide, from what's coming. But I'll be here to help you."

The tightness eased a little more.

She took my hand and squeezed it. "And quit worrying about Rick Davis. He won't learn anything I don't want him to."

"I'm telling you, the guy's a walking question mark. I don't trust anyone who asks that many questions."

An idea popped into my head. To get her mind off Rick Davis, I'd let her do her magick. She'd be so busy thinking up spells, she'd forget about talking to him. And what harm could one little spell do? I didn't believe in them, but she did.

"Tell you what, if it'll make you feel better, go ahead and do your thing with the candle and stuff. Just don't do it while I'm here. Okay?" I said, and smiled a weak smile.

"I'm not so old, young lady, that I don't know what you're doing." Abby leaned forward, her eyes narrowed. "You're trying to distract me. I'll do the spell because I'm worried about you, but I haven't given up the idea of meeting this Rick. You aren't the only stubborn one in this family."

I had just lost the battle.

# Three

After Abby left, I was glad it was Saturday and my day off. I felt out of sorts. In spite of how I'd acted around her, I believed her. Something was wrong. I might not use the same words as she did to describe my uneasiness, but it didn't make the feeling any less threatening.

Pacing back and forth in the kitchen, I hugged my arms to my chest and thought.

I didn't want to be involved in whatever was wrong. I didn't want my life to change. Stopping, I looked out the window and stared at the trees that ringed my empty backyard. Okay, so maybe my life was a little lonely sometimes, but I had my books, my pets. And I was safe. Safe from the demons that had haunted me four years ago. How hard would I fight to keep my life the same? Pretty damn hard.

But Abby said I didn't have a choice. I would be involved and my life would change. I resumed my pacing.

Poor Abby. I knew how much she regretted my decision not to learn the old ways. The knowledge wasn't passed down to every woman in the family. Only the chosen. And the chosen had to possess a gift, a gift to see beyond the world around us. That talent ran strong in our family living in the mountains of Appalachia; in a line, mother to daughter, grandmother to granddaughter, stretching back for over a hundred years.

It was a line of granny women, herb doctors, healers, white witches—women in my family had been called by many different names—but whatever the name, the training was the same. Each young woman, when her time came, would be taught about herbs, charms, potions, crystals, and the energy that vibrates all around us. She would learn how to use them as tools to heal and help, but never for her own profit, and never without the permission of the one she sought to heal or help.

The gift did occasionally skip a generation. It had skipped my mother and landed on me. No brothers, no sisters. An only child of an only child. I was the last of the line, the last of the chosen.

And I had walked away.

Chewing on my lip, I thought about my options. Could I use the gift to protect Abby from Rick? No, I'd made my choice. No turning back. So how could I keep Abby away from him? If he stayed in Summerset, he'd be sure to meet her. Could she keep her secrets and our family's past from someone as nosy as Rick without my help?

I stopped suddenly. What if, somehow, he found out about what happened to me after Brian's death? About the doctors? My name was never mentioned in the news articles written about Brian. And no one in Summerset, other than Abby, knew. But this was the age of the Internet. All kinds of information floated in cyberspace. What if he came across something about Brian and it led him to me? Then everyone in town would know. I wouldn't be able to stand the stares, the whispers, if the town learned my secret.

All the thoughts spun in my head like a hamster on a treadmill, around and around in an endless circle leading nowhere. The muscles in the back of my neck felt like rubber bands stretched taut. My stomach churned with anxiety and I felt the walls close in. I had to get out of the house. A walk in the woods with Lady would help me think, help me plan. I looked out the window; the sun was shining and the snow melting. The woods would be quiet and peaceful.

I'd changed from my bathrobe to a thick sweater and jeans. After combing my fingers through my hair and pulling it back, I was fastening a scrunchy around the loose ponytail when a strange car appeared in the drive. For a person who valued her privacy, I certainly was getting a lot of visitors. I watched from the window while the driver got out. Damn it all to hell—it was Rick Davis.

He knocked on the door. Today he was dressed again in jeans, with a red turtleneck sweater under the same leather jacket. From where I was standing, he couldn't see me unless he glanced at the window. If I refused to answer the door, maybe he would assume no one was home and go away. He took one step back and Lady started barking. Rick turned toward the sound, and I jerked back from the window. Too late, he spotted me. I had no choice but to open the door.

"Hi. I hope you don't mind me dropping in like this. I would've called, but your number wasn't in the book. I found this lying in the street," he said, handing me my billfold. "I thought you might be looking for it."

"Oh gosh," I answered, taking the wallet from him. "Thanks. It must've fallen out of my backpack."

I flipped the billfold opened and searched for my driver's license and credit card. Whew, they were still there. Frowning, I tapped the billfold in my hand. What do I do now? The man had just helped me out.

"Something wrong?" Rick asked, interrupting my thoughts. "Is something missing?"

"Ahh, no, no. It's all here," I said with a pained look, watching Rick linger on my porch.

Abby always said there was no excuse for bad manners. But if I could have thought of a reason to leave him standing there, I would've used it. But now I owed him, and I couldn't shut the door in his face. So I had to invite him in.

When I did, Lady, the shameless hussy, was all over him like a rash.

He squatted down and ran his hands over Lady's head. "Great dog," he said, admiring Lady's face. "What's her name?"

No, he wasn't going to worm his way past my defenses by winning over my dog.

I frowned. "Lady. But you'd better be careful. She may act friendly, but she can get mean."

Lady, of course, made it obvious I lied by looking at him with total adoration, while Rick scratched her favorite spot under her chin. If a dog could have smiled, she would've.

Queenie meandered in from the general location of the living room. She rubbed against his leg, and when he reached down to pet her, she rolled on her back, paws waving. Rick raised his head, his eyes gleaming.

"I suppose your cat is mean, too?"

Even from where I stood, her purr sounded like a refrigerator humming. Thanks to my unfaithful pets, Rick was laughing at me. I did not dignify his remark by answering.

"Please, come into the living room," I said, showing

him the way, while Lady and Queenie padded silently beside us.

He stopped at the door and surveyed the room. It was my favorite room in the house. Littered around it were books from the many bookcases lining the wall. My latest needlepoint lay on top of the old afghan on the couch, my treasures clustered about on the tables. The room looked cluttered and lived in. It was all very personal. I knew immediately it had been a mistake to bring him in here.

Rick wandered over to my books. "You have an eclectic taste in reading, don't you?"

"I'm a librarian. It's my job to know what's being published."

"True. Have you read all of these?"

Remember, Jensen. The man did you a favor. Be nice.

Trying to look composed, I smiled. "Other than dropping off my billfold, I'm sure you didn't drive over here to discuss my reading habits." I sat down on the couch and picked up my needlepoint. "Is there something else I can do for you?"

"No. I know we just met, but I was concerned about you yesterday. You were so upset when you left. I wanted to make sure you were okay." He watched me intently, the way he had the previous day.

What lie could I tell him now? I'd heard the best lies always contain a grain of truth. "I don't like talking about this, but I guess I do owe you an explanation for my behavior," I said, stalling for time. What explanation could I give him? I plucked at my needlepoint while I searched for a reason. Nothing. Suddenly, I had a flash of inspiration. "Umm, I suffer from panic attacks."

"Really?" he asked, tilting his head to one side.

"Yes, and I'm a little afraid of storms, so this one was worse," I said, nodding rapidly while I stared at the needlepoint in my hand.

Did that sound believable? Best stop before I made a mess of it. I plucked the needlepoint harder. Rick sat down facing me, and I felt like a bug under a microscope.

"Are you feeling better today?"

"Yes, much."

"Great," he said, shifting his eyes away from me and scanning the living room again. "This is a nice house. Have you lived here long?"

"Umm . . . about four years."

"Yesterday, you didn't mention you have family in Summerset. Your grandmother lives here, right? Is that why you took this particular job?"

Uh-uh, I wouldn't let the conversation go down that road. Abby was not a topic I cared to discuss with him. The less he learned about her, the better.

"Not really," I said, lying again. "It was a coincidence."

The look on his face said he didn't believe me, but when he didn't call me on it, I continued.

"Are you from a small town?" I asked, trying to look interested. Maybe my question would lead him away from asking me about Abby.

"No, I grew up in Minneapolis. Now about your grandmother—"

"Why are you so interested in my grandmother?" I interrupted.

"When I was playing pool at Stumpy's Bar and Billiards last night, your grandmother's name came up," he said, shrugging a shoulder.

"They were talking about my *grandmother* in a bar?" My eyebrows shot up.

Rick chuckled. "No, it wasn't like that. Stumpy mentioned her during our conversation. She sounds like a nice lady."

"She is. She's the best," I said, daring him to argue.

"He said she runs a greenhouse, and I thought some of our products might appeal to her. Several greenhouses do use our fertilizer."

Duh, he's a chemical salesman. Of course he'd assume Abby might buy something from him. But he assumed wrong. Abby didn't believe in chemicals. She used other methods to get her plants to grow. Hey, wait a second, narrowing my eyes and watching him, I didn't believe he *was* a chemical salesman.

"So what do you do for fun?"

"Me? Fun?" The sudden shift in conversation caught me off guard and my eyes widened in surprise.

Rick laughed. "Yeah. Fun. You do have fun, don't you?"

"Well, yes, I have fun," I stammered.

"Doing what?" he asked, tilting his head to one side.

"I don't know. I've never thought much about it. Watching old movies." I pursed my lips while I thought about the question. "Reading, naturally."

"Yeah," he said, nodding. "I enjoy reading, too." He gave a quick smile. "But you know that, since I begged you to give me a library card. What do you have about the French and Indian War? It's one of my favorite subjects."

"We have a few," I said while I ran through the titles in my head.

"Terrific. Maybe Monday I'll stop by and you can show me what the library has."

Showing him books on the French and Indian War sounded like a job for Darci. I'd pawn him off on her.

But instead of telling him my thoughts, I gave him a tight smile. "Sure, no problem."

Having exhausted the things we had in common, the room settled into silence. But sounds from the outside world drifted in. In the distance, I heard the train as it rumbled through town. A car drove by my house with the base on its radio loud enough to make the decorative plates on the wall vibrate. Down the street my neighbor's dog barked a series of staccato yips.

With my hand, I smoothed the needlepoint I'd been plucking and stole looks at Rick. When he caught me looking at him, he'd give me a friendly smile, but say nothing. Evidently, he didn't feel the need to end the silence.

My looks became bolder, till I was downright staring at him, trying to figure him out. But my stares didn't seem to bother him. He was too busy looking around the room, picking a piece of lint off his pant leg or petting Lady, who had taken a position by him, to notice me.

He sat in the chair, the ankle of his right leg resting carelessly on top of his other knee. Just a guy hanging out, at ease with himself and his surroundings. His eyes were bright, and I noticed they had little gold flecks in the irises. My eyes wandered down to his mouth. Lips—not too thin, not too fat. He should've looked arrogant, but instead he managed to appear both boyish and sexy at the same time. I should've felt comfortable; there wasn't anything about his attitude that was threatening. But while I watched him, I couldn't shake the feeling that I was missing something about him. But what?

"You're an unusual person, Ophelia Jensen."

At the sound of his voice, my eyes snapped back to his. "Huh?"

"I said you're unusual. Most people can't tolerate silence, and they'll do anything, say anything, to fill it."

"And you wanted to see if I started chattering to fill the void?" I asked, not knowing whether to feel angry or flattered.

Rick gave me a wide smile. "I doubt if you've ever chattered in your life. That doesn't fit my image of you."

The words tumbled out before I could stop them.

"What is your image of me?" I asked.

"You don't fit the mold and you're something of a puzzle." He stopped briefly, thinking. "But I'm a salesman. Part of my job is studying people, so I'll figure it out sooner or later."

I squirmed a little at the idea of Rick Davis studying me.

"Well," he said, slapping his leg and standing. "I'd better go. I'm sure you have a lot to do. But I'm glad you're feeling better."

"Thanks. And thank you again for finding my wallet," I said, standing and walking him to the door.

When I opened it, he started to leave, but turned at the last moment. He looked down at me and grinned. We were only inches apart, and it made my senses vibrate like strings on a harp. Rick made a move to touch my hand holding the door. When I drew back, his grin faded.

"Did I mention I like puzzles?" he said casually.

Not waiting for my answer, he strolled out the door and down the steps. At the bottom, he turned and waved at me.

I smacked myself on the forehead. Like I don't have enough problems? Great. Now I'm a puzzle. I'd never get rid of him.

# Four

Monday morning when I arrived at the library, who should be waiting patiently on the top step but Rick? He removed his sunglasses and grinned at me as I hurried up the steps. I slowed my pace and sighed. So much for pawning him off on Darci. She wouldn't be arriving for another hour.

"Hi," he said when I reached the top step.

"Good morning," I replied, shifting the books I carried and rummaging in my bag for the keys to the door. "You're up early."

Not paying attention to his response, I dug deeper in my bag. Dang, where were those keys? I hadn't left them at home, had I?

Rick noticed my struggle and held out his hands. "Here, let me hold those for you."

"No. I got it," I said as my fingers curled around the keys in the bottom of my bag. Pulling the keys out, I dangled them in front of my face.

After unlocking the door, I turned the knob and pushed the door open with my hip. Not waiting for Rick, I shifted the weight again, hitting the light switches on my way to the counter. Once there, I stowed my bag and grabbed the card files, setting them on top of the chipped Formica.

"You look nice today," he said, observing me from the other side of the counter.

I looked down at my clothes—linen jacket, tailored blouse, and navy Dockers. My hair was pulled back in a neat twist and I actually had on makeup. "More like a librarian?" I asked, raising an eyebrow.

He gave me a sheepish grin. "Yeah."

"Thanks." Passing from behind the counter, I walked over to the alphabetical card file. "Is there a particular book about the French and Indian War you're looking for?"

"Yes, there is," he said relaxing against the ledge. "*America's First, First World War—the French and Indian War, 1754–1763,* by Timothy Todish. I haven't been able to find it anywhere."

"Hmm," I said, and pulled out the first drawer. "That title doesn't sound familiar." I quickly leafed through the A's, and not finding it, pulled out the drawer marked S–T and did the same thing. "Nope. Sorry, we don't have it. Any others?"

Rick straightened. "I don't know," he said with a twitch of his shoulder. "What do you have?"

Tugging on my jacket, I made my way past Rick to the shelves containing books on military engagements. "Right here," I said, pointing to the middle two shelves. Pulling out one of the books, I handed it to him. "This one is about the Fort William Henry massacre."

"I had breakfast at Joe's Café this morning," he said absentmindedly while he read the table of contents. He gave a slight shake of his head and returned the book to the shelf.

I guess reading a book about a massacre and talking about breakfast didn't go together.

"Well, it's a good place to hang out if you want to learn about Summerset. A lot of the older farmers eat there." I pulled out another book and gave it to him.

"Yeah. The talk was all about the anhydrous thefts," he said while he studied the title.

I moved down the row to a different section. "For now, maybe."

He placed the book in the empty spot on the shelf. "What do you mean?" he asked, his brows knitting together.

"Oh, until something else unexpected comes along," I said nonchalantly.

"Like what?" he quizzed.

"Someone dying suddenly, news leaking out of a couple's affair, whatever." I shrugged while I ran my finger along the spines of the books. "It's the way small towns are—everyone knows, or thinks they know, their neighbors' business."

"But no one knows, not even the sheriff, who's stealing the anhydrous."

"According to Darci, they think it's someone from Des Moines." I tilted my head and read the word "French" on one of the spines.

"Do you agree? You don't think it could be a local?"

"I guess, maybe," I said, grabbing the book and opening the cover. "I don't know. I don't waste a lot of my time thinking about these things."

"You're not interested in the rumors?"

"Not really," I said, snapping the cover shut. "Here, what about this one? It's been checked out a lot." I held it out so he could see the title.

Rick glanced at the cover. "I've read that one," he said.

Okay.

I shoved the book back before reaching for the one beside it. "This one?" I said aloud.

"Read it."

Silently, I held out the next book.

He shook his head no. "What *are* you interested in?" he asked, following me as I made my way down the row.

"Finding books for hard to please customers?" I replied, offering him the last book in the row.

"Okay, I get your point," he said, his eyes twinkling as he took the book from my outstretched hand. "I haven't read this one."

Thank goodness. I'd exhausted our supply of military books, and to say nothing of how tired I was at playing twenty questions.

"I'd still like to read the Todish book," he said when we reached the counter. "Is there any way you could get it for me?"

"I can try," I said, flipping the cover open, pulling out the card, and stamping the due date inside. Maybe a little harder than I should have. Smiling, I slid the book toward Rick. "There. All set."

"This is great." He picked up the book and weighed it in his hand. "I appreciate your help this morning. Can I buy you a cup of coffee?"

"No, not necessary," I said, and filed his card. Scooping up the pile of returned books from the shelf, I laid them on the counter. Holding the first one open, I stuck its card inside the jacket, and then scooted it to the side.

"Dinner?"

I stopped, my hand hovering over the next cover. "Really, it's my job to help customers, Rick."

"But I'd like to show my appreciation. I—"

The chime on the library door interrupted him.

"Hi guys," Darci said, bouncing in.

Yes. Literally saved by the bell.

By mid-afternoon I felt like pounding my head on the wall. I'd called every library in neighboring towns, went through every book catalogue we owned, and had been to every book vendor on the Web, but could *not* locate the Todish book. My last hope was WorldCat, the national and international listing of books owned by specific libraries.

"Wouldn't you know, the book Rick wanted had to have one of the longest titles I'd ever seen?" I muttered while I hunched over the computer keyboard and typed in *America's First, First World War—the French and Indian War, 1754–1763* for the hundredth time. I was rewarded with a hit—a library in Massachusetts had a copy. "Hurray," I said, and spun my chair around.

"Are you talking to yourself, dear?"

I stopped mid-spin to see my grandmother standing in the doorway. "Jeez, Abby. You shouldn't sneak up on people like that."

She grinned and took a chair at the corner of my desk. "Sorry, but you looked busy."

I turned back to the screen. "Yeah, Rick Davis asked me to find a book for him, and now, three hours later, I have. Give me a minute to copy this information and send the Regional Library in Council Bluffs a request to borrow it."

I quickly wrote down what I needed and sent the library an e-mail request. Finished, I turned my chair toward Abby. "Now. What's up?"

"Nothing—really. I came to town to have lunch with Edna Walters, so I thought I'd stop by and see my favorite granddaughter."

"Your only grandchild," I said, and laughed.

"Be that as it may, you're still my favorite." Abby winked at me.

A little bubble of skepticism formed in my mind. Why was Abby acting so nice? She'd been here at least two minutes and hadn't teased me or brought up performing a spell once. I narrowed my eyes and studied her. Dressed in a flowing skirt, its folds floated over her legs and down to the floor. She sat on the edge of her chair, her feet tucked to the side and her hands resting in her lap. Her face wore a look of total innocence.

That look of wide-eyed ingenuousness gave her away—my sweet grandmother was getting ready to scam me.

"Okay, what have you been up to?" I asked, watching her with wary eyes.

Abby's eyes widened. "Whatever do you mean?"

I rolled my eyes. "Abby, you're buttering me up before you drop your bomb."

"Oh all right," she said, settling back in her chair. "I did some scrying yesterday."

Great. She'd been at it again. Scrying was the ability to receive images or impressions by staring at an object—a bowl of water, a mirror, a crystal, or a candle. The ritual performed was lengthy and required both the witch and the room to be purified first, usually by smudging. And since her zodiac sign belonged to the element of fire, Abby always used a candle.

"And what did you see?" I asked, shaking my head.

"I didn't really 'see' anything. But I did receive impressions. Impressions of you and Rick Davis sitting in your living room."

"No surprise there," I said, throwing up my hand. "We sat in my living room Saturday, after you'd left. I'd dropped my billfold and he returned it."

"I didn't get the feeling it was something that had already happened." Abby paused and tapped her chin. "The impression was very strong that the event lies in the future."

"Can't be. I have no intention of ever inviting him to my house. The guy makes me nervous." I frowned. "He's hiding something. I know he is."

"But—"

A rap on the door stopped her from finishing.

Darci opened the door and stuck her head in. "Excuse me, Ophelia. Didn't you want me to go to the post office and mail back the books from the traveling library?"

"Oh gosh, yes. What time is it?" I looked at the clock on the computer. "They close in twenty minutes. I'll be right up to watch the counter, then you can leave."

Darci started to pull the door shut, but Abby stopped her.

"Darci, wait, come in," Abby said, waving her into the room. "I have a question for you. You're a pretty astute judge of character. What do you think of Rick Davis?"

Darci astute? I looked at Abby in surprise, but she was watching Darci's reaction.

Darci smiled shyly at Abby's compliment. "He's very good-looking. Smart," she said, pondering Abby's question. "Umm—I think he's one of those people who seem to sail through life without a lot of problems. So he hasn't had to spend much time in self-examination."

My eyebrows shot up. Wow, I was surprised at Darci's response. But Abby wasn't. She nodded thoughtfully at her description of Rick.

"Because of his looks and intelligence, he's used to getting what he wants," Darci continued. "But I don't think he's a jerk. He just expects life to be easy, without even being aware of how he feels." She paused again. "And I think he asks too many questions to be a chemical salesman."

I gave Abby a knowing look. "See what did I tell you? Darci thinks he's lying, too."

Darci grinned like she'd just passed a test. "No one's at the counter, so I'd better get back upstairs. I'm ready to go to the post office whenever you want, Ophelia. I'll see you later, Abby." Wiggling her fingers in a wave, she sauntered out of the room.

When I was sure Darci couldn't hear me, I said to Abby, "I didn't think Darci paid that much attention to people."

"I think you underestimate the girl. But back to what I was about to say—"

"Please," I said interrupting her this time. Sighing, I massaged my eyes with my fingertips. "I'm tired of thinking about spells, evil circles, and Rick Davis." I dropped my hands and looked at her. "You know he asked me what I did for fun and I had a problem thinking of something? Isn't that sad?" I leaned forward and placed my hand on her knee. "Do you think we could table all of this for now? Let's do something fun. I read in the paper that the Cinemax in Des Moines is running a special old movie series. One of the movies is *The*

*Thin Man*. And I've never watched it in a movie theater. I thought about driving into Des Moines to see it. Would you like to go?"

Abby patted my hand. "Yes, dear, I'd love to."

"Great," I said, sitting back in the chair. "Maybe we can go to dinner first? We haven't done that in a long time."

"Sounds wonderful," she said, standing and smoothing her skirt. She leaned over and kissed the top of my head, squeezing my shoulder as she did. "Be careful, dear," she murmured against my hair. "I don't want to lose you. And I know you don't want to hear this, but I have to warn you. The reason I knew the impression I received hasn't happened yet—you and Rick were surrounded by an aura of danger."

She squeezed my shoulder and left.

# *Five*

Rick Davis had been in town less than a week, but by Tuesday everyone thought he was wonderful. He'd met people at Stumpy's, Joe's Café, the post office. Everywhere people gathered, Rick Davis—and his questions—was there. His curiosity seemed to be admired. *"Isn't it nice he's taking such an interest in the town?"* they were all saying. The ladies in town were talking about him—both young and old. *"What a nice young man." "Isn't he charming?" "Such nice manners." "Those brown eyes are to die for."*

Either I was hearing about him or the man himself was haunting the basement of the library. He spent so much time in the archives, I thought about charging him rent. It was no surprise to me when I found him once again in the basement on the computer.

"Back again, huh?"

Rick shut off the computer, making it revert to the original settings and clearing the history. He raised his head and looked at me. "Yeah, just reading about all of the thefts. I can't believe the sheriff doesn't have any clues."

He gazed up at me like I knew something he didn't.

"Bill? How would I know? I'm not in his confidence. You're staying at the bed and breakfast, aren't you? Why don't you ask Georgia? She dates Alan, one of Bill's deputies."

Rick gave me a lopsided grin. "Georgia does seem to know everything that's going on in town, doesn't she?"

I straightened the magazines on the table. "Georgia has a reputation for two things: cooking and being one of the biggest gossips in town. Be careful what you say to her. She repeats everything."

"I've already figured that one out." Rick leaned back in the chair and watched me. "Darci said your grandmother knows a lot about the town, too."

Placing both hands on the table, I slanted forward. "Darci's wrong. Abby minds her own business, just like I do. What do you care who knows what about this town?" I said, with too much force. I took a deep breath and started again, this time with my voice under control. "I thought you're here to sell fertilizer, not to do a history of Summerset."

Rick lifted his shoulders in a careless shrug. "It helps my sales pitch if I understand the community. And I find all these thefts fascinating. How can someone manage to steal all this anhydrous and not get caught? Aren't you curious about it?"

"No, it's Bill's job to figure that stuff out, not mine. And speaking of your sales pitch, exactly when are you giving this *pitch*? It seems to me that you're either here or busy ingratiating yourself with the townspeople. Mrs. Walters can't say enough about you after you helped her to the car with her groceries." I crossed my arms and stared at him.

"Come on, she's had hip surgery."

I rolled my eyes. "The hip surgery was two years ago and she's as strong as a horse. She played you for a sucker."

Rick cocked an eyebrow. "I don't mind. It got me an invitation to dinner."

"You should go. That is, if you don't mind hearing all the gruesome details of her surgery over the mashed potatoes and gravy. By the way, how much longer do you plan on staying in Summerset?"

"I don't know. It all depends," he said, fiddling with a pencil lying beside the computer.

"Depends on what?"

"Oh, this and that," he said as he watched me with a slight grin on his face.

Silence. Picking up the magazines again, I gave them one final tap to straighten them and glanced at the clock. "Well, as fun as this may be, I have work to do. Don't you have someplace you should be?"

"Are you trying to get rid of me?"

"Not only ingratiating, but quick, too," I said, walking past him into my office.

"Wait a second, I have one more question. And then I'll leave, I promise." Rick followed me.

I sighed. "What is it?"

He leaned casually against the door frame while I sat down at my desk.

"Who's Jake Jenkins?"

"Why do you want to know?"

"I was reading the letter to the editor he wrote about gun control."

"You mean his diatribe?" I frowned, picked up some papers lying on my desk and studied them. "Umm— Jake works at the co-op."

"And you don't like him."

"What makes you say that?"

"Even from here, I can see the page you're reading is upside down."

Putting the papers down, I looked over at Rick. "Okay, you're right, I don't like him. I think he's an idiot."

Rick laughed. "Why don't you tell me how you really feel, Ophelia?"

I grimaced. "Yeah, well he is. Lady doesn't like him, either. She goes nuts whenever she sees him. And she's an excellent judge of character."

"I agree. Did you notice how much she liked me?" Rick said, grinning.

"Ha, you're the exception to the rule. Just because—"

"Excuse me, Miss Ophelia," someone behind Rick said. "Don't mean to bother you, but Miss Darci said to ask you if there's anything else for me to do."

Damn! Benny. Jake's brother. Poor guy—almost as wide as he was tall—he had one speed, slow and ponderous. Darci told me it had taken him six years to complete high school. And now, in addition to farming rented land with his brother, he did odd jobs around town to supplement his income. How long had he been standing there? Had he heard what I said about Jake? I might not have cared about Jake, but Benny did. He worshiped his brother, and I wouldn't want to hurt his feelings.

"Benny, I'm sorry. I didn't know you were still here. No, there isn't anything else. But the shingles on my garage need to be repaired. Would you have time to look at them?"

"Sure thing, Miss Ophelia, but not today. Maybe Friday." Benny's round, earnest face stared back at me.

"That would be fine, Benny."

After Benny waddled off, I covered my face with my hands.

"I don't think he heard you," Rick said.

"Jeez, I hope not. Benny thinks Jake can do no wrong, and I wouldn't want to hurt Benny. He's harmless."

"But his brother isn't?"

"Look, I've already said enough about Jake Jenkins. And I really do have work to do."

"Okay, last thing—thank you for ordering the Todish book for me."

"No problem," I said, booting up the computer on my desk.

"Darci said it was. She told me you spent a couple of hours tracking it down."

Staring at the computer screen, I wished Darci hadn't told him that.

"No big deal. It's part of my job," I said, waving my hand in dismissal.

"I appreciate you ordering the book. I really would like to take you to dinner as a thank-you."

"It's not necessary," I said, not taking my eyes off the screen.

"Why don't you want to have dinner with me?" he asked abruptly.

I tore my eyes away from the screen and looked at Rick, the doorway framing him. "Okay, Rick, let me be direct. I'm not your type and I don't think it would be a good idea to have dinner with you."

He shoved his hands in his pockets and nodded. "That's pretty direct."

"You asked," I said, and started to type on the keyboard. "I need to have this report done today, so—"

"One more second," he said, interrupting me. You

said you weren't my type. What kind of woman do you think *is* my type?"

"I don't know," I said, squinting at the screen. "For a man who looks like you, a beauty queen, maybe a model. Someone cute."

"And you're not cute?"

"Oh, hell no." I clapped my hand over my mouth, but it was too late. The words were out.

Rick grinned. "I didn't think librarians swore."

"They don't. I don't. Well, maybe sometimes. But not a lot." I could feel the heat building in my face. My God, the man had me stammering. And he stood in the open doorway, watching me, with a big grin on his face. He had to leave before I said something else stupid.

Embarrassed, I looked up at him. "Please, I really do have things to do."

Rick gave a big sigh and said, "Okay, I guess my only option is to have dinner with Mrs. Walters, but I want you to know, I have a weak constitution. And listening to tales of her hip surgery . . . aaah." He groaned and grabbed his stomach. "The dinner could end badly. Don't you feel just a tiny bit sorry for me?"

Honestly, he was putting on such an act, sounding so pitiful, that I chuckled.

"Nope," I said, still smiling.

"Okay," he said dropping the "Oh, I'm sick" act. "See you around." And after a quick wink, he was gone.

But by the afternoon my mood matched the gray weather. The low hanging clouds had dumped big fat drops of rain on the ground all day. From the high basement windows, I could see the flashes of lightning. They were followed instantly by the rolling thunder.

First a snowstorm. Now this. It seemed Mother Nature couldn't make up her mind what season it was. Or was the order of nature disturbed the way Abby had said? Thinking about it gave me a headache.

Tired of staring blankly at the computer screen, I wandered upstairs. Darci stood simpering at the counter. Across from her stood Larry Durbin. He wore a ripped T-shirt under his denim jacket. His blond greasy hair was pulled back from his pallid face in a tight ponytail. A pair of dirty red tennis shoes—no socks—completed his outfit. A look of disgust crossed my face.

Out of the corner of his eye, Larry saw me. With his head down, he mumbled something to Darci and left.

Darci was still smiling when I reached the counter.

I frowned. "Honestly, Darci. Why is he hanging around here?"

"Oh, Larry's not so bad. He wasn't always like this. He used to be pretty hot, but the drugs have really screwed him up. I feel kind of sorry for him."

"Not that it's any of my business, but you don't go out with him, do you?"

"No, not now. We dated a little in high school, before he messed up. He knows I don't approve of his lifestyle, but he stops by here every now and again to talk."

"I don't like drug users hanging out at the library. It gives us a bad image. Tell him if he wants to talk to you, to meet you somewhere else, not here."

Darci's smile faded. "Don't you think you're overreacting a bit, Ophelia? Larry and me were just talking."

I blew out a shaky breath. "You're right. I'm sorry. I didn't mean to sound so harsh or be unkind. I have a lot of things to think about right now."

Darci scowled. "Did Rick upset you?"

"Rick? Why do ask?" I said, rubbing my temple.

"I saw you talking with him earlier. And he's been asking me a lot of questions about you. Wanted to know where you worked before moving to Summerset, where you'd lived, who your friends are. All sorts of questions."

"Really? And you told him what?" I stretched my neck, trying to loosen the muscles that cramped tighter with each word Darci said.

"That you spent summers here with Abby when you were a kid, but you grew up in Iowa City and worked there before moving here. And you've been in Summerset about three or four years. That was okay, wasn't it?" she asked, sounding worried.

"That's fine. It's okay," I said, dismissing her answers with a wave. "He's asked me a lot of the same questions. But I do resenting him questioning you."

Turning on my heel so Darci wouldn't see the irritation in my face, I stomped down the stairs to my office.

The rain stopped by closing time, but the damp it left behind seemed to sneak under my coat while I closed the door. It made me shiver.

"Ophelia."

I whipped around, almost losing my balance on the top step.

"Rick, what do you want now?"

"I stopped by to ask you if you'd have a beer with me at Stumpy's. It might help me handle Mrs. Walters's stories," Rick said while he watched me with a cheeky grin on his face. "And you didn't say no beer, just no dinner."

"No," I said, hurrying past him.

The ground squished under my shoes as I marched to my car. Suddenly, I wasn't cold anymore. The anger that had simmered all afternoon after talking to Darci erupted. Snooping into my life, asking questions about Abby, asking me to dinner after I'd said no once. This guy really pissed me off.

Rick ran down the steps and followed me to the car.

"Hey, it's just a beer," he said quickly.

I whirled around. "We've already been through this—I'm not your type—so, no, I won't have beer with you. Thanks anyway."

"That's right. I forgot. You're not cute," he said, grinning.

"Ha ha, very funny. Take your charm and go have dinner with Mrs. Walters," I said, yanking open the car door.

"Wait, why are you so angry?" he asked.

I glared at him. "I don't like people snooping around in my personal life. Asking people I work with questions about me."

"Darci—"

"Yeah, Darci. My life isn't any of your business," I said sternly, and made a move to get in the car.

"Hold on," he said, and raised his hand to stop me. "I'm sorry if I crossed any lines. I told you, I'm a curious kind of a guy and you interest me, Ophelia Jensen."

I gave him a skeptical look, but before I could comment, he held up his hand again.

"No, listen. I know you think you're not my type, but I swear," he said, placing his hand over his heart, "I've only dated one beauty queen my entire life. And she was kind of nasty."

I felt a smile tug at the corner of my mouth. As Abby would say, "This guy could charm the socks right off a person, without even taking off their shoes." But I couldn't afford to be charmed. There were too many things going on in my life, and I didn't have the time or the energy to deal with Rick Davis. And I still didn't trust him.

"Rick—"

He took a step closer to me. "Yeah?"

I backed up against the open car door, and when I did, Rick stepped back. I looked at him then, really looked at him. My gosh, Darci was right, he was an incredibly handsome guy. And my heart stuttered in my chest a little. Most women would rush to accept an invitation from him. But I wasn't "most women." Too many secrets and too much pain.

I shook my head sadly. "I'm sorry, Rick. I can't."

He took another step backward, away from me. "All right. Well then," he said slowly, "I guess it's Mrs. Walters and tales of hip surgeries. Have a good evening, Ophelia, okay?"

"Thanks. I will," I said as Rick turned and walked away.

# Six

The cupboard was bare. I was out of dog food, and I
hated being out of dog food. The best place to buy it
was the co-op, and I hated going to the co-op—it's one
of the last good ol' boy clubs in town. Everytime I went
there, I felt as if I had entered a time warp and it was
1955 again. The farmers, in coveralls and boots with
manure clinging to the soles, hung out at the co-op.
They sat around, drank coffee, and gossiped about the
latest rumor, the weather, and what was wrong with the
country. All the steel-corrugated building lacked was a
big potbellied stove to prop their dirty boots on while
they passed around the gossip. Since it was too wet to
work in the fields, everyone would be there today.

The parking lot was full when I drove in. About
every truck in town was there, and I had to pull into a
space at the opposite end of the building. After exiting
my car, I walked up the sidewalk and through the door.

The smell hit me immediately and I stopped. The
aroma of the sweet, dry feed mixed with the stink of
the manure-caked boots in the air, enveloping me. It
would cling to my hair and my clothes. It would haunt
my senses for the rest of the day. While I scanned the

room, I saw Jake Jenkins standing at the counter holding court. I had never met a man who liked the sound of his own voice as much as Jake.

"So, Jake, what do you think the co-op should do about all these anhydrous ammonia thefts?" one of the farmers was saying. "The sheriff don't seem to be able to stop them. Ed wasn't happy this weekend when he found his tank had been siphoned off."

"If we had a sheriff with any balls, he could've stopped them," Jake replied. "Those damned druggies are ruining this country. Someone ought to take 'em out and shoot 'em. That'd make those scum think twice about making meth."

To call Jake a Neanderthal was to insult that extinct species. But I noticed that all the men were nodding sagely at his sentiments. All but one, that is. Rick Davis stood against the wall, arms folded, listening and observing. He saw me hesitate at the door and arched an eyebrow.

"I heard they cut the line going from the tank to the applicator."

"Yeah, they must have drained it into something."

"Must have been something pretty sturdy, not like that guy up North who used a plastic milk jug. Jug exploded and the anhydrous hit him in the pants. Heard it really did some damage, if you know what I mean," the farmer said with a wink.

"Ouch, that'd hurt."

They all laughed except Rick. I felt as if I were in the middle of the boys' high school locker room. The testosterone hung in the air like ozone. It was too much for me. I strode over to the counter where Jake stood.

"Well, honey, what can I do for you?" Jake asked with a smirk.

"I need a forty pound bag of dog food, please," I said, frowning at the "honey" and ignoring the smirk.

"Sure thing, honey. That dog of yours sure eats a lot," Jake said, and looked around to make sure his audience was paying attention. "Must 'wolf' down her food."

Was that a joke? I didn't laugh, and neither did anyone else. The tension I felt whenever I was near Jake began to gnaw at the back of my neck. I couldn't get out of there fast enough. Couldn't he hurry up and give me the dog food, instead of making stupid jokes?

"Get it? Wolfs downs her food?" Jake's smirk slowly faded.

"I got it," I said. "You're referring to the fact that Lady is a wolf mix and that she consumes large quantities of food. You were making a play on words."

He looked disappointed. "It's not funny when you say it that way."

"Trust me, Jake, it wasn't funny the way you said it, either," I said, not looking at him as I signed the ticket.

A farmer chuckled. Jake heard him and gave me a stony look before he plopped the bag on the floor at my feet.

"Do you need help with the bag or can you get it yourself—honey?"

"I'll manage. Put it on my bill," I said, grabbing the heavy sack and lifting with all my strength.

Another farmer opened the door for me. "Are you sure you don't need help?" he asked, watching me lug the heavy bag out the door while he held it open.

He grinned when I boosted the bag higher with my knee and shook my head no. Jake wasn't popular with many people, and the farmer had enjoyed our little exchange. I knew the story would be told and retold over coffee at Joe's that afternoon.

"You sure?" the farmer asked.

"No, really, I can carry it. Thanks anyway."

I got the sack as far as my car and propped it against the bumper. Wiping my forehead, I looked at the heavy bag. How would I hoist it into the trunk? After my "I'm a capable woman" routine, I'd leave the bag in the parking lot before I'd go back inside and ask for help.

"So how are you going to lift it into the trunk?"

I jumped. Rick was standing behind me.

"I can manage," I said, tugging on the sack.

"No, you can't. That sack's almost as big as you are. If you let me help you, I promise I won't call you 'honey.' "

"Be my guest." I stepped back and watched him easily lift the heavy bag into the trunk.

"Thanks," I said, closing the lid. "I could've done it myself, you know."

"You are stubborn, aren't you?" Rick crossed his arms and slouched against the car. "I know you don't like Jake, but you were pretty abrupt in there. What's the story?"

"You know, Rick, your questions are getting old."

"I did get the dog food in the trunk for you and saved you from the humiliation of asking one of those farmers—or even Jake—to help. I figure you owe me at least the answer to one question."

"Oh, okay." I paused. "Jake tried to hurt Lady."

"How?" Rick jerked out of his slouch.

"He tried to hit her with his truck. She had chased a squirrel out of the yard. And she was running back across the street as he came around the corner. I watched him speed up and swerve to hit her. He missed her by this much," I said, holding up my thumb and forefinger about an inch apart.

"What did you do?"

"Jumped in my car and chased him till he stopped. Then I got out told him what I thought of him."

Rick chuckled. "I bet he didn't like that."

"No, he didn't. Jake is not used to anyone standing up to him." I gave Rick a steely look. "But nobody messes with my dog and gets away with it."

"No wonder Lady doesn't like him."

"Yeah. So now, every time I run into him, he tries to annoy me."

"He succeeds, too."

"Yes, he does. I told you, he's an idiot. See that truck over there? It's the one he drove when he tried to hit Lady."

Rick looked at the beat-up old pickup in the parking lot. It had deer antlers attached to the hood, a gun rack in the back window, and a bumper sticker that said, YOU CAN TAKE MY GUN WHEN YOU PRY IT FROM MY COLD, DEAD HANDS.

"That belongs to Jake? He *is* a member of the NRA, isn't he?"

"What was your first clue? He also likes to play war games with paint balls. Jake's only redeeming virtue is his loyalty to Benny. I don't know if you've noticed, but Benny's kind of slow. Jake protects him. If Jake's not around, the kids in town call Benny names."

"What do the kids call him?"

"Oh, no," I said, trying hard not to smile while I fished for my keys. "You said one question, and now you're over your limit."

"Come on, be a sport."

I walked to the driver's side of the car and looked across at Rick.

"They call him Dickey-Do."

"Why Dickey-Do?"

"You've seen how round Benny is. His stomach sticks out farther than his—well, you figure it out."

I glanced at my watch as I ran up the steps of the library. Damn. I was late. When I walked in the door, Darci hit me with it.

"Ophelia, did you—"

"Save it, Darci," I said, hurrying to the counter. "I was just at the co-op, buying dog food from Jake Jenkins."

I watched Darci while I shoved my backpack under the counter. Her mouth tightened when I said Jake's name. She didn't like him, either.

"I heard all about it. Ed Johnson had anhydrous stolen from his tank last weekend."

Her face fell when she heard that. But all at once, she perked up.

"Bet you don't know about the newspaper office. I just found out myself from Georgia. I can't believe no one said anything. Georgia dates Alan, Bill's deputy, you know. So she has the inside scoop."

"Yes, I know—Georgia, Alan, hot romance. What happened at the newspaper?" I asked, making a circle with my first finger, nudging her along.

"Well," Darci said, warming to her subject, "someone broke in last Saturday night. Georgia said Alan said—and you know how Alan—"

"Yes, yes, I know Alan likes to talk. Try and stay on track, Darce," I said, smiling. "You were telling me about the newspaper?"

"Okay, okay. Somebody broke in to vandalize the

office. But first they started a fire in the wastebasket, and the smoke detector went off. They had to leave before they could finish, or they would've got caught because of all the noise the smoke detector made. Alan said it was pretty stupid. They should've trashed the place first and then started the fire. Not too much damage was done, except for the wastepaper basket, of course."

A fairly concise rendition, for Darci anyway. The criminal element in Summerset had been busy lately. I hated to ask, but I couldn't help myself.

"Does Alan have any suspects?"

"No, he thinks it was probably a bunch of kids with nothing better to do."

I had a feeling Alan was wrong, but I kept it to myself. Was this the beginning of the trouble Abby had seen? I didn't want to know.

I looked up at Darci. She was watching me with a knowing look in her eye. She wasn't finished with her gossip yet.

"Georgia also mentioned Rick Davis was at your house on Saturday," she said, dropping the bomb. "Why didn't you tell me when Abby asked me about Rick?"

Peachy. That Georgia was just a fount of information. Someone must have seen Rick's car in my driveway. That's what I get for living in a small town.

"I think he likes you. That's why he's asking all those questions. And he dropped this off this morning," she said, and handed me an envelope.

Oh, brother, what now? I thought, ripping it open. Inside were two tickets to *The Thin Man* and a gift certificate to one of the nicest restaurants in Des Moines. Included was a note. *Thank you for the book.*

"See. I told you," Darci said, peering over my shoulder. "He likes you. Are you going to invite him to go with you?"

"Don't be silly. I can't accept this gift," I said, and stuffed the envelope in my pocket.

"Why not?" she asked.

"Because I don't accept gifts for doing my job. And, ahh . . . ahh . . ."

"You'd feel obligated?"

"Well. Yeah," I said, shifting my weight.

"And you don't like feeling obligated?" Darci looked at me thoughtfully.

"No, I don't." I shifted back.

"I think what he did is very sweet," she said, emphasizing the *sweet*. "And it wouldn't kill you to go out with him. You might be surprised and have a good time."

Darci was a hopeless romantic. For the past three years, she had tried to fix me up with every unattached man in town, usually her rejects. No matter how hard I tried to convince her I wasn't interested, she always persisted. This was all I needed, Darci manufacturing a romance between Rick Davis and me.

"He sure spends a lot of time here. You know, if you would put more effort into your appearance, you would have a lot of guys asking you out. You're pretty, you just need a little work," she said, sizing me up.

I snorted. There wasn't anything wrong with the way I looked, but I've never considered myself pretty. My smile's nice, and I'd been told before my eyes are expressive, but the guy who told me that just wanted sex. No, I'm strictly average. Average height, average weight, average everything.

"I know you're trying to be helpful, and I appreciate

it, but give it up. I'm not interested in Rick Davis, or anyone else for that matter. I don't have the time."

"Well, you should make the time. No one should be alone."

Yes, they should, especially someone like me. But I couldn't tell Darci that without explaining. And that was something I had no intention of doing.

# Seven

It was turning out to be a rotten day. First, the scene with Jake at the co-op, now I had to sit through an end-less Chamber of Commerce meeting that was being held at Joe's Café. Joe's had been a fixture of down-town Summerset for as long as I could remember. In fact, it had been here so long, the local joke was—Noah ate lunch at Joe's right before the flood. About twenty years ago, Joe decided to go out on a limb and do some remodeling. The walls were covered with fake wood paneling and the floors had cheap vinyl tile. The suspended ceiling tiles were yellow from twenty years' worth of cigarette smoke. Around the room, pinned to the paneling with thumbtacks, were colorful, card-board turkeys—the kind you buy at the dime store. I suppose it was Joe's attempt to give the place a festive tone for Thanksgiving.

Claire Canyon, the president of the library board, in-sisted I attend the meeting with her in case she needed my help with her summer reading program presenta-tion. And you didn't say no when Claire insisted. It had always amazed me how much energy and intensity could be packaged in such a small person. Her causes were many and her passion for each one was great. Plus, she had a habit of peering over her glasses in a way that made you want to find the nearest rock and crawl underneath it. So rather than look for a rock, I let myself be dragged to the meeting.

If the atmosphere at Joe's was lacking, the food made up for it. The turkey, mashed potatoes with gravy, and dressing had been wonderful. I wish I could say the same for the meeting. Talk, talk, talk, all without one single decision made.

Abby was also at the meeting, and I sat between her and Claire. They both listened politely to each speaker. But not me—I only pretended to listen. Actually, I was amusing myself by counting the number of dots on the ceiling tile. Joe's Café had a lot of them. According to my calculations, there were 2,355. I was so intent on my math that I missed Claire's comment.

"Ophelia, pay attention," she whispered.

"To what? Agnes McPhearson's report on the how many petunias were planted this year at the city park, or the one Mr. Collins will give on how much money the dunking booth made at the Korn Karnival?" I whispered back. "Honestly, I'd rather you force me to drive back and forth across Nebraska. It couldn't possibly be any more boring than this."

"Hey, I was born and raised in Nebraska." Claire peered at me over her glasses.

Oh no, the thing with the glasses, and I squirmed in my seat. "Oops, sorry."

"Never mind," she said, settling the glasses back on her nose. "We need the business community's support for the reading program at the library, so we have to tolerate this minor inconvenience till they reach us on the agenda."

She was right. With the cutbacks in state spending, support from the local merchants would make all the difference as to whether the program stayed open. Claire hoped her pitch for backing from the chamber would be rewarded in the form of cold, hard cash.

"So, exactly when will we be called on to speak? After the report on the petunias, or after the one on who got dunked?"

Claire chuckled at my remark, but Abby jabbed me in the ribs.

"Shh," she said without turning her head.

Claire briefly touched my knee. "Be patient," she said. "Adam is getting ready to shut Agnes off."

Adam Hoffman, the chamber president, had the same glazed look in his eyes that I did. He interrupted Agnes and smiled tightly.

"Thank you, Agnes, for your very informative report. And may I say, I hope the park looks as lovely next year as it did this year."

Agnes preened at his praise and sat down. I had to give Adam credit; he was smooth, almost too smooth. He had this habit of looking at a person without really seeing them. And he always had a smile on his face, but his eyes seemed flat. He reminded me of a politician or an old-fashioned snake oil salesman, not a bank manager. No one else in town agreed. They all loved him, and they treated him like everyone's favorite uncle.

When I looked around the room, I saw Ned Thomas, the editor of the *Summerset Courier*, hunched over in his chair, staring at the floor. Ned appeared as bored as I felt. Maybe he was counting the cracks in the floor, instead of the dots on the ceiling. He looked up at me and smiled. I smiled back.

When Ned mouthed the word "boring," I stifled a

giggle. He noticed and his smile broadened. My smile grew wider. Another jab in my ribs from Abby and a look from Claire got my attention.

"Would you quit making eyes at Ned? We're next," Claire said.

My face felt suddenly hot. Even though Ned was single, I didn't want him to get the wrong idea. Or Abby and Claire to think I was flirting. I looked back quickly at Adam Hoffman, sitting at the front table. From the look on his face, I knew he had been watching me. My face turned a deeper shade of red.

Finally, it was Claire's turn. In the end, she didn't need me after all. By the time she finished with her impassioned report, the chamber voted unanimously to make a contribution to the reading program. The only thought in my mind was to get out of there and go home, but Ned had other ideas.

"Ophelia, would you like to have a cup of coffee with me?"

"Gee, Ned, I really need to get home. This was a long meeting and I'm pretty tired." I looked longingly over my shoulder at the door.

"Well, a cup of coffee will perk you up, and I'd like to talk to you."

"Okay." After one last look at the door, I followed Ned.

We made our way to the back booth, past the crowd, and sat down. Joe came over and took our order. I fiddled with my spoon while I tried to think of something to say.

"I was sorry to hear about the fire at the paper. Was there much damage?" I said after Joe brought our coffee.

"No, not too much. They started the fire first, which

was a good thing, I guess. It made the smoke alarm go off. Alan figures the noise scared them and they ran."

"Did anyone see anything?"

"No, unfortunately. The funny thing is what they burned. They found all the pictures I had taken this fall of the Korn Karnival," Ned said, gazing into his cup. "They dumped them in the wastebasket, along with the negatives, and set them on fire." He lifted his head and looked at me. "Why do you suppose anyone would want to burn them?"

"Got me. Maybe it was the first thing they found."

"Yeah, you're probably right. Alan thinks a bunch of kids did it, but the fire isn't what I wanted to talk to you about."

"Ophelia, Ned, mind if I join you?"

I turned to see Adam standing over my right shoulder.

"Of course not, Adam," Ned said.

When Adam sat down, the scent of his cologne overwhelmed me. Evidently, he'd never heard of the saying, "Less is more." Trying not to wrinkle my nose, I scooted as close to the wall as I could to get away from the smell. Wedged in the corner, I watched both Adam and Ned.

"Ned, I was very upset to hear about the fire," Adam said. "I don't suppose the sheriff has any clues?"

"No, there wasn't much for them to go on," Ned replied.

"You're being very understanding. Personally, I think there have been too many incidences of vandalism and crimes here in Summerset recently," Adam said, settling back on the bench. "The city council should be addressing this problem instead of making excuses for the sheriff's department. Summerset needs its own police force."

"Well, if the rumors are true, and you run for mayor, that statement would make a good campaign issue."

"Ned, you've lived here all your life. You ought to know better than to believe rumors." Adam smiled another of his flat and lifeless smiles.

Ned leaned forward and met Adam's smile with one of his own. "I've also been a newspaperman long enough to know some rumors are based in fact. My instinct tells me this one might be true."

The smile left Adam's face, and he stared down at his hands and steepled his fingers. His face was serious when he looked at Ned. "This is strictly off the record. I'm only telling you this because I trust you. The truth is, I have been approached by several concerned citizens and asked to run for mayor. They don't like the direction the town is heading. Too many things have happened recently, and they feel the sheriff hasn't been as effective as he should've been. I've made no secret that I agree with them, and I'd love the chance to clean things up. However, my family comes first, and Nina's health is a big concern. She's so fragile, and I don't know what the stress of a campaign might do to her. Until I talk to her doctors, I won't make a decision."

Both of them seemed to forget I was sitting there. While I listened to their conversation, I twisted the paper napkin in my lap back and forth. I fiddled with the coffee. Being this close to Adam Hoffman made me nervous, and I didn't care whether or not he ran for mayor. It was nothing to me. I wanted to think of a polite way to excuse myself and go home. It had been a long day.

Looking over the back of the booth, I saw Abby standing by the door talking to Claire. Maybe if I caught her eye, she'd rescue me. I stared at her, willing her to glance my way. When she did, I made a slight jerk with my head. But instead of walking to the booth, she waved and resumed talking to Claire. Defeated, I turned back to Ned and found them both watching me.

"Excuse me? Did you say something?" I asked, blinking with surprise.

The corner of Ned's mouth twitched as if he was trying to stop a grin. "Ophelia, Adam asked you about the vandalism."

"Me? I'm just the librarian. I don't know anything about what's going on."

Ned laughed. "He didn't ask if you knew anything, just what you thought."

"Oh, hmm . . ." I paused, picking apart the twisted napkin in my lap. "Well, it's unfortunate."

Adam turned his gaze to me and slid his arm across the back of the booth. I didn't think the smell of his cologne could get any sharper, but it did. And I crouched closer to the wall.

"That's it? Unfortunate? Don't you have any other opinion? Don't you care about what's going on in our community?"

His questions made me feel as if I were in seventh grade, when Mrs. Simpson called on me in class and I didn't know the answer. If I weren't an adult, I would've slunk under the table.

"Ah, I guess I trust Bill and Alan to figure it all out," I said.

A look of pure disgust crossed Adam's face at my lack of civic interest. Irritated, I sat up straighter in my seat.

"Actually, Adam, I do have opinions, but they're private. I don't believe in announcing them all the time the way some people do. And I prefer to make my political opinions known in the voting booth."

He pulled his arm back from the top of the booth and turned back to Ned.

"Well, Ned, Ophelia has made it clear where she'll be standing come election time. Now, if you'll excuse me, I must get home to check on Nina." Looking first at me, then Ned, he reached out to shake Ned's hand. "I know I can trust your discretion concerning Nina. I wouldn't want any rumors circulating about her health."

He stood, and I watched as he made his way through the room. As he did, he stopped to talk to people still gathered in groups. He shook some of their hands and gave a jovial pat on the back to others.

Boy, he sure knew how to work a crowd.

Scanning the room, I looked for Abby, but she had left. Now I couldn't use her as an excuse to leave myself.

I looked back at Ned and noticed him twisting a napkin back and forth.

"Ophelia, after you basically told Adam Hoffman to mind his own business, I probably shouldn't bring this up."

I glanced at his napkin, twisted in a tight ball now and lying on the table.

"Ned, it's late, just say what you want to say. If it isn't any of your business, I'll tell you."

"I heard Rick Davis was at your house last weekend."

"That isn't any of your business."

Ned grinned when I folded my arms and leaned back against the worn cushion.

"I'm not kidding, Ned, it isn't any of your business."

"See, I knew you'd say that. I'm not trying to be a snoop, I'm just curious as to what this guy is doing in town."

You and me both, Ned, I thought, but I couldn't very well voice that without giving something away.

"As far as I know, Ned, he's a chemical salesman."

Ned took a slow sip of his coffee while he appeared to be considering his next words.

"Do you really believe that?"

"Why shouldn't I?"

"Come on, I make my living at sifting truth from lies. You may fool some of the people in this town, but you don't fool me. You're an observer, just like I am. You watch and listen, and you keep what you learn to yourself. You don't get involved. You stay behind the wall you've built around your life. As far as I can tell, there are very few people you let inside that wall."

The shock must have been apparent on my face. I couldn't believe Ned read me so well. Evidently, I was slipping. The thought made me shudder. I had too many secrets to protect to allow that.

"Oh, don't worry. I don't think anyone else in town sees you the same way I do. Most people are content to take things at face value. It's easier that way. And I'm not interested in prying into your personal life—I only want to know about Rick Davis. Somehow, he bothers me."

Ned sipped once again on his coffee, and I tried to think of an answer. What did I know about Rick Davis? Nothing, really, so what could I say? He gave me tickets to go to a movie?

I took a deep breath. "I don't know anything, except what he's told me, Ned, that he's a chemical salesman. The only thing that struck me as different was his interest in the archives. That's it."

"Archives, huh? Do you trust him?"

"I don't know him well enough to trust him, nor do I plan to know him that well."

"Well, I don't trust him. The guy is asking a lot of questions. And don't you think it's odd, he shows up, we have another anhydrous theft, and the paper gets trashed? All in the space of a few days?"

"It could be a coincidence," I reasoned. "We had thefts before he came to town."

Ned traced the rim of his coffee cup. "I don't think it is. The last one was a couple of months ago. My source in the sheriff's department said they knew who was responsible for those thefts—they were sloppy—but there wasn't enough proof to make the charges stick. Still, this last one was different. It wasn't sloppy. Someone knew exactly what he was doing."

"But that doesn't mean Rick Davis did it," I said, shifting in my seat.

"No, I suppose not, but I still think the whole thing is pretty fishy. I don't want to frighten you, but I think you should be careful around this guy. For all we know, he could be involved. If he is, he's dangerous."

Ned's warning sounded too much like Abby's for my peace of mind. Too bad for me, Ned wasn't finished yet.

"Another thing, Ophelia," he said, his voice low and intense. "If you learn something about him, don't do anything rash. Come to me first, and I'll help you."

Wonderful. What was happening to the nice little organized life I had carved out for myself? Warnings of impending doom from my grandmother, warnings of danger from Ned, and a stranger asking questions. I didn't need any of it. I wanted to go home, pull the covers over my head, and wish this whole situation away, and that was exactly what I planned to do.

# Eight

My plan didn't work. First, I couldn't find the right spot on my pillow, and then I couldn't find the right place to put my left arm. I finally fell asleep, but woke up hours later with a powerful thirst. I managed to get out of bed and stumble to the kitchen for a glass of water.

I gazed at the woods beyond the window while I stood drinking the water. The moon was waning—half dark, half light. Endings and beginnings, Abby had said. It was a "witching" moon. I could imagine broomstick riders flying across its face.

Lost in my fantasies, I didn't notice the shape at first. It caught my attention when it drifted toward the back of the yard near the trees. The figure was dressed in a white cowled robe like Abby sometimes wore. Damn it. Abby? She was out in the yard doing one of her goofy spells. I should've known she wouldn't leave magick alone. I wouldn't have that. Warnings of danger be damned. I was going to put a stop to that nonsense.

Grabbing a jacket and slipping it on over my flannel nightgown, I shoved my bare feet into an old pair of boots and stormed out the back door. The hem of my gown flapped against my ankles while I marched across my backyard.

But when I reached the stand of trees at the edge of the yard, she was gone. She probably went into the woods. Yes, there, I could see a faint glimmer of white ahead. I rushed after her. The branches and weeds tore at my hair and nightgown while I ran. The wind penetrated my gown and chilled my flesh. In the distance an owl hooted, once, twice. I still ran on, deeper and deeper into the woods. My side began to ache and my breath was coming in short, quick gasps, but I couldn't stop. I had to keep her in sight.

Suddenly, I heard a crash and the sound of running behind me. Someone else. In the woods chasing me? Instead of running toward something, something or someone was after me. I pumped my legs harder, but my nightgown tangled around them. Whoever chased me was slowly gaining. My foot caught on an exposed root and I sprawled facedown in the dry leaves and twigs. The pounding footsteps were coming closer and closer.

I scrambled to my feet and took off again, trying to put distance between us. I had never ventured this far into the woods, and I was lost. I looked around and could no longer see a white figure ahead.

I continued running. A stitch in my side ached every time my legs pumped. My breath burned my chest. I couldn't run much farther, but the footsteps remained right behind me.

Just when I didn't think I could go on, I saw a gate to my right. I ran for it. Maybe I could hide inside the fence. I grabbed the gate with both hands and pulled. It wouldn't open, as the hinges had rusted shut. I rattled the gate in frustration, wasting precious seconds. Whoever was pursuing me closed in. I could hear ragged breathing, but I couldn't get the old gate loose. I yanked at it once more. The hinges gave way, and I hurled myself through the opening. Then I fell, feeling a soft blow on the side of my head. Then nothing.

When I came to, I found myself lying faceup on the ground. The dry grass prickled my naked back.

Naked? What happened to my nightgown? And where the hell was I?

I sat up and looked around. Stones were tumbled among the dead weeds. Like soldiers fallen in battle, they lay at odd angles to one another. My nightgown? Nowhere to be seen. Nor was the person who'd chased me. I crawled over slowly to one of the stones. In the light of the half-moon, I could make out a name and date on its moss-covered face. It was a headstone, and I was in an old cemetery. Everywhere the stench of decay—dead leaves, rotting vegetation, and only God knows what else—floated in the night air. From deep inside, I felt my fear bubbling to the surface. What sounded like the scraping of sharp toenails against stone caught my attention. I looked up—into the hot red eyes of the biggest rat in the world. A scream tore from my throat when the howl of a timber wolf erupted from the woods. Our voices mingled in the night air until they were one—an endless sound that went on and on.

I bolted upright. My throat was raw from screaming. Lady sat at my side, her head tilted back. It was her howl that penetrated my dream.

Dream? Had it been only a dream? My body trembled while I brushed sweat-soaked hair from my face. Reality came into focus. No one had been chasing me. There was no white lady, no cemetery, and most important, no rat. I was in my own bed with my night-gown twisted around me like a mummy's wrappings.

The dreams were starting again. Last time that happened, it almost destroyed my sanity. I couldn't bear to go through that again. My sore throat became tight with unshed tears as my body shook again, not with fear this time, but because I was sobbing.

Lost in my misery, I jumped when my bedroom door burst open. Abby stood in the doorway, looking like an avenging angel. She rushed to the bed and gathered me in her arms the way she had when I was a child. I felt her cool hand stroke my hair.

"Why are you here?" I mumbled, my head resting on Abby's shoulder.

"I was half-asleep when I thought I heard your voice calling me. You sounded so lost and alone, and without thinking, I went in your old room to comfort you. You weren't there, of course, but I knew I wouldn't sleep until I made sure you were okay. I got in the truck and drove here." She hugged me closer. "You had a dream, didn't you?"

I nodded, and the scent of the baby powder Abby used every night before bed filled my senses. It took me back to a time when life was simple—before Brian's murder.

"Abby, I can't stand . . ." My voice cracked.

"There, there. It's all right, Ophelia. Go ahead and have a good cry."

I wrapped my arms tightly around the one person in the world I could touch without fear and cried.

The face peering at me from the mirror the next morning was not a pretty sight. Its owner looked like she had been on a three-day binge. My eyes were puffy and bloodshot, with bags underneath big enough to pack. My nose was the color of a ripe tomato. All in all, I looked bad, so bad I would scare small children if they saw me. How could I pull myself together for work? I had two choices—call in sick, leaving Darci to fend for herself, or wear sunglasses and a ton of makeup. I stood pondering my choices when Abby knocked at the bathroom door.

"May I come in?"

"Sure. You can help me figure out what to do about my face," I said while I patted the swelling around my eyes.

"Oh, my," Abby said after she took stock of my face. "Well, cotton soaked in witch hazel might help the swelling around the eyes. But the nose . . . there isn't much you can do for it. The redness will eventually go away."

"Great. Oh well, I guess my face is the least of my worries, isn't it?" I turned my attention from the mirror to Abby.

She didn't say anything. She calmly set a cup of coffee on the vanity next to the wash bowl and rubbed my shoulders.

"I'm afraid so, dear," Abby finally said, sitting down on the vanity bench.

I turned back to the mirror. My face was a mask of bitterness. The corners of my mouth turned down and deep lines of worry etched my forehead.

"It's not fair. It's starting all over again, isn't it?"

Abby didn't answer me.

I slammed my hand against the sink. "Damn. I don't want anything to do with this."

Angry tears welled in my eyes. I wouldn't allow myself to cry. I'd done enough of that the previous night. Crying wouldn't solve anything.

"I know you've only seen vague images and you aren't clear on who, what, or when, but can you at least tell me why I'm involved? And don't give me a bunch of 'it's my destiny' stuff."

"I'm sorry. I truly am. I know how you feel about all of this, but things happen for a reason. Whether we can see the reason or not. There's a cosmic justice, you know. You don't believe it, but not believing won't change the truth. It must be you and you must accept it. Why you and not someone else?" Abby shrugged. "I don't have an answer for you."

"Well, that's just peachy, isn't it? What exactly is it I'm supposed to do?"

"Fight the evil, of course."

I groaned. "And how am I supposed to fight this evil?"

She smiled.

"Oh, no you don't. Not with any of that hocus-pocus stuff. I absolutely refuse to get involved in that. I'll figure out something else."

The next question lingered in the corner of my mind. I knew I had to ask it, but her answer might be frightening.

After several long minutes I said, "You said evil. Does that mean someone's going to die?"

Abby's face was full of compassion when she looked up at me, silently answering my question. My knees wobbled and I slowly sank to the floor in front of the sink. Throwing my arms around my knees, I hugged them to my chest.

"It's already happened, hasn't it?" I asked, resting my forehead on my knees.

"Yes," Abby said softly.

"Who?" I asked, looking up at her.

"I don't know. I got a fleeting image of a man—a dangerous man—lying faceup near water. He hasn't been found yet, but he's somehow tied to what's happening here. I think you need to tell me about your dream, Ophelia. Dreams aren't hocus-pocus. Everyone has them, and it might answer some questions."

Abby put a lot of stock in dreams. She didn't believe they were random thoughts of the subconscious released in sleep. It was pointless to argue with her.

"Okay." I closed my eyes and willed myself to remember. "I got out of bed for a glass of water. When I was standing at the window, I saw someone in white in the backyard. I thought it was you doing some kind of spell, so I went out to stop you. But you went into the woods."

"Someone in white? White would represent someone you felt you could rely on. What happened next?"

"I followed you into the woods, but someone started chasing me." I opened my eyes and looked at Abby. "I can figure that one out on my own. Running means escape. I'd like to escape what's happening right now."

"Anything happen while you were running?"

"Just stumbling, panting, that kind of thing. No, wait, an owl hooted."

"Were you running toward the owl or away from it?"

"What difference does that make? I was running away from it."

Abby frowned. "That's not good. Running away from a hooting owl means disappointment, reversals."

"Abby, this is stupid," I said, and scrambled to my feet. "Do you know how ridiculous this all sounds? Hooting owls, white figures. I don't want to talk about this anymore."

I walked from the bathroom to my bedroom, intending to dress for work, but Abby had other ideas.

"Ophelia," she said from the doorway, "this is important. I need to know what happened in your dream."

"Oh, all right," I said, flopping on the bed. "In the dream, right before whoever was chasing me could catch me, I came to a gate. It wouldn't open. I struggled with it. My pursuer was right behind me. Then the gate opened. I fell. The next thing I knew, I was lying in the grass. Naked. And yes, I know what that represents, too. Vulnerability. I looked around and found myself in an old, abandoned cemetery. The stones were broken and toppled. And there was a huge rat sitting on top of one," I said, feeling goose bumps march up and down my spine.

"A rat? You poor thing," Abby said. "You've always been so terrified of them. Did you wake up then?"

"Yes, I think so. No, I heard a howl right before I started to scream, then I woke up."

Abby crossed over to the bed and sat beside me. She took both of my hands in hers.

"Ophelia, I want you to listen to me very carefully. I know what I'm about to say will be very hard for you to accept. Especially after what happened four years ago. You *are* in danger. This dream was a bad one. The symbol of the rat and the cemetery were bad signs. It meant danger, opposition, adversity. There wasn't any resolution at the end of the dream. It showed the end hasn't been determined yet. If you're going to win, you have to quit running from your past. Use what's been given to you."

"No." I jumped to my feet and looked down at her. "I'm not joining the 'family firm.' I refuse to practice magick. It's okay for you and the others in the family, but not me. I've chosen a different road. If I have to, I'll go to the sheriff, let them solve this whole mess."

Abby smiled. "And tell them what, dear? You had a bad dream and your grandmother told you there's a dead man somewhere near water? That the stranger in town, Rick Davis, makes you nervous?"

"Okay, so I can't go to the sheriff, but I can snoop around, ask some questions. If I find anything out, then I'll go to the police." Satisfied with myself, I walked to the closet and began rummaging for something to wear. Abby sat on the bed and watched me while I pulled a pair of linen pants and a sweater off the hangers.

"Who are you going to ask these questions? Rick Davis? Do you expect him to tell you the truth? Can you trust him?"

Not answering her question, I tossed my clothes on the bed. "I'm going to be late for work," I said, glancing in the dresser mirror. "I've got to do something about my face and get dressed. And I need more coffee. I know you're worried, but we'll talk about this later."

Abby got to her feet and placed both hands on my shoulders. "You're going to be fine, Ophelia," she said, and kissed my cheek. "I've got to get back to the greenhouse. If you need me, call."

"I will," I said, nodding.

With a quick squeeze, Abby left.

While I dressed, I thought about Abby's question. It was the second time in less than twenty-four hours someone had asked me if I trusted Rick Davis—it all came back to him. I'd start there, with Rick. I'd find out about him and what he was doing in Summerset. *How?* I asked myself, pulling on my pants. And the answer came to me: I'd open the conversation by thanking him for the tickets and gift certificate.

I grabbed the tickets off the top of the dresser and shoved them in my pocket.

I could handle it. I could be polite. As long as he didn't tease me. After thanking him for the tickets, I'd lead him around to talking about his "job." A rotten liar myself, I should be able to tell when someone else was lying, shouldn't I? Ned said I was observant, so how hard could it be?

After I'd finished getting ready, I marched into the kitchen, and the smell of fresh brewed coffee tickled my nose. Pouring a cup, I silently blessed Abby for making it before she left. I felt good, I decided, while I sipped my coffee. Better than I had in days. I had a plan, one that didn't include magick. If Abby were right and I had no choice, fine, then I'd be involved. It would, however, be on my terms.

My confidence was short-lived. My stomach knotted. And the taste of coffee turned bitter in my mouth. Dizziness swept over me when I saw it. The water glass was beside the sink just where I'd left it last night, in my dream.

# *Nine*

By the time I finally made it to work, my face looked like I had taken makeup lessons from a clown. My eyes were the worst, and no amount of makeup would help them. I resorted to wearing sunglasses. A little odd for November, but what the hell, I wasn't in the mood for curious looks. The water glass by the sink had shaken me. When I called Abby and asked her if she had used the glass, she said no. She used the coffeemaker and the two cups. Unwilling to start another discussion about magick, I let the subject drop. I would worry about what it meant later. There had to be a logical explanation.

My mind churned when I entered the library. I needed time to plan my strategy, but I wouldn't get it today. A pile of returned books sat neglected on the desk. Darci was in front of the self-help books, helping Nina Hoffman, who read at least two of those a month; in my opinion, with little result. I opened the first book and began the tedious job of checking it in.

"Umm—excuse me, Ophelia," a timid voice said.

I looked up from the book to see Nina and Darci standing there. Nina was pale and wan. I had understood what Adam meant when he described her as fragile. She looked like a wraith. Her pale blue eyes darted back and forth nervously, as if she were afraid.

"Nina, can I help you?"

"Umm, umm." Nina stared at the floor, not looking at me. "There's a new book out on self-esteem. Darci remembers a new self-esteem book coming in, but we can't find it."

"Do you know the name of the author?"

"No."

"What about the title?"

"No," Nina said, shifting her eyes to me and blinking rapidly. "But it was reviewed in the *Des Moines Sunday Register*. I'd know the title if I saw it."

"I'll have to look at the new listings on the computer in my office. Why don't you see if there's another book you might like while I check," I said, and headed for the stairs leading down to my office.

Darci took a step to follow me. "Ophelia, Rick—"

"Not now, Darci," I said, waving her off. "I'll be back in a minute."

I hurried down the stairs toward my office in the corner of the basement. Maybe after I found the book for Nina, I could hide out down there for the rest of the day. When I rounded the children's section, I saw the door to my office open. I heard a voice coming from my office.

"People I've met so far? Nice, friendly."

I stopped to listen. It was Rick. He was using my phone.

"No, I haven't made contact yet."

He paused.

"That's not good. It could mean trouble if they find out I'm here."

Who was he talking to?

"I've tried to blend in, and I don't think I've aroused any suspicion."

Ha. He'd aroused mine.

"No, I'll be careful."

Why did he need to be careful?

"Who? The librarian?"

Me? Why was he talking about me? I edged closer to the door.

"I don't know, but I don't think so. She's definitely smart enough."

Well, that was a boost to my ego.

"Yeah, but she isn't the type." Rick paused, listening to the other voice.

"Oh, she's sort of prissy, real tight-lipped. Likes to boss people around."

Prissy? Tight-lipped, huh? I guess the old adage might be true: People who eavesdrop seldom hear good of themselves.

Rick laughed. "Not her. Nothing about her is typical. I've never met anyone quite like her. And I can't decide how much she knows. What?" He stopped talking for a beat. "Nope, she won't go." He stopped again. "Hey, I tried, but it didn't work."

If I took another step, would I be close enough to see him? Would he be able to see me? I craned my neck and peered at the door while I tried to decide if I could get closer.

"She's kind of pretty, but you have to get past the prickly personality."

Pretty was nice, but prickly? I'd show him prickly.

"Right. She's a loner—doesn't seem to have many friends. There's definitely something going on with her. It's like she's afraid of something. It may take a while, but I'll figure it out."

I'd heard enough. I chewed on my bottom lip, thinking. What could I do? March in there, demand to know what he was doing in my office? If I did, he'd know I'd been listening. No, I'd be sneaky, just like him. One problem: I'm no better at being sneaky than I am at lying.

"Don't worry. Everything will be okay. As soon as I get what I need, I'm out of here. You just take care of things on your end." Rick paused. "Okay, 'bye."

Damn, any minute now he'd walk out the door and see me. I had to do something. I'd run back to the stairs and pretend to be coming down them. Unfortunately, my foot caught the book display. The books fell like dominoes, each one thumping into the next. The sound bounced off the basement walls. A second later Rick walked out of my office.

"Rick, I didn't know you were down here," I said, bending down to pick up the fallen books.

He walked toward me, wearing his boyish grin.

"Hi, Ophelia." He motioned toward the office. "Darci said it would be okay to use your phone. I had to check my voice mail and my cell phone's dead. I hope you don't mind."

Voice mail, my Aunt Fanny. You don't talk back to voice mail. While I picked up the books, I tried to gather my thoughts. Think, Ophelia, think. Try to be charming. When I stood, I felt the envelope in my pocket.

"I don't mind," I said, plastering a fake smile on my face. "And, Rick, thank you so much for the tickets. It was so very sweet of you."

"You're welcome," he said, looking perplexed.

"How are you this morning?" I asked, my voice overflowing with concern.

"Ah . . . fine. And you?" He eyed me suspiciously.

"Oh. Fine, fine," I said, while my mind scrambled for ways to charm him. Too bad charm isn't one of my skills. What was the plan? Oh yeah, get him to talk about his job. "Rick, I wanted to ask you—"

"By the way, nice sunglasses. Rough night out on the town last night?" he said, interrupting me.

"Oh, *whatever*," I replied, slamming the books on the table. Well, so much for the plan.

Rick laughed. "Ha. I knew it wouldn't last. Trying to be nice was killing you."

"I was being nice," I snapped. "It's all your fault if I failed. All you want to do is give me a hard time."

"My my, rather cross this morning, aren't we?"

"No. We aren't cross this morning, we just aren't in the mood for bullshit." The situation was impossible—I couldn't be in his company for more than a minute without his teasing getting to me. I gave up and turned to leave.

"Wait, I'm sorry. I always irritate you, don't I? I don't mean to. Can we start this conversation over?"

I paused, turning around. If I left, I wouldn't learn anything. "Okay, you go first."

He smiled again.

"Good morning, Ophelia. Thank you so much for allowing me to use your phone," he said politely. "You look lovely this morning—with your sunglasses and all that makeup. Going for the circus look?"

"That's it. It's impossible to have a civil conversation with you. You always have some smart remark. And why do you keep popping up everywhere? Why can't you just go away and leave me alone?"

"I don't want to go away. Believe it or not, Ophelia Jensen, I like you. Teasing you is the most fun I've had since I got here."

"Well, go someplace else for your fun. I don't exist for your amusement."

Rick stepped closer.

"You know when you get mad, you're very pretty?"

"Oh brother, what a line," I said, putting a hand on my hip. "Is that the best you can do?"

He took a half step. "Why don't you have dinner with me tonight and find out?"

The sarcastic reply died on my lips when I looked over and saw Darci and Nina at the bottom of the basement steps. Nina's mouth hung open and her pale blue eyes stared at my face without blinking. She reminded me of a cornered rabbit.

Rick stood inches away from me, smiling. My rudeness had no effect on him at all, and his confidence irritated me. I tried to stifle my reaction but failed. My control was slipping. I had to get away from him before I escalated to anger.

"No, I won't have dinner with you tonight," I said through clenched teeth.

I knew Nina and Darci were soaking in every word. This would be all over town before lunch. I had to end this before it got worse.

"I have work to do. If you need anything else, Darci can help you."

I headed for the stairs, but before I could move, Rick's hand closed over mine. The heat from his palm seemed to burn my skin. I couldn't bear it. The control I'd struggled to maintain slipped.

"Get away from me and leave me alone," I said, and twisted away from him. "I've made it very clear I want nothing to do with you. I think you're the most arrogant, self-absorbed jerk it has ever been my misfortune to meet. And, I'm tired of all your questions, all your jokes. Now, just go away."

Even as the words rushed out of my mouth, I knew I was overreacting again. But I couldn't stop them. Fear, worry, and mistrust ricocheted around in my brain, clouding my common sense.

I watched Rick's smile drop, driven away by my outburst. Nina and Darci were quiet, their eyes wide and their lips pressed in tight lines. The room was deadly silent, and my dignity lay shattered at my feet. I had to leave. They were all staring at me, and I couldn't stand it, their faces full of pity. *Poor Ophelia, she's lost it again.*

I pushed past Nina and Darci and ran up the stairs.

# Ten

The car tires sprayed gravel when I whipped into Abby's driveway. I'd made up my mind. We were both leaving town until this whole thing was finished. And she was coming with me, whether she liked it or not. I wasn't going to let Rick Davis's snooping ruin Abby's life.

"Abby? Abby? Where are you?" I called, my voice echoing through her large farmhouse.

"Ophelia, whatever is the matter?" Abby said, coming from the kitchen.

She had on a dark red cowled robe, and the faint aroma of simmering clove drifted from the kitchen.

Terrific. She'd been stirring up a little something in the kitchen. Hmm, red robe, cloves—she'd been doing a spell for safety. As if some stupid spell would protect us. I had a better idea.

"Come on, go pack. We're going to visit Aunt Rose in Cedar Rapids for a while."

"What's happened now?" she asked as I rushed by her.

"Nothing much, just made a fool of myself in front of several people. Now, I'm getting the hell out of Dodge, before it happens again," I said from the bottom of the stairs. "And you're coming with me. Rick Davis is asking too many questions about us." I glanced at Abby over my shoulder.

She wasn't moving. She stood with her feet planted slightly apart, her arms crossed over her chest. "Don't be silly. We're not going anywhere," she said.

I glared at her. "The hell we're not." I grabbed the banister and started running up the stairs.

"*Ophelia.*" The tone of her voice stopped me dead. "You stop your swearing and listen to me."

Abby hadn't used that tone of voice with me since I was six years old. I turned to look at her.

"I tried to explain to you this morning, you have no choice. You have to stay and see this through."

"Oh, yeah. Who says?"

"Quit being childish. You know the answer to that."

"Oh, of course, it's my fate, right? Just like it was my fate four years ago. Only four years ago, things didn't go very well, did they? I wasn't able to change anything, was I?"

I sat down on the step. She joined me.

"Abby, you know what happened to me, don't ask me to do it again. I've worked hard to straighten out my life, put the past behind me. But now it's starting all over again—the dreams, a dead man. I've had two fits of nerves in the past few days. I don't want to lose control again. Not when I finally have my life pulled together."

I bowed my head, staring at the pattern on the stair runner.

"Ophelia," Abby said gently, "you haven't pulled your life together. You've shut down and dropped out of life. Whatever happened to the girl who was bright as a new penny? The one who loved life, loved being with people?"

I lifted my head to look at her. "She was an ignorant child who thought life was a game, until she lost the game and reality slapped her in the face. Too bad someone had to die to teach her that lesson." I didn't feel the tears on my face until Abby reached over and brushed them away.

"I've told you, Brian's death wasn't your fault, Ophelia."

"Tell that to Brian's family." I clenched my fists. "I'm damn well not going to do it again. I won't. I don't care if it's fate, cosmic justice, or whatever else you want to call it. And you can't make me. I'm leaving." I stood and hurried down the stairs.

"Ophelia Mette Marie Jensen, you stop your whining this instant."

I looked up at Abby, who stood on the stairs, her face angry and stern.

"Whether you like it or not, you're one of the chosen. It's time for you to stop running and deal with it. You were not raised to be a coward, and I expect you to stop acting like one."

She walked down and past me then, her head held high, leaving me alone and ashamed.

After leaving Abby's, it took me fifteen minutes to reach Roseman State Park. It was one of my favorite places in the world. I spent a lot of my childhood roaming those woods with Abby, looking for wildflowers—Dutchman's-breeches, sweet william, and bloodroot. She taught me plants had the power to help, or to harm. Nettles would blister the skin when touched, but inhaling smoke from the dried, burning leaves helped bronchitis. Foxglove could stabilize an irregular heartbeat, but too much would cause the heart to stop. There'd be no plants in the woods today. Only dead, wet leaves scattered about. Abby's wildflowers were asleep now, waiting for spring. I envied them.

I parked my car and headed into the woods. The air smelled cold and clean, and it felt good against my flushed face. I had to stop my life from spinning out of control. But how? Abby's spells hadn't helped me four years ago. All the magick in the world hadn't saved Brian.

Brian . . . he would've loved a day like today—fall was his favorite time of year. I could see him striding across the campus, his plain face animated while he talked to his students. He enjoyed life so much. It wasn't fair it ended so soon. No matter what reason Abby gave me—fate, karma, whatever—it was all bullshit. I would never accept his death. Brian was my best friend, and he had been murdered. When the murder was never solved, I lost all faith in Abby's cosmic justice, in Abby's magick.

My dark thoughts were interrupted by the snap of a twig behind me. I spun around to see Rick standing there.

"What are you doing here?"

"Darci and I saw you fly by the library in your car. She was worried and asked me to find you, so I followed you here," he said, trying to read me. "Why are you so upset?"

"You. I'm upset with you." I picked up a twig and broke it. "Boy, you're hard-headed. Don't you get it, Davis? I'm tired of this game you're playing and I don't want anything to do with you."

"It's not a game. I like you," he said. "You're such an easy mark, and I never know how you're going to react to my jokes. It keeps me off balance. And that's a new experience for me." He scuffed the leaves at his feet with the toe of his boot. "I'd like to be your friend, Ophelia. That's all, just a friend. I don't think I've ever met anyone who needs one more."

"No thanks," I said stubbornly. "Now go away, and this time permanently."

"You know, I'm going to start thinking you don't like me if you keep this up," he said, smiling.

"You'd be right, I don't like you."

"Sure you do. Everybody likes me. I'm a likable kind of guy," he said, still smiling.

"Ha! I don't know who told you that, but they were lying," I said, putting my hand on my hip and glaring at him.

His teasing wasn't going to work. I was mad, and I intended to stay mad. It was safe being mad. And I wore the feeling like a cloak, protecting me from other feelings I didn't want to think about.

Rick studied me for a moment, his smile slowly fading. "Yeah, well, I know a lot of liars. Even though I like you, I happen to think you're one of them. But I can't figure out what it is you're lying about. And why you're so afraid of people."

I moved two steps away from him. "I'm not afraid of people, and you're crowding me."

"Okay, okay." Rick held up his hands in mock surrender and took a few steps back, increasing the distance between us. "I know by now you don't like to be crowded. Look, can't we have a normal conversation?"

"One that involves you asking a lot of questions, no doubt," I said sarcastically.

"I've told you before, I'm curious. Also, I like solving puzzles, and you're a puzzle, Ophelia Jensen."

"I don't understand what gave you that idea. I'm not a puzzle. What you see is what you get."

"And which Ophelia is that—the prim and proper librarian, or the screaming shrew who swears—or is it someone in between?" Rick smiled. "Would the real Ophelia Jensen please stand up?"

I turned to leave. "You know, you aren't nearly as funny as you think you are."

"Oh, come on. Lighten up. Talk to me. Please."

I stopped with my back toward him. "What is it you want to talk about?"

I could hear the muted footsteps on the wet leaves when Rick came forward, but he stopped before he came too close.

"You know, normal things. Tell me about your life, what it's like living in a small town, and I'll tell you about my life. Stuff like that. I promise I won't pry into any secrets."

Could I believe him? Could I find out some of his secrets and still keep mine? If I could, it might help me.

I turned around and rolled my shoulders, trying to relax. "Okay, what do you want to know?"

Rick laughed. "That's one of the things I like about you, Ophelia, you don't beat around the bush. Okay, I know your parents are retired professors and you grew up in Iowa City. Do you have any brothers and sisters?"

"Only child. Do you mind if we walk while we're doing this? It helps me think."

He laughed again. "You need to think about your answers? Why? Afraid you'll tell me too much?"

I shrugged. "I'm not very good at small talk. I'm a little out of practice."

"It doesn't surprise me. I had you figured for a loner. But it's okay, I like being alone sometimes, too."

Unbelievable—Rick Davis alone? In the short time I'd known him, he seemed to thrive on being with people. The feeling was mutual. People were drawn to him. Ned appeared to be the only other person in town who questioned why he was here.

"I doubt it," I said.

"Doubt what? That I like being alone sometimes? I do, even though I come from a large family."

"I don't believe you. You're too comfortable around people to be the type of person who enjoys being alone. I've seen you in action, remember? I've witnessed you worming your way into the town's good graces. Everyone thinks you're wonderful."

"Including you?"

An unladylike snort slipped out before I could stop it.

"Well, that answers that question."

Rick stopped and turned toward me. He stood there, his hands in his pockets. His eyes were full of humor. Self-confidence hung around him like an aura.

It almost made me jealous. I couldn't imagine what it would be like to be that comfortable in your own skin, to accept who and what you are without question. I kicked at the wet leaves in front of me while I walked away, mumbling to myself.

"Yeah, and I bet you were voted Most Popular when you were in school, too."

Rick had followed me, and now his laughter echoed in the empty woods. "I heard you, and yes, I was. It annoys you, doesn't it?"

"Don't be silly," I said as he caught up. "Why should it annoy me? Those are empty titles. The Most Likely to Succeed from my class is on welfare now and has six kids. Didn't exactly become the ball of fire everyone expected."

"Okay, tell me the truth. What is it about me that

pisses you off so much? You've already told me I'm an arrogant self-absorbed jerk. Anything else?"

"The list is endless."

Rick looked down at the ground and shook his head.

"You're determined not to like me, aren't you? I've never met anyone who resists friendship as much as you do. Why is it? What happened? Did someone hurt you, let you down, disappoint you?"

He was getting too close to the truth. If he learned about Brian, he would figure the rest out. The whole ugly story was in the police report at Iowa City and in the old newspapers. Thanks to that snoopy journalist, anyone could read about the murder in the papers, and the part I had played in the investigation. I tensed.

"I thought you weren't going to pry?" I said.

"All right, I won't pry. You don't have to tell me anything you don't want to. But that does seem to cover a lot of subjects. What *is* safe for us to talk about?"

The conversation was going around in circles. I lost my temper. Again.

I whipped around to face him. "I don't understand any of this, Mr. Rick Davis. Just who are you, anyway? You blow into town and ask a lot of questions—not normal behavior for a chemical salesman. Oh, you're smooth enough to be a salesman, but I don't believe you are. Who are you and what are you doing here? Maybe if you tell me the truth, I'll answer some of your questions."

Of course, it was a bluff. I had no intention of telling him anything.

He had stopped walking and stood staring at the trees. It was his turn to be uncomfortable. I could see by his expression that he was struggling to think of an answer. For once, I felt I had the advantage. My tension eased. Maybe I could do this, after all. I tilted my head back to look at the sky, trying to think of a way to press my advantage. Buzzards were making lazy circles in the air above me. Rick saw them, too.

"What are those?" he asked.

"Turkey buzzards. Means there's something dead nearby."

Dead, oh no, Abby's vision. I started running across the packed leaves, toward the river.

"Ophelia, where're you going?" Rick called out behind me.

I skidded to a halt when I saw the body. The buzzards, startled at my sudden approach, took flight. The bile rose in my throat at the sight before me. I fought to keep it down. A man lay faceup on the damp leaves. His eyeless sockets stared at the cloudless sky. Even from where I stood, I could tell he'd been there a few days. The buzzards hadn't been the only ones to find him. Bones protruded through the raw, puffed-up flesh where the coyotes, wolves, and other carnivores had been at him.

And the smell. Oh, Lord. The smell. Since the surprise snowstorm, the temperature had been above freezing, and now the stench of a rotting body was thick and cloying. Every breath I took drew the stink inside my lungs. I could almost taste it in my mouth. My stomach heaved, and grabbing the nearest tree, I vomited.

When I raised my head, Rick was nearby, his face blanched. He walked toward me as I stood doubled over, leaning against the tree and hugging my rebellious stomach.

"Stop." I held up one hand, afraid if he touched me, I'd lose the battle with my stomach and wretch again.

"Ophelia——"

"No, I'm okay. Give me a minute." I slowly uncurled my body, still gripping my sides.

"Do you know him?" Rick asked almost hesitantly.

"I don't think so, but I don't intend to get close enough to find out. We need to notify the sheriff. My cell phone is in the car."

I took one step away from the tree when the world tilted and darkness descended.

# *Eleven*

I floated in darkness that washed around my body like warm water. From a great distance I heard a shuffling noise. It stopped when strong, gentle hands picked me up. They were hot and they clutched at me. I felt their heat traveling over my body. Ripples of it drifted over my skin, warmer than a hot breeze. My flesh seemed to absorb the heat through every pore until it not only covered me, but was inside me as well—just below the surface. It flowed through my body, touching each nerve along its way. My muscles melted like chocolate left in the sun. Somewhere, in the corner of my mind, I wondered if I might be dying—would the warmth stop my heart from beating? I didn't care. It felt so good—I would die happy, here on the waves of soft, dark heat.

The waves tumbled about me, but I was anchored by the hands that held me. Their pace was sometimes fast, sometimes slow—-sometimes rough, sometimes smooth. The heat expanded and contracted around me. The breath would whoosh from my lungs when it squeezed, only to rush back in when the grip of heat relaxed. It seemed to toss me about like a cork, only to change and caress my skin with a whisper. I wanted it to go on forever, but too soon the ebb and flow of heat stopped.

An abrupt noise pierced my warmth and darkness. I tried to shut it out, but it kept pulling at me, pulling me away from the darkness where I floated. I didn't want to leave, but the sound wrapped around my mind and tugged. Other harsh sounds pressed against the edges of my mind. There were too many, and I couldn't shut them out. Hands, no longer gentle, tapped at my face. They were cold, and they chased the last of the warmth away.

"Ophelia! Wake up!"

I scrunched my eyelids tight, refusing to open them. I fought to return to the darkness, to sink once again into the heat. It was gone. I opened my eyes and found Rick kneeling next to me, his face inches from mine. I jerked upright and, in the process, bumped heads with him.

"Jeez, Ophelia, you've got a hard head," Rick said while he rubbed his forehead with the heel of his hand. "Are you all right?"

"Yeah-yeah." I scooted backward like a crab across the hard ground.

"Sorry, but you'd better let me check you out," a voice to my right said.

It was then that I noticed the medical examiner's car parked next to mine, the sheriff's car on the other side. The ambulance was some distance away. I remembered what we'd found and my stomach threatened to revolt again. I put my head between my knees and drew in great, gasping gulps of air.

"Lord, you're not going to faint again, are you?" Rick asked.

I raised my head and gave him a hard stare.

"Of course not, I never faint."

"That's funny. What do you call what happened in the woods? I had to carry you all the way back. You were dead weight, too."

His tone of voice was light, but he repeatedly ran his fingers through his hair till it stuck out in tufts. His expression was puzzled. "And you made these strange snuffling noises."

I felt the blush spread over my face like a red stain. The EMT on my right saved me from explaining.

"I need to check her out now, sir. I think Bill wants to talk to you."

"The sheriff will have to wait," Rick said. "I'm not leaving until you make sure she's all right. It's not normal to be unconscious for such a long time."

Normal? What around here was normal anymore? During the last few days, it was as if I'd been transported to the middle of some really bad movie.

Rick's face was still white; his dark brown eyes looked like a pair of shiny marbles. Was the cause concern for me, or the awful sight we had seen down by the river?

"Don't worry, sir. I'll take good care of her. We go way back, don't we, Ophelia? She was my babysitter when I was a kid."

I looked up at Jerry, the EMT, and gave him a weak smile. This was humiliating. I had babysat for his parents when I was fourteen and visiting Abby for the summer. He had been an ornery little devil and tormented me relentlessly. And he was going to examine *me*? What next? Abby riding in on a white charger and telling the sheriff she knew all about the dead man?

"Go on, Rick," I said, "go talk to Bill. I told you I'm fine."

Rick frowned at me, but at least he walked away, over to where Bill stood talking to one of the deputies.

I turned my attention to Jerry.

"You're not going to put a worm down my shirt or anything, are you, Jerry?" I said, shifting uncomfortably on the ground.

He laughed. "Come on, I was only seven. I've changed."

I lowered my head and tried to block Jerry touching me from my mind while he took my blood pressure. After he pronounced me well, I stood, ignoring the hand extended to help me to my feet. Somehow, on unsteady legs, I managed to join Rick and Bill.

"You stopped at the line of trees and didn't approach the body?" Bill asked.

"That's right." Rick's eyes darted away from Bill's face.

"Good, maybe the crime scene is still intact. If we're lucky, we might get a shoe print, but I doubt it. The leaves are packed hard. How are you feeling, Ophelia?"

I wished everyone would stop asking me that question. I was getting tired of telling them I was fine. "I'm fine, Bill. Do you know who the man is yet?"

"No. No ID on the body. His one hand is chewed up pretty bad, but we might be able to get a set of prints off the other one. Have to wait and see. Since you were here before Mr. Davis, Ophelia, did you see any strange cars or anything unusual?"

"Sorry, nothing out of the ordinary."

"Okay. I don't have any more questions. Mr. Davis answered everything I have for now. You two can leave, but if I think of something else, I'll call. Where did you say you're staying, Mr. Davis?"

"The bed and breakfast."

"Georgia's place? My deputy spends a lot of time there, so if I have any more questions, Alan will be around to ask them."

He glanced toward the woods, his attention captured by two deputies carrying a body bag followed by the medical examiner. I turned away from them. I didn't want to think about what was in the bag. The best place for me was home, with the doors locked and the phone off the hook.

I walked to my car and left Rick rooted to the spot, staring intently at the men carrying their gruesome load. He didn't notice I was gone.

First, it was Abby. So much for locking my doors and taking the phone off the hook. A moat and drawbridge wouldn't have kept her out.

"Are you all right, Ophelia?" she said, wrapping her arms tightly around me.

"Yes." I looked Abby straight in the eye. "It would've been nice if you'd have warned me about this, though."

Abby released me and strode into the kitchen. I had no choice but to follow her. She walked to the table and sat down.

Eyeing her cautiously, I joined her.

"Any more little surprises? More dead bodies? Another bad dream? Mysterious strangers? No, let me guess, those images are vague, too," I said, shaking my head.

"This will help; give me your hands," Abby said, and reached across the table.

Before she could touch me, I pulled my hands back and tucked them under my legs. "Uh-uh, no you don't. Not going to do it, no way."

"Come on, don't be such a baby," she said, wiggling her fingers. "You know it doesn't hurt."

"I don't like my psyche poked and prodded."

"I'll get a clearer picture of what happened to you today."

"I was passed out most of the time," I said, and lifted an eyebrow. "So there isn't any picture for you to see."

"That's not true. Even when we're unconscious, the mind continues to receive energy and impressions from what's going on around us. It will help." Abby's hands were still outstretched.

"You're not going to give up, are you?" I asked. When she didn't answer me, I reluctantly placed my hands in hers. "This is—"

"Shh, I need to concentrate."

Abby turned my hands so they lay palms up in hers. Her eyelids drifted shut while she used her thumbs to stroke the center of my palms. It had a hypnotic effect. My mind became sluggish and dull. My eyes closed. Images of the riverbank passed through my mind as if on a movie screen, but without any of the sickening horror. The same dim rustling sound I had heard after passing out came back to me. It was followed by soft thudding footsteps. I sank deeper into my mind. All I felt was the rhythmic stroking of my palms.

When I opened my eyes, it took me a minute to get my bearings. Abby watched me with a funny look on her face.

"Interesting. It's nice to know you haven't repressed everything."

Wonderful, my seventy-three-year-old grandmother now knew what I'd felt while Rick was carrying me. Abby ignored my embarrassment.

"You didn't touch the body or any personal belongings of the dead man's?"

"My God, no. You saw in my mind what the body looked like."

"Too bad, I might've been able to pick more up if you had. Oh well, when I meet Rick Davis, I'll see what I get from him. He touched the body."

"What do you mean?"

"I mean, he touched the body. Searched the dead man's pockets while you were passed out and lying by the tree. I told you the subconscious continues to register information, even though we're not aware of it. It was the shuffling sound you heard."

"Gross," I said, making a face.

"Yes, it was, rather. I'd really like to get my hands on whatever it was that young man took from the jacket pocket. Personal items always carry so much energy."

"You're kidding, right? Rick couldn't have removed something from the body. That's illegal."

"I've got a feeling this Rick isn't overly concerned about legalities. I really need to meet him." Abby stood to leave. "I'm going home and concentrate on this, maybe I'll see something else." She settled her jacket around her shoulders and walked to the door.

I stumbled behind her, shocked at what she told me about Rick. I needed a dose of sarcasm to get my equilibrium back.

"Sometimes, Abby, I think you missed your calling. You should've run away when you were a kid and joined the circus. You could've spent every day telling people stuff they didn't want to hear." I looked at Abby and gave her a smart-ass grin.

Abby gently patted my face. "But then I'd have missed having a granddaughter like you, dear."

Abby sailed out the door and down the sidewalk.

One last parting shot. "Going to use a crystal ball, are you?"

She turned. "No, a circle of salt and a candle work just as well. Oh, look. Here comes Darci. Have fun, Ophelia."

# Twelve

It sucked—all the attention. If it weren't for Abby calling me a coward, I'd run away and join the circus myself. Madame Ophelia, she sees all, knows all. It could work. I could pull it off. Maybe.

Darci approached the house holding a big basket of fruit and a potted mum. Great, now I had to be sociable. The strain would probably kill me. I thought the plant and the basket of fruit were over the top. Those were usually reserved for a serious illness or when a death occurred in the family. I wasn't sick, and I certainly wasn't dead. It was the poor guy on the riverbank who was dead.

"Darci, what are you doing here? And who's running the library?"

"Claire is taking care of things. After I heard what happened, I had to come by and see how you were."

"It's all over town?"

"Of course it is. Something like this hasn't happened in Summerset since the Hart boy went crazy and shot Ed Barns. Ed lived, so this is much worse. It'll keep the liars' club going for weeks." She shoved the basket of fruit into my arms.

The liars' club met every morning and afternoon at Joe's for coffee. All the retired men in town belonged and the gossip flowed faster than the coffee. What an honor, I was going to be the prime topic of discussion. I felt like beating my head against the door.

Darci stood waiting for me in the hallway.

"This is really nice," she said, looking around. "I don't think I've ever been here before."

She hadn't—we'd worked together almost four years and I'd never invited her. Never wanted to invite her. This was my home, and I've never liked intruders. In the past few days too many people had invaded my private world. I hated it.

"I'll put this plant in the kitchen. Is it back here?" Darci waved her hand toward the back of the house.

I nodded and followed her down the hall to the kitchen. When I reached the doorway, she had already placed the plant on the table and was turning it this way and that, checking which side looked the best.

She turned and smiled. "Doesn't it look great? Matches your kitchen perfectly."

"Really, Darci, this wasn't necessary. I'm not sick. I had a bit of a shock, that's all." I set the fruit on the counter.

She shivered. "A shock? I'd say it was more than a shock. They said you were unconscious for a long time."

Oh yes, the mysterious "they." Summerset was full of "theys," but no one ever knew exactly who "they" were. My life wouldn't be worth living till "they" quit talking about the dead body.

"I'm fine."

"Can I make you some tea or something? You know, you should be resting. Why don't you go lie down while I make you some hot tea?"

"Darci, listen, I said I was fine." My jaw clenched to stop my teeth from grinding. "Go back to the library. And if anyone else tells you they're coming to visit, tell them not to bother. I don't want any visitors."

How much more direct could I be?

"Oh, I'm the only one. No one else is coming." Darci walked to the first cupboard and opened the door. She carefully placed two cups on the counter. I watched in amazement. She hadn't heard a word I'd said. Talking to her was like spitting into the wind— the words blew right back in your face. Nothing penetrated her peroxided head. I tried one more time.

"Good, I don't want the whole town parading through my house with fruit baskets and plants. I'd rather be left alone."

"Don't worry, they won't come. You intimidate them."

My eyebrows shot up. "I do?"

Darci saw my look of surprise and grinned. "Yeah, but not me. Which cupboard did you say the tea is in?" She opened another cupboard door.

"For curiosity's sake, why don't I?"

"Why don't you what?"

"Try and stay with me here, Darce. Why don't I intimidate you?" I spoke slowly, enunciating each word, as if speaking to a toddler.

"Silly, I know what a nice person you really are."

"I am not." I glared at her. Over the past four years, I've worked hard at maintaining a cranky image. It kept people away from me, and now Darci was trying to slip past that image.

"Yes, you are. Look at what you did for old Mrs. Walters when she broke her hip. You visited her every day and read to her."

"I was sucking up. I thought she was going to croak and leave all her money to the library. But she didn't, she got well."

"Oh, you were not. You're teasing. How about when you helped Mickey Dahl with his science fair project?"

"The kid was a pest, didn't know how to do research or experiments. Only experiment his folks ever do is count how many beers they can drink before they pass out. I helped him so he'd quit hanging out at the library."

"Oh, and when he won, that's why you put his picture from the newspaper on the bulletin board." Darci shook her head. "Deep inside, you're a nice person. You only act this way because you're lonely. You need a friend."

What was this? Why were all these people analyzing my character? First Ned, then Rick, now Darci—it was downright annoying.

My annoyance got the better of me and I gave Darci an icy stare. "You'll excuse me if I don't break into a rendition of 'You Gotta Have Friends.'"

Darci's lips trembled and tears sparkled in her eyes. Oh God, I wasn't nice. I was mean and nasty. And I felt as if I'd just kicked a puppy. Crossing the space between us, I almost reached out and touched her shoulder, but I stopped myself in time.

"I'm sorry. I'm really sorry. I didn't mean to insult you. I've been under a lot of stress lately. And sometimes I say things without thinking."

Darci sniffed and gave me a weak smile. "It's okay. Dad says I let my feelings get hurt too easy. If I were you, I'd be grouchy, too. All this stuff is happening to you, Rick Davis asking questions about you, finding a dead body. You're in the middle of things I don't understand. What does Abby say about this?"

I frowned. "What do you mean?"

"Well, since she's a clairvoyant and a witch and all. I thought she'd be the one to help you."

I caught the chair to stop my slow slide to the floor.

"That's it, breathe deep," Darci said, while her hand rubbed the spot between my shoulder blades. "You'll be okay."

I stared off into space. Nothing registered in my brain. I didn't even try and avoid her touching me. A chant reverberated in my mind. *She knows, she knows, she knows.* What do I do now?

"Let me make you some tea. Okay?"

"O-Okay."

Darci crossed to the cupboard by the stove. "Which one?"

"On the left."

My wits were jumbled and I couldn't string more than three words together. We were always so careful about Abby's secret. How in the world did Darci, of all people, figure it out? I watched her while she made the tea. Darci, with her tight jeans, tight sweaters, and cotton candy hair. The original good-time girl, the town crier. If she knew, how long would it be before others knew? This was too much for my mind to process.

Darci placed the tea in front of me.

"Here, drink this. You'll feel better."

The hot tea warmed the cold spot deep in my gut.

"Abby's secret is safe with me. I've known for a long time, and I would never tell. I think Abby's awesome, and I'd never do anything to hurt her. You can trust me."

My eyes narrowed when I looked at Darci standing there. Could I trust her? The last person I trusted was

Brian, and he died. Abby was the only one I trusted now. Darci squirmed under my scrutiny.

She sat down. "I mean it. You can trust me."

"How did you know? You're not—"

"Involved with witchcraft? In a coven? No."

"Abby doesn't belong to a coven," I said quickly.

"I know, she does folk magick. She would be called a wise woman or a shaman in some parts of the world."

"How do you know all this?"

"About shamans and folk magick? I read a lot."

I must have looked skeptical.

"Well, I do," she said defensively. "I'm disappointed in you, Ophelia. All most people see is the blond hair and big boobs in a tight sweater, especially guys. They don't see past the way I look, like they don't see past the way you act. They automatically assume I'm stupid. I thought you were different. I may like to laugh and have a good time, but it doesn't make me dumb."

"You're right, it doesn't," I said, nodding.

I was the stupid one. I'd worked with Darci for almost four years and never given her much thought. I'd been so wrapped up in my own world, my own pain. How many other things had I missed?

"So tell me, how did you find out about Abby?" I asked, leaning back in my chair.

Darci tossed her head. "I always knew there was something special about Abby, even when I was little. She is so in tune with the world around her. And there's her knowledge of herbs. Everyone knows she has a green thumb. Anyway, I was reading this book about Appalachia one day. It talked about wise women and how they used natural remedies to cure illness, how many of them were considered to be clairvoyant. Then it hit me. Abby's one of them—a witch."

"I'd better get rid of that book. Someone else might figure it out."

Darci smiled. "They won't. Everyone sees Abby as this sweet, little old lady who's a great gardener, and that's it. No one around here will question it." She paused and frowned. "But Rick Davis might. He sure is asking a lot of questions, especially about you. I tried playing dumb to see what he'd tell me, but it didn't work."

"You play dumb on purpose?"

"Sure." Darci's face lit up. "You'd be surprised what you can find out that way, plus guys fall all over themselves to help you out. Why, I haven't raked the leaves in my yard or had to change the oil in my car for five years."

"You little manipulator," I said with a big grin.

She shrugged. "So? If they can't take the time to see the real me, I figure they got it coming."

I didn't know what to say. It seemed Abby and I weren't the only ones with secrets. Darci had her share, too.

"Another thing, I pretend not to pay attention. Like earlier, I knew you didn't want me here; you were trying to get rid of me. I heard every word you said, but I knew if I acted like I didn't, you'd give up and let me stay. I really wanted to stay. I like you and I've been worried about you. You've acted so strange lately." Darci leaned forward.

This was bizarre. Darci and I sitting at my kitchen table having a heart-to-heart. My life was taking so many unexpected turns, and I couldn't keep up with them.

"I'd like for us to be friends."

Before I could answer, the sound of a vehicle backfiring outside caught our attention. We went to the living room window and looked out. Benny Jenkins sat in my driveway in his old rattletrap of a truck. I'd forgotten I'd asked him to come by and fix the shingles on the garage roof. I couldn't deal with this now.

Darci read the expression on my face.

"You go upstairs and rest. I'll take care of Benny. He'll do whatever work you wanted, plus anything else I think needs to be done. And I guarantee, it'll be free." With a wink, she sauntered out the door to befuddle poor Benny.

Life is full of surprises.

# *Thirteen*

When Darci said I intimidated people, she shouldn't have included little old ladies. They're not only snoopy, but bloodthirsty, too. Give them all the details and make sure to include the gore. They showed up at the library all week, alone, in pairs, dressed in sensible shoes and polyester pantsuits—all wanting information about the dead body. First they tried softening me up with brownies and cookies. I think they thought if I was on a sugar high, I'd talk. When it didn't work, they became assertive. A top prosecutor couldn't have grilled a witness any better than they grilled me.

Edna Walters and Viola Simpson caught me putting away books in the reference section.

"Ophelia, how are you?"

"Fine, Mrs. Walters, and you?"

"Well, my hip bothers me some when the weather changes, but . . ." She paused. ". . . I'm more concerned about you. I heard about the shock you had. It must have been awful for you."

Mrs. Simpson stepped forward. "Yes, dear. Imagine coming across something like that. No wonder you fainted. Did you get a good look at the dead man before you passed out?" The blue highlights in her silver hair glinted under the fluorescent light.

I looked at Mrs. Simpson. "Well—"

"Do you know how he died?" Mrs. Walters interrupted, her double chins quivering from excitement.

I turned to Mrs. Walters. They were tag-teaming me like a couple of wrestlers in a "wrassling" match—*over to you, Edna*. Why weren't they zeroing in on Rick Davis? Oh, that's right, Rick had disappeared—not as in vanished, but he was keeping out of sight. I hadn't seen him all week. At times I almost missed him.

"Is it true there wasn't much left of the man's face?" Mrs. Simpson asked.

I got dizzy, pivoting my head back and forth between them. I had to end this.

"Really, ladies, I don't think Bill wants me to talk about it. There is an ongoing investigation, you know." I tried to return to putting the books back, but they weren't ready to give up.

"But, Ophelia, so many rumors are circulating. If Edna and I knew the facts, we could set the story straight," Mrs. Simpson said.

Yeah, right. By the time the two of them got done embellishing the "facts," whatever I told them would be unrecognizable.

"We brought you some brownies?" Mrs. Walters said hopefully.

"I'm sorry, Mrs. Walters, Mrs. Simpson, but I simply can't talk about it."

Momentarily defeated, they wandered off to plan the next phase of their attack.

I'd finished putting the books away and intended to go hide in my office when Bill showed up.

"Ophelia, got a minute?"

"Sure, Bill. Why don't we go downstairs and talk in my office. That way no one will see or hear us talking."

Bill laughed. "They giving you a hard time?"

"Put it this way—I don't think the library has had this much traffic since Mr. Carroll wanted to ban the latest Nora Roberts book for being too smutty. After he lambasted the book, everyone wanted to check it out—for educational purposes, of course."

Once in my office, Bill got right to the point. "Have you remembered anything else?"

"No, I'm sorry, I haven't."

"That's what I was afraid of." Bill sighed. "I was hoping maybe you remembered seeing something. We don't have a shred of physical evidence. No footprints, no tire tracks, not even the weapon that struck the guy in the head."

"Is that how he died?"

"I suppose it won't hurt to tell you, since some guy in the medical examiner's office has already shot his mouth off about how the guy died. And your alibi is solid. Based on the decomposition of the body, the medical examiner said he'd been dead about a week before you and Davis found him. Murder probably happened on Saturday. You were seen that night having dinner at Joe's with Abby."

Surprise ripped through me. I picked up a pencil and tapped it on my desk.

"We had to check both you and Davis out. This isn't the first time you've been involved in a murder."

Of course, since he was the sheriff, Bill would know about Brian.

"But that doesn't have anything to do with this," I said. I didn't like the idea of my life being scrutinized. I tapped faster.

"I know. Look, I don't want to offend you, but we can't overlook anything."

"Okay, but I don't like being reminded of four years ago," I said. "Did Rick have an alibi?"

"Yes. Why do you ask?"

"Just curious."

"Davis was seen at Stumpy's till closing that night."

"So how did the man die?"

"Drowned."

I stopped tapping. "Drowned? But he was lying away from the river, on the bank."

"Yeah, he received a blow to the back of the head, not hard enough to kill him, just to knock him out. The medical examiner thinks the murderer dragged him down the bank and held his head under the water till he drowned. There's bruising on the back of the neck. The body was pulled back up the bank and left for the animals to find." Bill frowned. "Whoever did this is one mean sonofabitch."

Bill had given me way too much information, and it made my stomach turn. "Do you know who the man was?"

"No. We were able to get partial prints from one hand, and we're waiting for them to come back. Listen, I got to go. Didn't think you'd remember anything else, but it never hurts to ask. I'll talk to you later." Bill stood to leave. "One more thing. How well do you know Davis?"

"Not very." I frowned. Did he know something about Rick? Watching him, I searched Bill's face for a clue, a reason for his question, but saw nothing. "Why?"

He shrugged carelessly. "No reason, just wondering. He seems to spend a lot of time here."

After Bill left, I sat at my desk in a daze. Who could

be so cold as to knock someone out and then drown them? And why? Darci stuck her head in the door.

"I think it would be a good idea if you spent the rest of the day somewhere else. Mr. Carroll and Mrs. Anderson have joined Mrs. Walters and Mrs. Simpson. They're pretending to check the shelves for new books, but I know they're waiting for you so they can jump you."

"Great. I doubt I'd make it to the door."

"Don't worry, I'll run interference for you. I'll ask Mr. Carroll if he's read the new Sandra Brown book— he hates her almost as much as Nora Roberts. That'll be good for a five minute tirade, at least. The ladies won't want to miss out on that. You can slip out the back door."

Darci had been a mother hen all week. She had tried her best to keep the little old ladies away from me. Now she was more of an expert on their ailments than their doctors.

I grabbed my stuff and bailed, leaving Darci to the mercy of Mrs. Walters and Mrs. Simpson.

Walking relieves stress, but I didn't like the idea of walking in the state park anymore. So instead I thought I'd go to the woods behind Abby's. They were peaceful, and I knew them like the back of my hand.

I went home and threw on some old clothes. I thought about taking Lady for company, but pheasant season had started. Abby had No Trespassing signs posted, but you never know. I didn't trust some of the city boys who trespassed in her woods to know the difference between a dog and a bird. Some of them would shoot at any animal that moved. I grabbed a bright orange sweatshirt and was off.

I parked my car in Abby's driveway and headed for the woods behind her house. Abby was nowhere to be seen, and I didn't try to find her.

The woods stretched for several miles. When Grandpa and Abby moved here fifty-three years ago and bought this place, Abby said she put an ancient spell on the woods to protect the wildlife from hunters. By the time I was a teenager, local legend had it that the woods were haunted. But according to Abby, it was her spell.

Did I believe it? I don't know. I did know the woods were full of deer, squirrels, and birds. You could hear the chattering of the squirrels, the rustling of the animals while they foraged under the trees, and the birds singing—until a hunter with a gun appeared. Then the woods became deadly quiet with a silence so heavy that a person would feel it pressing down on them. In all the years Abby had watched these woods, not a single animal could ever be found by a hunter. After a while the local hunters gave up and left the wildlife alone.

It was a beautiful day. Still chilly, but no sign of rain. Had the rain after the surprise snowstorm caused the body to decompose faster?

No. I had to stop that. I couldn't think about it. Just enjoy the day and the walk in the woods, I told myself. I didn't want to think about death when I was surrounded by life. I could hear the squirrels scampering through the leaves, gathering the last few nuts to store away for winter. The miles disappeared beneath my feet. Soon I was far from Abby's house.

My mind kept drifting back to Bill and the dead man. Should I have told Bill about Rick taking something from the dead man's pocket? No, not a good idea.

Suddenly, I was pitched forward to the ground. Falling, I heard a pop followed by a loud hissing sound. Great clouds of yellow smoke swarmed in the air. The smell of sulfur stung my nose and the smoke billowed around me, making my eyes water. Covering my nose and mouth with one hand, I scrambled to my knees. I had to get away, but I was caught. My right foot wouldn't move. I threw myself down flat, still trying to block the smoke with my hands. But it seeped through my fingers and clogged my lungs while I lay there. I choked and gasped for air.

I don't know how long I lay trapped, coughing and sputtering, but finally the hissing stopped and I raised my head. The smoke no longer surged around me, but hung in wispy layers. When I pulled myself to a kneeling position, I found a thin green wire wrapped around my ankle. Attached to the end was an odd little metal piece, like some kind of pin. I unwrapped the wire from my ankle and tugged on it, but it didn't budge. It was tied to something. I crawled on my hands and knees and followed the wire to where its end was wrapped around a small tree. But where had the end with the pin been attached? I sat back, looking around till I saw a metal stake shoved in the ground with some kind of can wired to it. Yellow residue coated the stake and covered the ground around the stake in a wide circle.

Afraid to stand, I crawled over to the stake, but stopped at the edge of the yellow circle. Even from where I knelt, I could feel the heat. The metal cylinder attached to it looked similar to a bug bomb. A bug bomb that spewed smoke? This close to the stake, the smell of sulfur was overwhelming.

It was some kind of booby trap. Some unsuspecting fool—in this case, me—walks along, trips on the wire, and sets off the can of smoke. Why? It didn't seem intended to hurt anyone. The can itself didn't explode, just sent smoke and sulfur into the air. No flying shards of metal. Lucky for me. Was it someone's idea of a joke? Or was it more sinister?

Either way, I knew Abby would have a stroke when she found out about this. Should I tell her? If I did, she might come out here alone to drive away the intruders. That could be dangerous. But what if she decided to take a walk, like I did, and stumbled across another booby trap? Equally dangerous—a fall, a broken hip, exposure to the weather—the woman *was* seventy-three years old. If anything ever happened to Abby, I don't know what I'd do.

That reasoning was pointless. I could sit here in the woods on my butt for the rest of the day, wondering about all of this, and not solve anything. I pushed myself to my feet and started back toward Abby's.

The smoke had dissipated, and now the sun shining through the bare trees dappled the ground in sunlight. Little bits of metal reflected the light. The ground was littered with them. I bent down and picked one up. It was a shell casing, but not from a shotgun. It was about the size of my little finger and made of brass. What kind of a gun shot shells like this?

What was going on?

# Fourteen

When I reached the edge of the clearing behind Abby's house, the scene before my eyes was one I had seen many times, but it still amazed me. Abby was tucking her bee colonies away for the winter. The slight breeze lifted the tendrils of white hair peeking out from her head scarf and swirled them around her face. And her clogs rustled the dry grass while she moved slowly around each hive. Her old flannel shirt—one that had belonged to my grandfather—hung loosely off her shoulders.

While she worked, insulating the tall white supers, she murmured soft sounds—old sounds. She was thanking the bees for their gift of honey and promising them, come spring, gallons of sugar water would be waiting for them. I could almost hear the humming and buzzing while the bees gathered in a tight ball around the queen to protect her from the harsh winter ahead. Many would die in the months to come, especially those farthest from the queen, but the colony would survive.

Two deer, a buck and a doe, lay not five feet away from where Abby worked. Their big brown eyes watched her, their ears perked to catch the sound of her voice. I stood downwind from them, so they hadn't caught my scent. I doubted it would matter if they did, they were so intent on listening to Abby. They had no fear in their eyes. The deer seemed to pulse with a quiet energy. I hesitated, not wanting to spoil the peace that existed in the clearing. I almost believed in Abby's magick.

I wanted to stand there forever and let the tranquility wash over me. Lord knows, after the past few days, I needed some, but I couldn't. Abby had to be told about what I found in the woods. I only hoped I could talk her out of going there herself.

I stepped forward. In unison, both deer looked at me, and before I took another step, they were gone, their white tails bobbing as they ran for the woods.

Abby saw me, too. She held up her hand, for me to stop. I couldn't enter the clearing until she was done. She lingered at each beehive in turn, whispering. After she finished with the last hive, the energy seemed to slowly slide away, until it was gone. Then she turned, head down, and walked to where I stood. When she lifted her face, she wore an expression of contentment and peace. Her eyes met mine, and her expression changed.

"What's happened?" Abby reached out and touched my arm. "Oh dear, this isn't good. Come to the house and tell me what you found."

"You know?"

"No, but I felt your distress. What happened?"

I pulled the small shiny casing from my pocket and handed it to her.

"I found this in the woods, along with some kind of booby trap. A trip wire had been strung between a tree and a stake. When I tripped on it, some kind of smoke bomb was set off. Did you see it—the smoke?"

"No. Were you hurt?"

"No, but I don't know what this all means. Have you heard any gunfire?"

"Of course not, no one hunts those woods anymore."

"Abby, that's where I found this casing. Someone's been shooting, about three miles from here, near the old Jones place."

"Benny Jenkins farms that, doesn't he?"

"You think he did it?" I stopped walking, and she did, too.

"No, Benny's not like his brother. There's no hate in his mind." She looked at the shiny object in her hand and rolled it around in her palm.

"What are you getting from that?" I asked, watching her closely.

Abby shook her head. "Nothing. Whatever the feelings were of the person who shot this, they're gone now. You could show me the spot and I'll try and see what I pick up."

"No. That's not a good idea. What if the person who shot these shells came back and caught us snooping around?"

Abby's eyes narrowed. "That is my property, and I don't appreciate trespassers."

"Listen." I grabbed her arm. "You can't go charging out there, especially by yourself. Promise me you won't."

Abby stood, eyes still narrowed, and stared at her woods. I could almost see the thoughts racing around in her mind.

Suddenly, she smiled. "All right. I won't go out there. Come on, I'll make you coffee."

That wasn't good. Abby had given in too quickly. But before I could question her, she marched toward the house. I caught up with her at the back door.

"What have you got planned?"

"Nothing," she said innocently.

I followed her to the kitchen and waited while she made the coffee.

"Abby, I know you're planning something. It's not like you to give in without an argument. Are you going to tell the sheriff about this? Is that your plan?"

"No, I think the less people who know, the better. We don't know who's involved." She handed me a coffee cup. "But I think I can keep strangers out of those woods." She smirked.

Now was as good a time as any to tell her about Darci. "Ahh, did you know Darci knows about your secret pastime?"

"And what pastime would that be, dear?" she asked, laying a hand on my shoulder and smiling down at me.

"Oh, nothing much, just that you practice magick," I said, watching her reaction.

Instead of the shocked look I expected, Abby shrugged.

"That doesn't surprise me. Darci's a smart girl. People tend to underestimate her."

"She's one of the biggest gossips in town. Doesn't it upset you that she knows?"

"No, Darci may like to gossip, but she's also very loyal. She would never do anything to hurt me."

"Yeah, that's what she said." I stared at the coffee cup. "You trust her?"

"Yes, I do. You'd do well to trust her, too, Ophelia. You could use a friend. You've stayed inside your shell far too long. It's time to start trusting people again."

"Abby, I don't want to talk about what happened four years ago. We have enough new problems without bringing up old ones."

"Yes, and have you ever considered Darci may be able to help? She knows everyone in town, and as you pointed out, she likes to gossip. Maybe she's heard something, knows something, has a piece of the puzzle."

"Okay, I'll ask her to help. How do I do that without telling her everything?"

"You mean about you?"

"Yeah, I don't want to do a lot of explaining."

"Then tell her part of the truth. She'll probably sense you're hiding something. Like I said, she isn't stupid. But I think she'll do everything she can to help you."

"How do we know Darci isn't involved in this?"

"She isn't. Trust me, there's no harm in the girl."

"Okay, I'll talk to her. I don't really see what she can do to help, but we're not getting anywhere on our own."

"Good." Abby smacked the table and winked at me. "That's the best thing I've heard you say in a long time."

When I returned home, I called Darci and invited her over for pizza and beer. Maybe the beer would help my usual reticence. It wouldn't do, however, to get plastered and tell too much. It had been so long since I'd tried to be friends with anyone; the whole thing made me jittery. By the time Darci arrived, my entire house was clean and the pizza was in the oven.

Darci arrived at six o'clock, a twelve-pack in one hand and a chocolate cake in the other. Beer, pizza, and chocolate, does it get any better than this? Maybe the evening wouldn't be so bad after all. She followed me to the kitchen. She put the cake on the counter and the beer in the fridge.

"The pizza will be done in a few minutes. Would you like a beer?"

"Sure." Darci's eyes traveled around the kitchen. "I see your plant hasn't died yet."

I handed her the beer and glanced at the mum. "No, so far I haven't killed it. I don't seem to have the same touch with plants that Abby does." Whoops—that statement could lead the conversation in a direction I didn't want to go. "Ahh—would you like a glass?"

Darci smiled. "No, this is fine. This is hard for you, isn't it, Ophelia? Having company, I mean." She tipped the beer back and took a long drink.

I checked the pizza before I answered her. Do I get right to the point? Or try and make polite conversation first? Right to the point won. I picked up my beer and pulled out a chair across from Darci.

"I'm sorry. Yes, this *is* hard. I never have made friends easily. During the past four years, I haven't even tried."

"That's okay. I understand," she said, her voice kind.

"No, I don't think you really do. Have you ever wondered why I left my job at the university and moved to Summerset?"

Darci shrugged her shoulders. "I always thought it was to be closer to Abby."

"Well, that too." I picked at the label on the beer bottle with my finger. "Four years ago I became ill and had to be hospitalized for three weeks. When I was released, I couldn't go back to the job at the library. Abby suggested I move here and find a job. I needed a different environment, a different life—so I came here."

"Three weeks? That's quite a while to be in the hospital."

Half the label was peeled off and I was working on the other half. A little pile of shiny wet paper formed at the base of the bottle.

"I wasn't on a regular floor, Darci; I was in the psych ward."

"Oh."

The buzzer on the oven stopped any further explanation. I took the pizza out, cut it, and placed it on the table. It was so quiet that I could hear the clock above the cupboards humming. I understood Darci's silence. What does one say to someone when they announce that they've been hospitalized for mental problems?

"Would you like another beer, Darci?" I asked stiffly. I didn't want to look at her, didn't want to see what was written on her face.

"Yeah, I think I'd better. The pizza looks good, Ophelia," she said in a cheery voice.

And the moment passed.

The aroma of the hot pizza pervaded the kitchen. Darci chatted while we ate, carrying on the conversation without much help from me. Finally, she put her pizza down and looked at me.

"Would it be prying to ask why you were in a psych ward, or would you rather not talk about it? I mean, you seem pretty sane to me, and if you don't want to talk about it, well . . ."

She looked so kind, so sympathetic, that I smiled. "It's okay. Thanks for the vote of confidence about my sanity." The smile vanished while I thought about four years ago. "It is hard for me to talk about. The whole experience made me feel weak and helpless. I hated it." I exhaled a shaky breath. "I was diagnosed with post-traumatic stress syndrome."

"What was the trauma?" she asked, cocking her head to one side.

I took a deep breath. Okay, Ophelia, you can do it. Just blurt it out.

"My best friend, a professor at the university, was murdered—the case was never solved."

"Oh, my gosh. That's terrible." Darci's hand darted across the table toward mine but hit the bottle of beer instead. The bottle wobbled, then tipped. Foamy beer sloshed over the table and down to the floor.

Darci made a dive for the bottle, while I grabbed a towel and began mopping the spilled beer.

I felt relief at the distraction. The next part would be hard. How did I tell her about the garbage collectors finding Brian's broken and mutilated body in a Dumpster, as if he were trash? How did I tell her, when the investigation began, I'd been their prime suspect?

The humming clock sounded louder. Standing, I stared at the half-eaten pizza and the snippets of shiny paper littered on the table.

Darci shook her head sadly. "I'm sorry for your loss. It's hard losing someone, but to lose them that way—"

"That's not all, Darci," I said, picking up the plates and carrying them to the sink. "It was bad enough that Brian was murdered, but they didn't have any suspects." With my back to her, I flattened my hands on the counter. "I was the last one to see him alive."

"They didn't question you, did they? They didn't think you had something to do with it, did they?"

"Well, yes, they did, at first. They even searched my apartment. Oh, man," I said, rubbing my face. "It was a mess. Brian had stopped by my apartment after his last class. He wanted me to go to a local hangout with him, but I was busy. I told him I'd meet him later, but he wasn't there when I arrived." I crossed to the table and sat down. "In fact, he hadn't been there at all. His body was found four days later. When the police questioned me, one detective thought I was hiding something. They questioned me over and over. They had this stupid idea I was in love with Brian and he had rejected me. Those idiots. Brian was gay. I tried to tell them, but they wouldn't believe me."

I amazed myself. I sounded so calm, telling Darci the story. None of the fear or the terrible sense of helplessness I had felt crept into my voice. I had been so scared, and the police were so sure I was hiding something. They were right, but I wasn't going to tell Darci that part of the story.

"What a nightmare."

"It was, but it got worse. A reporter picked up on it. The police weren't giving any information to the press, but somehow this one reporter learned I was being questioned. He wrote a rather vague story about the police investigating my connection to Brian's murder. The story made my life even more miserable than it had already become. I had lost my best friend, the police were at me all the time, and everytime I turned around, there was the reporter." Suddenly, my throat felt dry. I finished my beer in one swallow. "Would you like another beer? Mine seems to be gone."

"Sit still, I'll get them."

Darci handed me another beer. The next swallow eased my tight throat.

"What finally happened?"

"The police entered Brian's murder in the national crime database. Two weeks after Brian's death, they received a report. A murder had been committed in Illinois two years before with the same M.O. as Brian's. And before that, one in Ohio. The police decided they were after a serial killer who preyed on homosexual men. And that was it—they were out of my life."

"What about the reporter?"

"Oh, a serial killer makes a much better story than a lust-crazed librarian, so he left me alone, too."

"Was that when you had your breakdown?"

"Yeah, my nerves were wrecked. I kept asking myself, 'Why didn't I go with him? Maybe if I had, this wouldn't have happened.' I felt so guilty. I couldn't go back to the library after I was released from the hospital, so Abby suggested I come here. Take the job at this library."

I picked up my bottle of beer; it was empty. When did I finish this one? Darci got two more.

"And now there's another murder," Darci said, and tipped her bottle back.

I shuddered. The image of the body by the river played through my mind. I knew this man had nothing to do with Brian's murder, but once again I was involved.

"So, you talk to a lot of people," I said. "What does the town think of all this?"

Darci shrugged. "Last week the big news was the fire at Ned's and the anhydrous thefts. Now it's the body you found. Of course, town gossips think kids set the fire at the newspaper office and the murderer was from out of town. Nobody in Summerset would commit murder. If we didn't believe that, we might have to start locking our doors. Do you suppose Ted Bundy's neighbors thought the same thing?"

"You think someone in Summerset is involved?"

"Who knows? But think about it—Rick Davis comes to town, and in the space of two weeks we have more thefts, the newspaper office is vandalized, and a dead man is found in the state park. A little odd, isn't it? Things like that have never happened before."

"Do you really think Rick could be involved in this?"

"I'd hate to think so," Darci said, and shook her head. "Rick Davis is too cute to be a bad guy, but hey, you never know."

Her eyes narrowed while she sipped her beer. She set her bottle down, folded her arms on the table and leaned forward.

"There is definitely something off. Rick seems to be real easygoing, easy to talk to, but have you ever noticed how any conversation with him is all one-sided? You don't think about it while you're talking to him, but later, if you replay the conversation, it hits you. You did most of the talking. His conversation consists of asking questions. He never shares any information about himself. And he's so smooth, you don't even realize what he's doing."

How could I have ever thought Darci was stupid? Boy, did she have Rick's number—one of the few people in town who did.

"So why do you think he's here?"

"I don't know," Darci said, getting two more beers from the fridge and placing them in front of us. "Has he told you anything?"

"No. He did mention he came from a large family, but that's it."

"Well, that's a worthless little tidbit. What do you think? You've spent more time with him than anyone else in town. What's your impression?"

"You mean other than he annoys the hell out of me most of the time?" I said, and chugged my beer.

Darci laughed. "Yeah, he likes doing that, doesn't he? I meant something we can use, some indication of what his motives are."

I glanced around the table. Where did all those empty beer bottles come from? Did we drink all of them? Must have, it was the only excuse for what I did next.

"If I tell you something, Darci, you have to swear you won't tell anyone."

"Not even Georgia?"

"Especially not Georgia, she dates a cop. According to Abby, while I was unconscious, Rick went through the dead man's pockets."

"Yuck."

"No kidding, yuck. And Abby says he took something."

"How does Abby know?"

"How do you think?"

"Oh. *Oh.*" Darci's eyes went wide. "I see. Cool. What did he take?"

"I don't know, but I'd love to find out," I said while I peeled the label off the last beer bottle. I was too far gone at the time to notice the sudden gleam in Darci's eyes.

# Fifteen

I had this tiny headache, right behind my left eye, and my mouth felt like the inside of an old leather shoe. What had I been thinking? I'd pay the price most of the day. While I drove to the library, the sun was a little too bright and the sounds were a little too loud. Darci was waiting inside the door for me when I opened it.

It was disgusting; her skin was smooth, her eyes clear, and nothing of last night's excess showed on her face. The words "bubbly" and "perky" sprang to mind as I watched her. I didn't think I could handle bubbly and perky right now.

"I have to talk to you. I had the most brilliant idea last night walking home," she said, her body bouncing with anticipation.

"Darci, most ideas someone gets when they're loaded aren't brilliant." I walked to the desk and hung my coat on the rack.

"This one really is." Darci's eyes darted to the right then to the left, as if to make sure no one was standing too close. Her voice dropped to a whisper.

"We'll search Rick's room. See if we can find what he took from the dead man."

"Are you crazy?" I almost shrieked.

"Ssh, someone will hear you."

"Okay." I dropped my voice a few decibels and smoothed the lapels of my corduroy jacket. "Are you crazy? That's breaking and entering, and it's illegal."

Darci grabbed my sleeve and pulled me around the corner of the desk. "Not if you have a key."

"How are you going to get a key? Pick his pocket?"

Bad mental image. I didn't like the idea of Darci going through Rick's pockets.

" 'Course not. I'll get it from Georgia."

"Georgia is not going to give you the key to Rick's room. That wouldn't be very good business, giving out the keys to her customer's room." I tried walking past Darci to the counter, but she wouldn't move. "Come on, we've got work to do. We can't go around planning to break into someone's room, even if it is Rick Davis. And for Pete's sake, did you forget Georgia dates a cop? Alan would arrest us in a second for this."

"Look, I told you it wouldn't be breaking and entering, not with a key. And I know where she keeps the duplicates. I help her with the cleaning sometimes on the weekends. She keeps the extras in a drawer behind the counter. It would be so easy to borrow the key to his room and put it back after we're finished."

I stood there, hands on my hips, glaring at her. This was stupid. We'd get caught sure as the devil; maybe not arrested, but there'd be a lot of explaining to do. But Darci wasn't giving up. I could feel the excitement pouring off her in waves.

"Darci—"

"No, listen, I've got this all figured out. Here's what we do. I snag the key from the drawer, you come with me to Georgia's, and while she's busy, you sneak up the back stairs to Rick's room. I'll keep her busy in another part of the house. When you're done, sneak back down the stairs and out the door. See, easy," she said, her eyes dancing.

Oh, yeah, easy. And what happened to the *we*? If someone got caught, who would that someone be? Not *we*, *me*.

"It seems you've forgotten one small thing. What about Rick? Where will he be while I'm conducting this search? Hmm?"

Darci's eyes lost some of their sparkle while she contemplated the glitch in her plan.

"Oh, I didn't think about him." She brightened. "I'll figure something out. We'll get somebody to keep him busy."

"And how are you going to do that? Tell someone *'Oh, by the way, planning a little break-in tonight. Could you keep Rick busy so he doesn't catch Ophelia going through his stuff?'*"

"I'll think of something. Don't worry, trust me, I won't let him catch you."

"Darci, when somebody says, *'Don't worry, trust me,'* the first thing I do is worry. This is a bad idea, and I'm not going to do it." I walked around her to the counter and picked up the returned books.

Darci didn't move. Out of the corner of my eye, I watched her. From the look on her face, I could tell she wasn't ready to give up on her plan. But she didn't have any choice because I was not going to search his room.

"Okay, if that's how you feel," she said as she picked up another pile of books.

"Good, I'm glad you're being reasonable. There has

to be another way to find out what he's up to." Satisfied, I turned to place the books on the shelves.

"Fine. If you don't want to, I'll ask Abby."

The books hit the floor with a loud thud.

"She'd be better at it anyway. Maybe she could pick something up from handling his stuff." Darci walked over to the mystery section and began putting the books in order.

"Darci," I whispered harshly, "you are not going to involve my seventy-three-year-old grandmother in this scheme."

"Okay, so when do you want to do it, then?" She paused and thought for a moment. "I think today after work would be best. The sooner, the better. We can pick up my car at your house and drive to Georgia's. You'll have to hide in the backseat till I can slip you the key," Darci said, sliding *Murder on the Orient Express* next to *Nemesis*.

I stood there, my eyes unfocused, and wondered what customers would say if they walked in and saw me trying to shake some sense into Darci.

## *Sixteen*

Later that day Darci's big plan played over and over in my mind while I filed the overdue notices. I was going to burgle someone's room. I'd have a key, but that was rather a fine point—it was still breaking and entering. Well, maybe not breaking, but certainly entering. If I were caught, would I be able to talk my way out of it? Would Georgia press charges?

"Ahem."

Raising my head, I saw Ned standing there, watching me.

"You seem lost in your thoughts."

I couldn't meet his eyes; if he only knew. Would Ned be writing a story about me for this week's paper—Librarians Stage Burglary of Local Bed and Breakfast? It would give the liars' club a new topic of discussion.

"Ned, what can I do for you?"

"I need to talk to you, in private. Could we use your office?"

"Sure, right this way."

Ned's footsteps echoed in the stairwell while he followed me to the basement. My office was in its usual mess—books and magazines piled everywhere. I moved the largest stack from a chair.

"Sorry. Have a seat. What do you want to talk to me about?"

"Well, we haven't had a chance to talk since you found the dead body. How are you holding up?"

"Fine."

"That's good. I thought about calling you, but I didn't know if you'd welcome it."

Ned scooted forward on his chair.

"Is that what you wanted to talk to me about? How I am?"

"No. Well, yes, partly. Ahh, I heard the sheriff was by to talk to you. I wondered what it was about. You know how snoopy journalists are."

He smiled, his green eyes crinkling in the corners. His smile—boy, did he have a great smile. So friendly, so understanding. How could I not tell this man anything he wanted to know? I fought the inclination to spill my guts.

"You have a source in the department. I imagine they could tell you more than I can."

"Yeah, but they're not talking. The whole department is stonewalling me, even my source. Haven't gotten anything since it slipped how the guy was killed."

"You know as much as I do."

"But you saw the body. I didn't. Anything specific you remember about it?"

"You mean other than it made me sick and I fainted?"

Ned's friendly smile faded and he squirmed in his chair. "I didn't mean to sound uncaring. I'm sure it was gruesome, but I need all the information I can get."

"You're going to have to get it someplace else. I

don't know any more than what I've already told you and the sheriff," I answered, staring at a spot on the wall above Ned's head.

"But, I know how observant you are. Surely, there must be something you remember about the body. Maybe if you thought about it." Ned leaned forward, forcing my attention to shift to him.

"You want me to relive that whole scene in my mind? Is that what you're asking me to do?" I asked, frowning.

He pulled his hand through his hair and leaned back. "I know that sounds tough, but I've got to find out what's happening to this town."

"I'm sorry, I can't help you."

"Okay, then can you tell me what you were doing in the woods with Rick Davis? I told you he might be dangerous."

I stood. "That isn't any of your concern. If the only reason you wanted to talk to me was to pump me for information, like I said, I just can't help you. Now if you'll excuse me—"

"Sit down, I'm sorry. Davis was by the office this morning, asking a lot of questions about the Korn Karnival, and I don't know why. Do you?"

I sat, leaned back in my chair and crossed my arms. "What kind of questions? Like how many funnel cakes the Methodists sold at their food stand or what?"

Ned cocked his head and frowned at my sarcasm.

"Of course not. He asked me how many people were there and how many of them were strangers, even asked if I had any pictures from this year's celebration. I told him most of them were destroyed in the fire set in the wastebasket. What do you remember about the Korn Karnival this year, anything important?"

"Are you kidding? The only thing I remember is it rained during the parade. And it made the colors of crepe paper on the co-op's float bleed together. Their giant yellow and green ear of corn looked like this soggy, greenish, phallic symbol. I doubt that would interest Rick Davis."

Ned didn't like my answer. His eyes narrowed again while he glared at me.

"Come on, think, you have to know something. You've been spending a lot of time with Davis. What does he ask you about?" His eyes scanned the room restlessly, as if he were searching for proof I was lying. "I know you're holding out on me. Why? Have you fallen for his line of bullshit like everyone else in this town?"

"Okay, that's it." I stood again, looking down at him. "I've tried to be polite, but I'm not going to allow you to harass me. I've got work to do. Go find someone else to badger."

"That's how it is, huh?" Ned surged to his feet. "I thought you cared about this town, too. I guess I was wrong."

The door to my office hit the bookcase behind it, bouncing, when Ned shoved it out of his way.

I was still standing in the same spot when Darci peered around the corner.

"Are you okay? I saw Ned storm out of here. What happened?"

"Oh, he thinks I know something that I'm not telling him."

"Well, you do. You know Rick took something from the dead man."

"Right, and I'm going to tell him that?"

"Guess not. Then you'd have to tell him how you

know. Anyway, forget about Ned. It's time to close up. Are you ready to go?"

"Yeah, let me shut off the computer." I walked around the corner of my desk, clicked the mouse, and the computer powered down.

"I went to Georgia's for lunch today. Here, you'll need these."

I glanced over my shoulder to see Darci holding up a key in one hand and a pair of rubber gloves in the other.

"Are you nuts?" I said, shoving the key and gloves back in her hands when she tried to give them to me.

Darci pushed the gloves and the key in my hand. "That's the second time today you've asked me that."

"No, the first time I asked you if you were crazy," I said, refusing to move.

"Come on, we've got to hurry, I changed the plan. I'll tell you about it on the way to your house."

I allowed Darci to hustle me out of the library. Once in the car, I stole a look at Darci while I drove.

"Okay, so what's your modified plan?"

"I snitched the key when I had lunch with Georgia today. The gloves are hers, too. She uses them to do dishes. Anyway, I checked around, and Rick is playing pool at Stumpy's. He'll be there for the next hour and a half, so you need to hurry."

"How do you know he'll be there that long?"

"'Cause I paid Johnny Tucker twenty bucks to keep him there," Darci said, her voice full of satisfaction.

It would be pointless to ask her again if she were crazy, I knew the answer. But who really was the crazy one? Darci or me? She thought this whole scheme up, but I was the one who allowed myself to be suckered into it. I'd say it was a toss-up.

After picking up Darci's car, the drive to Georgia's was silent at first. Darci wanted me to dress like some covert operations specialist—black jeans, black turtleneck. I refused, pointing out time was limited and we didn't want to waste it arguing about making a fashion statement. We were on the way to the bed and breakfast within fifteen minutes.

"All right," Darci said, "here's what you do. Right before we get there, you need to slump down in the seat so no one can see you. I'll go inside and tell Georgia I stopped by to pick up some of her homemade pickles. They're in the basement, and while she's down there, I'll let you in the back door. Watch for my signal. I'll park in back, but stay scrunched down in case someone comes too close to the car."

Like maybe Georgia's boyfriend, Alan the deputy? I didn't ask her how I was supposed to see her signal if I were hiding in the bottom of the car. Silently, I sat cursing myself for being a fool.

"Once you're inside, I'll keep Georgia busy while you go up the back stairs and search Rick's room. It's the second door on the left. Oh, and when you're going up the stairs, watch out for the third step from the top, it squeaks."

Ten minutes later I'm twisted in the shape of a pretzel in the bottom of the car, peeking out the window, with only the top of my head visible—I hoped. Finally, I saw Darci waving frantically from the back door. Should I crouch and run like the swat teams do on television? Or calmly walk to the door, like I wasn't planning on searching someone's room? I searched my pocket and found the key. Grabbing the gloves, I was out of the car in a half walk, half saunter to the house.

"Hurry up. Georgia's going to be back any minute."

When I reached the door, I thought about making one last plea for sanity. The look on Darci's face told me it would be a waste of time—time we didn't have. Her face glowed and there was an air of excitement about her. She seemed to quiver while she whispered her last minute instructions.

"Hurry, you have about an hour left. When you're done, sneak back down the stairs. I'll keep Georgia in the parlor, it's in front."

"How will you know when I'm done?"

"Drop the gloves by the back door. Go on, hurry, and remember about that step."

I crept quietly up the stairs. Did Darci say third door on the left and second step from the top—or second door on the left and third step from the top? Damn, I couldn't remember. When the third step creaked, the sound rang in my ears. It was so loud Darci and Georgia must have heard it. Do I stay where I am or creep back down the stairs? I listened for the sound of rushing footsteps, but the house was silent. The sudden noise had solved my problem—third step, second door.

I tiptoed up the two remaining stairs, so afraid I'd put my weight on the wrong spot. My fingers felt cold and numb, and the gloves made it hard to find the key in my pocket. Every second while I struggled to fish the key out, I expected hands to grab me from behind and spin me around.

While my shaking hands grappled to fit the key in the lock, I expected to hear an angry voice yelling, *"What in the hell are you doing?"* My nerves were taut, and the hair on the back of my neck prickled as if someone were watching. Finally, the blasted key went in the lock. I swung the door wide and hurled myself into the room.

After shutting and locking the door, I stood there, my hand on the doorknob, my forehead resting against the closed door. My breath came in short bursts, and my heart drummed a rapid beat. All the while the clock was ticking. Rick would be back soon. I had to do this—now.

I turned and surveyed the room. In the fading light, it was hard to see. Soon it would be pitch-dark, another reason to hurry.

Rick's room seemed to be orderly, no tripping hazards that might cause a loud crash to be heard in the front parlor. Where to start? If I were Rick Davis, where would I hide something? He was so confident, it would be in plain sight, and he would never expect anyone to search his room.

From what I could see, the room was large, but the shadows were growing. The bed faced a fireplace across the room. Two wing chairs with a table between sat near the window. To the left of the door I leaned against was another door, which I presumed to be a closet. A large gentleman's dresser with a mirror was to my right. Okay, let's try the closet.

Rick's suitcases were stacked neatly on its floor. It would be a good place to hide something. I took them out one at a time and opened them. Nothing—nothing in the pockets—nothing in the sides. It would have been nice if Abby could have given me a hint what to look for. What about his clothes? His shirts hung in a straight row. I caught the subtle scent of the cologne he wore while I rummaged through them. Another bust, I only found two candy wrappers and a toothpick. Must've been at Joe's recently.

The light continued to fade; I had to get out of there. My pulse jumped. The dresser was my next choice.

Jeez, I'd be pawing through his underwear. I wondered if he wore boxers or briefs. The thought made an insane giggle catch in my throat. I'm rummaging around his room and thinking about his underwear. Get a grip, Jensen.

The question was answered when I opened the first drawer—definitely a boxer kind of a guy. I removed one pair at a time and laid them carefully on top of one another. I would stack them in reverse order when I put them back. And then there it was, at the bottom of the drawer.

I pulled the pristine Ziploc bag out of the drawer. Holding it carefully with two fingers, I opened the bag and sniffed the contents. The smell of decay burned the inside of my nose and sent me staggering back. Quickly resealing it, I turned the bag over in my hands while I studied its contents.

The bag held one of the town's less brilliant marketing strategies—a matchbook, its edges curled and stained. But the printing was still legible. The council had printed several thousand of these, and all the merchants were told to push them. Unfortunately, the demand for the matchbooks was less than anticipated and a few thousand were left over. They were recalled and would be used again next year. Luckily for the town treasury, the council had been smart enough not to print the date, just the words: *Korn Karnival*.

# *Seventeen*

This was it—Rick had removed these from the dead man's pocket. This was the reason he had been asking Ned all the questions about the Korn Karnival and wanted to see pictures. Did these matches somehow connect the dead man to the vandalism at the newspaper? Should I tell Darci about them? If I did, would she want to break into the newspaper office? Somehow, the Korn Karnival was tied in to all of this, but how?

First things first, time was almost up. I needed to get out before Rick came back. Placing the bag on the dresser, I put the boxers in reverse order back in the drawer. When I picked up the last pair, I heard the sound—creak.

Oh God, what now? Rick would walk in the door any second and I'd be standing there with a pair of his boxers in my hand and the Ziploc bag lying on the dresser. How guilty would that look? I shoved the boxers in the drawer and quickly shut it. But I forgot the Ziploc bag—it was still lying on top of the dresser.

Muffled steps were coming down the hallway. I had to hide. But what about the bag? Should I waste precious seconds burying it under the boxers? When a key rattled in the lock, I panicked. Snatching the bag and cramming it in my pocket, I ran for the closet. Trite, but isn't that what all good burglars did, hide in closets? I prayed, when I shut the door, that Rick wasn't the type to immediately hang up his coat. If he were, it would be all over for me. I saw the light come on from the crack underneath the door and heard footsteps cross the room.

My palms were clammy in the rubber gloves, so I peeled them off and wiped my palms on my jeans. The nervous perspiration wasn't limited to my palms. My shirt grew wet under my arms and I could smell my own fear. Thoughts of Rick's possible involvement with the dead man bounced through my head. What if he was involved in the man's murder? What if he opened the door and saw me? Would mine be the next body on the riverbank? The sound of my own heart pounded in my ears in the silence of the closet.

Where in the hell was Darci? Some watchdog. Didn't she know Rick was back, or was she too busy with Georgia to notice? If I survived this—if Rick wasn't a murderer, if I didn't die from a heart attack brought on by fear—I was going to kill Darci for getting me in this predicament. Maybe not kill, but there are things worse than dying.

A knock at the door to the room made me jump. I grabbed the stacked suitcases before they toppled. Footsteps again crossed the room to the door.

"Darci, I didn't know you were here," Rick said.

"I stopped by to pick up some of Georgia's pickles. I saw your car outside and thought I'd come up and say hi."

More footsteps crossed the room. The next sound I heard sounded like bedsprings squeaking. Oh no, please don't let Darci's newest plan be to seduce Rick so I could sneak out. A faint noise signaled the door shutting.

"Haven't seen you around the library lately. What've you been up to?"

"Oh, you know, this and that. How's Ophelia doing? I haven't seen her since we found the body. I wanted to call her, but you know how she is. Figured she'd tell me to go away and leave her alone."

"Yeah, she hates people making a fuss. She's had problems at the library. All the little old ladies keep trying to question her. Bill and Ned have been there, too."

Shut up, Darci, you're giving him way too much information. I pressed my ear against the door.

"Really, both Bill and Ned? I know Bill planned to talk to her again, but what did Ned want?"

Darci giggled. "I don't know. They were in her office for a long time. I've always suspected Ned has the hots for her."

"Yeah? Does she have the hots for him?"

"How would I know? Ophelia keeps to herself. Never tells anyone anything. I keep telling her if she would try a little harder, Ned would ask her out."

"Try harder?"

"Yeah, fix herself up more, instead of running around in jeans and those silly T-shirts with the sayings on them. She could wear a little makeup once in a while. If she did, she'd be really pretty. And she should try flirting a little."

"I don't know; I think she looks great the way she is, and I don't think Ophelia knows how to flirt," Rick said. "Not to change the subject, but what's everybody in town saying about the dead man?"

"Everyone wants to hear all the gruesome details, of

course. Lots of speculation about who he is—or who he was, I should say. Some people are locking their doors now, but most think the murder doesn't have anything to do with Summerset. Just some stranger murdered by some stranger."

"No connection to the anhydrous thefts?"

"No, why would they be connected? Is that what you think?"

"I don't have an opinion; I'm just an outside observer."

I smiled in the dark. Right. A very curious outside observer.

"I did have a reason for coming up here, Rick, other than just to say hi."

Oh Lord, here it comes, the seduction. I could see Darci in my head, sitting on the bed, batting her eyelashes while she glanced up shyly at Rick. Maybe patting the bed next to her. Rick watching with this predatory male look on his face.

"When I went to the basement with Georgia, to get the pickles, I thought I heard something, maybe a mouse. You know how these old houses are. Georgia didn't want me to ask you, afraid it would be bad for business, mice and all. But would you go down and look? I'd do it myself, but mice give me the willies. I know I'd simply faint if I saw one."

Good job, Darci. I was so proud of her, appealing to his ego to get him out of the room and in the basement.

"Sure, no problem."

The bed squeaked loudly and a pair of footsteps crossed the room. I heard the door open and close. Seconds later the stair creaked. How long would it take them to reach the basement? Hopefully, Georgia would go with them. It was too dark in the closet to see my watch, so I started to count—one Mississippi, two Mississippi, three Mississippi. When I reached thirty Mississippi, I slowly opened the door. The room was dark, but with enough light to see that I was alone. I bolted out of the closet and out the door into the hallway, remembering to shut the door behind me. I managed to avoid the third step while I hurried down the stairs. I was almost there, around the landing and out the back door. The voices of Georgia, Rick, and Darci floated up from the basement when I reached the back door. I heard Darci giggle again. Even in my panic to leave, I had to admire her. No one played the fluttery female better than she did.

The distance to the car seemed farther than I remembered, but finally I made it and was soon safely hunched over on the passenger side of Darci's car. For the first time in over an hour, my heart returned to its normal rate and I could breathe again. Ten minutes later Darci joined me. We didn't speak till we were a block away from Georgia's and I was sitting, normally, in the seat beside her. Darci glanced at me.

"What'd you do with the gloves?"

"Damn." I closed my eyes and groaned. "There in the bottom of Rick's closet. Think he'll find them?"

"I don't know. What do you think? Does he miss much?"

I didn't appreciate the sarcasm.

"Forget about the gloves," Darci said. "Even if he finds them, no way could he know it was you. We'll deal with it, if it comes up."

The tension in my arms and shoulders seemed to leak away, and in its place came shaking, mild at first, but building. My teeth began to chatter. It was so noisy, even Darci could hear it. She glanced at me.

"Gosh, you must be suffering from some kind of shock. I need to get you home and get something in your stomach," Darci said, and drove faster.

Lady and Queenie met us at the door and followed me into the living room. By now the shaking had increased to the point where I had trouble walking. Darci covered me with my afghan lying on the couch and started a fire. I was so cold, and couldn't seem to get warm. Queenie curled up on my lap, but even her small warm body did nothing to dispel the chill.

Darci came back a few minutes later carrying a steaming bowl and a cup, also steaming.

"Drink this, then eat the soup. It'll warm you up," she said, handing me the cup and placing the bowl in front of me on the coffee table.

One whiff of the liquid in the cup was all I needed to smell the whiskey.

"Oh no. I'm not drinking this. Drinking two nights in a row is more than I can handle."

Darci stood over me. "Drink it."

I sipped the hot liquid and felt the heat all the way to my stomach. The shaking eased. I set the cup down and started on the soup. Darci sat in the wing chair across from me, watching me while I ate. Each of us seemed preoccupied and unwilling to start the conversation.

The fire cast warm shadows around the room, and the smell of wood smoke drifted faintly in the air. The cat was still curled in my lap, and Lady lay down in her familiar spot in front of the fire. A cozy scene to talk about murder.

"Okay, did you find anything?" Darci asked when I finished my soup.

"Yeah, these." I handed her the Ziploc bag from my pocket.

"This is one of the matchbooks from the Korn Karnival this year. Are you sure this is what he took from the dead guy?"

"Well, if you doubt me, open the bag and take a sniff. I did. Paper absorbs odors, you know."

"Umm, no thanks," she said, holding the bag away from her. "I believe you. What was the dead guy doing with these?"

"One of two things—either he picked these up somewhere, or he was in Summerset during the Korn Karnival. If it's the latter, it could mean he knows someone who lives here—"

"And that someone might be the one who killed him."

"Exactly. Rick thinks so, too."

"How do you know?"

"Ned told me Rick was at the paper asking all kinds of questions about the Korn Karnival. These matches would explain his sudden interest. He also wanted to know if a lot of strangers were in town this year and if Ned had any pictures. But of course, he doesn't, most of them were burned when the office was vandalized."

"It wasn't kids after all?"

I shrugged. "That's my guess."

"The killer. Maybe Ned had a picture linking him with the dead man, but how do we find out?" Darci tapped her chin, thinking. "I know, Agnes McPhearson," she said suddenly.

"Agnes McPhearson?" I looked at Darci in surprise. "What would she have to do with this?"

"She's always taking pictures, fancies herself quite the photographer. All we have to do is get all the pictures she took this year. Maybe we can spot the dead guy and who he was with."

I hated to disappoint Darci, but we had one slight problem. "We don't know what the dead man looked like."

"Why not? You saw him."

"The medical examiner said he'd been there for almost a week. Do you know what animals do to exposed parts of a dead body? I don't want to gross you out, but from what I could see, there wasn't much left of the guy's face."

Darci paled. "I never thought about it. I really don't want to think about it, either. Yuck."

"Yeah, well try seeing it firsthand. Even if we did know what he looked like, the chances of Agnes catching him on film are a long shot."

"Are you going to tell Ned about this?"

"No. All we have right now are assumptions. But what if we're right? We don't know who the players are, and if we tell anyone about this, the wrong person might find out before we have any proof."

"That would be bad."

"Yes. That would be very bad. Whoever it is isn't fooling around here. Whatever it is they're trying to hide, it's important enough for them to kill to keep it secret."

"And we have no idea who it is. It could even be Ned." Darci shook her head. "We need to think this over, come up with another plan."

"Another plan's right, but not one like tonight. No way am I ever doing that again."

"Okay, but let me think this over." Darci looked at the clock. "I'd better go. We've talked enough about murder for one night, and you still look pale. Go to bed; we'll put our heads together tomorrow."

Darci stood, grabbed her coat, and slipped it on.

"Shoot, where did I put those car keys?" she said, groping in her pockets. "I could've sworn they were in my coat."

"They're in the kitchen on the counter, next to the plant you brought me." I rubbed my eyes while weariness crawled through my body.

Darci's eyes widened. "How did you know that?"

"Know what?"

"That my keys are in the kitchen. You came straight in here; you haven't been in the kitchen."

I felt the blood creep into my face.

# *Eighteen*

I walked slowly toward the library. I knew Darci would be waiting for me, but I had no idea what to expect from her. Her reaction to the news that I was clairvoyant surprised me. *"Wow, cool,"* was not the normal reaction. People either wanted their palm read or thought you were a freak.

A week ago I wouldn't have cared, but our growing friendship was important to me. I hadn't wanted a friend since Brian, but things had somehow changed for me.

The first person I saw inside was Benny. He balanced precariously on a ladder, changing a fluorescent tube. He frowned when he examined the end.

"Hi, Benny."

Startled, he grabbed at the shaky ladder. "Hi, Miss Ophelia. Just changing the light."

"I see that. How are things going?"

"Oh, okay I guess. Me and Jake went to a sale last weekend, but Jake said the auctioneer was trying to rob everybody. So we didn't buy nothing. Too bad, too, had my eye on the sweetest little four wheeler. Woulda been perfect for getting around the farm and doing chores." Benny shook his head sadly. "Ed Johnson bought it."

"That is too bad. Maybe you'll find another one you like better."

"I don't think so, Miss Ophelia, this was—" Benny stopped and began to fiddle with the end of the tube. I looked over my shoulder to see Adam Hoffman headed straight for me. The aroma of his cologne preceded him by a good five feet.

"Ophelia, Benny, good morning," Adam said, smiling sanctimoniously.

"'Mornin'," Benny mumbled from his perch on the ladder. "'Scuse me, Miss Ophelia, Mr. Hoffman, this tube ain't working. Gotta get me another one."

Benny climbed down and lumbered off.

I turned to Adam. He was dressed in his banker suit, polished and buffed till he shone—not a single hair out of place. His face still wore his patented smile, and the cloying smell of his cologne made me a little nauseous. I stepped away, putting distance between us.

"I'm sorry, Ophelia. I didn't mean to run Benny off. It seemed you two were having quite the conversation, if one can have a conversation with Benny, considering how slow he is."

My temper flared and I took a small step toward him, trying to ignore the disgusting smell surrounding him. "Benny may be slow," I said frowning, "but he's a hard worker. You should know that. Doesn't Benny rent your farm?"

Adam placed his hands behind his back and rocked back on his heels. "Yes, he does. He does tolerably well, always on time with the rent, takes good care of the livestock, but I've never sought any conversation with him. But, apparently you do."

I decided to let that one pass and retreated a step.

"Was there something else you wanted, or did you come here to discuss Benny?"

"Funny. I simply wanted to stop by and express our—Nina's and mine—concern for you."

"Your concern for me? Why are you concerned?"

"That unfortunate incident, of course. It must have been terrible for you, finding the dead man. It would be enough to shake anyone's sanity."

"I assure you, it would take more than a dead body to shake my sanity." How's that for bravado? Why had he said that? He didn't know about my breakdown.

"Please, Ophelia, don't take offense," he said, spreading his hands wide. "I merely wanted to offer you our support should you need it. I know we haven't always seen eye-to-eye on matters concerning the town, but you have done an excellent job with the library. I would hate to see you leave."

"Adam, what are you talking about?"

"A lesser person might wish to move after finding something like that."

"I have no intention of moving. Did someone indicate to you that I might?"

"Well, Ned did comment how unsettling it had been for you. It led me to believe you might be thinking about leaving."

"Well, I'm not. Good day."

Adam stared at me, his smile still locked in place. I turned on my heel and left. The talk of me leaving— was it wishful thinking on his part, or had Ned said something? A phone call would answer the question. But before I reached the phone, Ned came up the basement stairs.

"I hoped you were here, Ophelia. When you weren't

in your office, I thought maybe you hadn't arrived yet. We need to talk."

"We certainly do. Here or downstairs?" I said, putting one hand on my hip.

"How about Joe's? I'll buy."

"No thanks. Here's good." I stepped forward till I was right in front of him. "What are you doing telling people I'm moving?"

Ned moved back. "Hey, I didn't say you were moving. Adam Hoffman asked me if I thought you might. I said I didn't know, I've always thought you were overqualified for this job, so it wouldn't surprise me if you did. Most people don't like finding dead bodies lying around. That's all. If Adam said anything different, then he misunderstood me."

Even though I wasn't convinced, I backed off.

"I'm very sorry about the other day. I shouldn't have blown up at you. Can you forgive me?"

"Fine, consider yourself forgiven." I crossed to the desk with Ned right behind me.

"I have only one explanation for my behavior—I'm worried about you and Davis."

"There is no 'me and Davis.'"

"Ophelia, how can you say that? After all we've been to each other?"

I spun around to see Rick lounging by one of the bookshelves, observing us with a casual air. A slight grin lingered at one corner of his mouth. The grin broadened into a smile when he wandered toward the counter.

"I take it you and Ned had a little tiff?"

"Oh, stow it, Rick."

"She really likes me, but hides it well, don't you think?" Rick whispered loudly to Ned.

By the expression on Ned's face, he didn't find Rick funny.

"I can see we won't have a private conversation here," Ned said. "I'll give you a call. Maybe we can have dinner. 'Bye, Ophelia, Rick."

Ned nodded stiffly and walked away.

"Sorry, didn't mean to interrupt," Rick said.

"Yes, you did. Now, where have you been? I haven't seen you since that day at Roseman."

"I thought you didn't want to see me. You've told me to get lost often enough. Now you're upset that I did?"

"No, I'm not upset. I wanted *you* to be the one to deal with the snoopy little old ladies, instead of me."

"I'm touched you wanted me around for any reason. Really, I'm surprised you noticed I was gone. From what I heard, Ned's been doing a good job at keeping you entertained."

"Oh, where did you hear that?"

"Somewhere, I forget now." Rick leaned against the counter. He picked up a pencil and began to doodle on a piece of paper. "One question: How long have you lived here? Three years?"

"Almost four. Why?"

"Oh, no reason. Doesn't it seem odd you've lived here this long, and now, all of a sudden, Ned's your new best friend."

"Ned is not my *new best friend.*"

He dropped the pencil and straightened. "That's right. Your new best friend would be Darci, wouldn't it? See you later." He strolled away from the counter.

I picked up the piece of paper with the doodles on it. Rick had drawn a glove.

\* \* \*

I was still staring at the paper when Claire showed up.

"Hi, Claire," I said, sticking the paper in my pocket before she noticed it.

"Ophelia." Claire grabbed the glasses dangling from the chain around her neck and shoved them on her nose. Pulling out a notebook from her purse, she flipped it open. "I need to talk to you about the next meeting of the library board. As president, I think we should put on the agenda—"

"Sorry, Claire," Darci interrupted.

Claire turned and peered at Darci from over the top of her glasses, but Darci ignored her.

"Ophelia, there's something wrong with the computer in your office. I tried to get it to boot up, but it won't. Would you show me what I did wrong?"

I hadn't noticed Darci approach.

"Claire, would you mind watching the counter?" I asked.

"No, but I do need to talk to you before I leave," she said, pushing her glasses back on her nose.

I followed Darci to my office.

"What's wrong with the computer?"

"Nothing. I haven't had a chance to talk to you all morning, so when I saw Claire come in, I decided now would be perfect. Claire can watch the counter while we talk."

Darci amazed me. She was so good at getting people to do what she wanted. And they never even suspected. I wondered how many times I had fallen for her carefully planned schemes.

I shut the door to the office, while Darci rearranged the books and magazines and pulled the chair closer to the desk.

"Okay, before you start, I want you to look at this." I handed her the paper from my pocket.

Darci looked at it, then at me. "So? It's a doodle of a glove. I told you to quit worrying about it. If you're drawing stuff like this, you're thinking way too much about Rick finding those gloves."

"I didn't draw it. Rick did."

"Oh. I guess he found the gloves and figured it out. Shoot," she said, stomping her foot. "I'd hoped he'd think Georgia dropped them. I bet he knows the matchbook's gone, too." She stopped and chewed her bottom lip. Finally, she shrugged and said, "He can't prove anything. He can't tell Alan or Bill about it without telling them about the matchbook. We're safe. And you could always do a spell."

I groaned. "Darci, I'm not a witch. I have a precognitive ability, that's all. That doesn't make me a witch."

"What about Abby?"

"What Abby does with her abilities is her choice. Her mother, who was a healer in the mountains, taught her the traditions. I've chosen a different path."

Darci leaned forward. "This is so cool. Tell me, can you predict the future, read minds, or what?"

How could I explain this? Should I tell her about what could happen when I touched someone? I retreated to sarcasm.

"No, I can't predict the future, and I haven't found a mind worth reading yet."

"Very funny. What can you do?"

"There are different kinds of precognitive ability. I have flashes, sometimes of the future, sometimes of the past. And I seem to be good at finding things."

"That's it?"

"Believe me, it's enough. When I was a child, it was

fun. I was a whiz at hide and seek, and there was no such thing as a pop quiz for me. I knew when the teacher had one planned. After I grew up, it wasn't fun anymore."

"Brian?"

"Yes," I said, and closed my eyes at the memory. "The first time I ever needed my gift, and it betrayed me—my friend died. I saw his murder, but I couldn't stop it. I tried. I ran to the bar where we were supposed to meet, but he wasn't there. Even now I don't know if what I saw had already happened or was about to happen. Either way, I was too late to change Brian's fate. It's haunted me ever since."

"Did you tell the police that?"

"Part of it. When I couldn't find him, I went to the police and told them I was afraid something had happened to Brian. They blew me off, said a missing persons report couldn't be filed for forty-eight hours. The next four days were pure hell, waiting for Brian's body to be found. After some garbage collectors found the body in a Dumpster, the police remembered my report."

"They wanted to talk to you, I suppose?"

"Oh yeah, they wanted to talk to me, all right. Why did I suspect something had happened to Brian? When was the last time I saw him? Did anyone see him leave my apartment? Did I talk to anyone else after I talked to Brian? Question after question. I couldn't tell them the truth—that I knew about the murder because I'd 'seen' it. They knew I was hiding something. It put me at the top of their suspect list, but they had no proof and couldn't hold me."

"And the reporter?"

"He could tell something was not quite right, but he

had no proof, either. His solution was to dog my every step. Question people at the library, my other friends, anyone who was connected to me at all. I lived in fear the whole time, but I've already told you how it ended."

"In the hospital."

"Yeah, and there I dreamed, over and over again, about Brian's murder. I saw it all. Everything the monster did to him, everything—except the monster's face."

Darci reached across the desk for my hand, and a piece of paper fluttered to the floor. It was an envelope. It must have been on the corner by the pile of books. I hadn't noticed it before. I picked it up and turned it over. My name was on the front, made from letters cut out of a magazine. I didn't have to open it to know what it was.

# Nineteen

My fingers tingled as I drew the single sheet of paper out of the envelope. The letters, cut from a magazine and pasted to the paper, were crude. The words they made, seemingly harmless:

**HOW LONG DO YOU SUPPOSE IT WOULD TAKE THEM TO HIRE A NEW LIBRARIAN?**

But it was the rough drawing that caused my heart to jump. Rough maybe, but there wasn't any doubt what it depicted—an old-fashioned headstone, the kind in every old cemetery. Only this one had my name chipped into it.

Darci watched over my shoulder while I read the note. Her gasp sounded in my ear.

"Oh, my God, this is awful. We need to call Bill or Alan."

I continued to stare at the note. "We can't. The first question will be: Why do I think I received it? Then, who do I think sent it? What do I tell them? Maybe Rick Davis? He knew we were snooping in his room and this is a warning?"

"Do you really think Rick was the one who left it here?"

"Who knows? This has been a popular place today. Benny, Adam Hoffman, Ned, Rick, and God only knows who else, has been down here today. It could've been anyone, but Rick is the only one who might want to warn me off. His little doodle of the glove proves he can draw."

Darci sighed. "Can you pick up any vibrations from this? You know, residual energy? I've seen psychics on TV shows do that."

"What, hold it up to my forehead and say, 'I think I see, I think I see a . . . a . . . '? Those are pretend psychics. I have flashes of insight, which is why I'm good at finding things. Sometimes, I pick up images from people when I touch them."

"That explains why you avoid touching and being touched. You see things when you touch people, don't you?"

"Once in a while. Depends on the person, how open they are. It always disturbs me, and I hate it. Abby's the one who receives visions from objects."

"Call her—now. I'll ask Claire to stay."

Abby must have broken the speed laws driving to the library. She rushed in the door, with Darci right behind her. They both sat down in chairs by my desk. Abby, instead of wasting time with words, took both of my hands in hers and closed her eyes.

"Where is it?" she said, opening her eyes.

"Right here." I motioned to the paper on the desk.

She picked it up and placed it between her palms. Her shoulders and head drooped while she rubbed the paper. All at once she jerked her head and the paper dropped. Her hands clenched and unclenched, twice. Then she ground her palms together as if she were trying to remove a stain. Abby looked first at me, then Darci.

"My goodness."

"That's it, 'my goodness'?"

"No, that's not it. You girls seem to be causing someone a lot of problems. And they don't like it."

"Who? Could it be Rick Davis?" I asked.

"I couldn't see the face, but they are very angry. They wear a mask to hide the evil in their soul. Hate is driving them. Hate, loss, and betrayal."

I slapped the desk. "See, Darci? You can *never* get a straight answer with this stuff. Everything is always couched in mystery that tells you *nothing*."

Abby stared at me. "I understand your frustration, but—"

"My frustration? My frustration?" I jumped up and started to prowl the small room. "Yeah, I guess you could say I'm frustrated. Some jerk is threatening me, and all you can say is 'they wear a mask.' Well, who the hell doesn't wear a mask?"

"Calm down—"

"I will not calm down." I stopped directly in front of Abby. "I want answers, and I want them now."

Tension seemed to crowd even the air from the room. Abby's face flushed red. I knew I'd made her angry. Well, I was angry, too. Poor Darci sat with her hands clasped in her lap, not looking at either Abby or me. Welcome, Darci, to the wonderful world of psychics.

"I wanted to teach you, guide you, the way my mother taught me. But no, you wouldn't allow it. You were so bitter about your grandfather's death," Abby said, her body stiff and straight. "You were so sure you could deal with your abilities in your own way. Well, maybe if you had let me help you, your understanding would be greater now."

"Would greater understanding have saved Brian?" I asked through clenched teeth. "It didn't save Grandpa."

She seemed to sag and tears gathered in her eyes. "Some things can't be changed, but sometimes understanding can help the pain."

I'd made my grandmother cry. How low is that? Ashamed of my outburst, I touched Abby's hand. "I'm sorry, I—"

"I know, dear," she said softly, and squeezed my hand. "I'm a psychic, remember?"

Abby's gentle reply seemed to drive the tension from the room.

"And remember, so are you, Ophelia. No, wait," she said, holding up her hand. "Before you start arguing, listen to me. I said some things couldn't be changed. You can't change who and what you are. You are born of a line of women who were blessed with a talent, a talent you share. Use that talent. Let it lead you to your answers."

"I don't know how."

"Yes, you do. It's there waiting for you. All you have to do is accept it, open yourself, your mind. You'll find the way."

"I've got it." Darci brightened. "All she has to do is touch everyone who was here today. She'll pick up their vibes and know who the bad guy is."

"She watches too much TV," I explained to Abby.

"Darci, I can't go around grabbing all the people here today. I told you it doesn't work that way."

"I don't see why not," Darci said with a pout.

"Because—"

A sharp knock at the door stopped me. The door swung open and Claire leaned against the door frame. Her glasses hung uselessly on their chain. Her face was pale and her eyes were puffed from crying.

"Claire, what is it?" Darci asked.

"Georgia was here looking for you, Darci. She heard it over the police scanner and called Alan. Doug Jones was killed when his car went off the bridge on Highway 6."

Darci gasped, and then a thick, heavy blanket of silence dropped over the room. We were stunned, and no words could describe our feelings—too private, too personal to share.

"He was only sixteen," Darci whispered. But even her whisper sounded loud in the quiet room. "Does anyone know what happened?"

Claire straightened and cleared her throat. "Georgia said they found meth in the car. They won't know if that caused the accident until they do the autopsy."

"Ophelia, I'd better go back upstairs with Claire," Darci said, walking to her and placing an arm around her shoulders.

Not speaking, I nodded in agreement and watched them walk away, leaning into each other.

From my position by the desk, I thought about Abby's reaction when she heard the news of the Jones boy's death. No glimmer of surprise crossed her face, no sudden gasp. She knew, she had seen it. I shook my head in bewilderment. Abby had called this talent blessed, but was it a blessing, this knowing of the pain that waited ahead?

\* \* \*

Sadness hung over the library like a transparent veil when everyone learned of the accident. People congregated in small groups, whispering in hushed and solemn voices. Behind the sadness, anger shimmered. Anger at a young life wasted, anger at the drug dealers who preyed on the weakness of others, anger at the police for their inability to shut down the meth labs. How many more young lives would be lost or ruined before these social vampires got what they deserved? They were sucking the lifeblood from our town by corrupting its youth. It had to be stopped.

All I could think about was going home, away from the sadness, into the safety and warmth of my home. Darci must have felt the same way; she was subdued and thoughtful for the rest of the morning and afternoon. We decided to keep the letter among the three of us. Bill and Alan had enough to deal with right now. There wasn't anything they could do but just tell me to be careful. No, it was better not to involve them.

I had my coat on and was out the door at five. The peace I thought I'd feel when I reached my house eluded me. Lady and Queenie, sensing my mood, stayed close to my side. But even their quiet presence didn't help me find the peace I sought. I tried working on my needlepoint, but after snarling the thread five times, I gave up. I popped a tape of *The Thin Man* with Myrna Loy and William Powell into the VCR. I might have missed seeing it in the theater, but I could watch it now. Getting involved in the movie would help me relax. Wrong. The snappy dialogue failed to hold my attention. Shutting the tape off, I wandered from room to room until I finally found myself in the kitchen.

What did I know that was so important that someone

would try to scare me? Did they think I knew something about the dead man? And what connection did he have to Summerset? Were the matches in his pocket a fluke, or had he been here during the Korn Karnival? How involved was Rick Davis in all of this? The trouble had started when he came to town. Another fluke, or was he somehow behind it?

I needed answers, and I needed them fast. It didn't take the note or Abby to tell me the danger was growing. I could feel it myself. A quiver of fear slid through me.

What had Abby said? Let my gift lead me to the answers? All I had to do was open my mind and myself? Yeah, right. I'd tried that one before. Problem was, I never knew what would pay me a visit. I'd sworn after Brian, I would never try again. Now I had no choice; I had to find the answers.

I went to my bedroom, changed into my nightgown, and crawled under the covers. Lady and Queenie stood vigil by my bedside. While I lay there, I emptied my mind and willed sleep to come. The last conscious feeling I had was falling.

I found myself floating aimlessly in a strange room. My nightgown billowed around my legs, but my feet didn't touch the ground. The room was large, with a shiny wood floor. Two walls were covered in full-length mirrors, but I cast no reflection.

One of the mirrored walls had a barre attached to the glass. At the barre stood a young girl—neither a child nor yet a woman. Her pale blond hair was pulled tightly into a bun on the top of her head. She wore a black leotard with a short flowing skirt attached. Her feet were encased in pointe ballet slippers, and the shiny ribbons crisscrossed her strong ankles and calves. She arched and stretched while she warmed her long lean muscles.

After she finished her exercises, she knelt and pushed the play button on a small tape player. The haunting music swam through the room. I had heard the music before, but I couldn't remember the name. The girl swayed to the rhythm. Suddenly, she was flying across the room in elegant leaps. She twirled and spun on her toes while her arms circled her body in great sweeps. The music surrounded her and she moved to it effortlessly. Her form was controlled, yet there was so much freedom in her movement. My heart hurt from the poignancy of the girl's dance.

With one huge leap it was over as a single note echoed in the empty room. The girl crouched on the floor with her head bowed. When she lifted her face, she wore a smile of complete joy. I could feel the girl's happiness, and I knew this was her purpose in life.

The scene shifted, and we were in a bar. Young men in uniform gathered along the bar and in the corners. The girl was on the dance floor with her friends. Once again the music carried her away, as it had in the dance studio. Only this time the music was the hard, throbbing rhythm of rock and roll. She knew she wasn't supposed to be in the bar—she was too young. But she didn't care; she delighted in breaking the rules. From the corner of her eye she saw a soldier, a cigarette held between his thumb and forefinger, watching her. Turning to face him, with sensuous moves she rotated her hips in time to the music. The soldier's eyes grew wide in appreciation, and he blew out a long stream of smoke. She gave him a bold look and continued dancing, using all her skill as a dancer to keep the soldier's attention.

When the song ended, she left her friends standing on the dance floor and walked up to him, smiling. He threw an arm around her shoulder and handed her a bottle. Tossing her head back, she downed the contents in one gulp. Reaching up, she removed the cigarette from his mouth and, placing it between her own lips, took a drag. The soldier laughed and bent to whisper in her ear. She looked up at him, smiling, and—

The rage hit me and slammed me against the wall, clouding the vision of the girl and the soldier from my mind. It wasn't my rage I felt, but someone else's. The soldier's? It was dark, and it roiled through the room in angry waves sweeping me with it. I was caught in the vortex, and it was pulling me deeper and deeper into the depths of hate, vengeance, and grief. I knew if I didn't free myself quickly, I would be lost forever in its dark tortuous mass. Like a swimmer struggling toward the surface, I kicked free.

I jolted awake. My body was covered with drops of sweat. Disoriented, I pulled myself up and looked around the room. Familiar objects surrounded me, and I sighed with relief. I was in my own bed, in my own house—back where I belonged.

Queenie crawled on my lap, her purr rumbling in the quiet room. I stroked her absentmindedly while I thought about the dream. The music was familiar, and the melody fluttered and teased in my head. I was close, so close, to remembering, but it evaded me. I knew I had heard that song before, but where and when? I had never seen the girl before in my life. Who was she?

# *Twenty*

"What happened to you?" Darci said when I approached the counter the next morning.

"Thanks, and you look nice, too," I replied, smiling tightly.

I didn't need to be reminded how awful I looked. I already knew. I had spent most of the night trying to remember the song from my dream, vision, or whatever it was.

No matter how hard I tried, it wouldn't come. It was driving me nuts. My eyes had dark circles under them and were red from lack of sleep. I felt out of sorts and hoped today would be calm. I needed time to regroup.

"I'm sorry, did you have a bad night?"

"Yeah, I did. Things are spinning out of control, and I don't know what to do next. I tried to do as Abby instructed last night, but I don't know if it worked or not."

"What happened?"

"I dreamed of a girl dancing, a ballet, to a familiar song, but I can't remember the name. Somehow I think it's important that I remember."

"Did you know the girl?"

"No, of that, I'm sure. But I can't shake the feeling she's somehow tied to the dead man I found." I rubbed my hand across my forehead. "I don't know. The situation is so complicated. Maybe my dream was some type of a vision, or maybe it was just random electrical firings from my subconscious."

"Hum the song for me, maybe I can help."

"Oh, please. I can't sing for sour apples, and that includes humming."

"Try."

I hummed the tune. "There, happy? Bet you didn't recognize it, did you?"

She shook her head. "I'm sorry."

"What's this? A sing-along? Can I join?" Rick said, walking from around the corner of a bookcase and wearing his usual grin.

I eyed him suspiciously, while Rick looked back at me, the picture of innocence.

Who *was* Rick Davis? I'd known him for little over a week, but what I knew about him wouldn't, to quote Abby, have filled a thimble. Was he as innocent as he appeared? Abby said the person who left the note wore a mask. What if Rick's friendly attitude was a mask? A mask to hide the evil. A chill blew over my skin.

Rick squirmed a little. "What?" he asked defensively. "What have I done now?"

"Nothing," I said, rubbing my forehead again. "Don't you have someplace else to go?" I asked, squinting at him.

"I'm glad to see you, too," he said, ignoring the hint. "You look a little rough today. Tired. Like you haven't been sleeping well. Have you been sleeping well?"

This guy doesn't give up, I thought, rolling my eyes and shaking my head.

I turned my attention to Darci. "I'm going to my office. And I don't want to be disturbed by anyone," I added, with a pointed look back at Rick.

"But we weren't finished talking."

"Oh yes we were."

"No," he said slowly. "I want to know why you're having trouble sleeping. When someone can't sleep, it's because something's bothering them. Is anything bothering you?"

"You mean other than you?" I asked sarcastically.

"Ha ha, you're such a kidder. Sometimes a guilty conscience can keep people awake at night. Are you feeling guilty about anything? Would you like to talk to me about it?" he asked, tracing his finger back and forth along the edge of the bookcase.

When I didn't answer, Rick shifted his posture. His shoulders squared, and the affable manner he'd worn since I met him seemed to fall away like a snake shedding its skin. And I got a glimpse of the man behind the jokes and the teasing. A man with a strong will, who let very little stand in his way when pursuing his goal.

"You don't know what you're dealing with, Jensen," he said, looking me over.

"I—I don't know what you mean," I stammered, and looked down at my feet.

No, I would *not* let him intimidate me. I tossed back my head and met his stare. "The only thing I want to tell you, Rick, is to—"

"Good morning, Ophelia."

Damn, Abby was standing there. She was dressed in a gray linen pantsuit that made her eyes look even grayer. Her normal braid was wound not around the top of her head, but in an elegant knot at the base of her skull. And in her arms was a huge dried herb arrangement. I spotted goldenrod, eucalyptus, clover, and angelica. All arranged in a willow basket. Abby wasn't taking any chances—each one of the herbs, along with the basket made from willow, was to provide protection.

I stole a quick look at Rick, and I could almost hear his urbane facade click back into place.

"Abby, what a large arrangement," I said. "Is that for here?"

"Yes, dear, I thought you might need it."

Right, I bet she had the salt in her bag, and when my back was turned, it would be sprinkled all over our carpets.

"You haven't introduced me to your friend."

I grimaced. The inevitable had happened. "Abby, I'd like to introduce you to Rick Davis. Rick, my grandmother, Abigail McDonald."

"So, this is the nice young man I've been hearing about? I'm pleased to meet you, Mr. Davis." Abby shook his hand warmly.

"Please, Mrs. McDonald, call me Rick," he said, and turned on the charisma.

I found an interesting spot to watch on the floor. I knew what Abby was going to do to him. He might have thought he was irresistible but wait till she finished with him. His brain would be scrambled for about five minutes.

"You must call me Abby. I've wanted to meet you, Rick. I would like to thank you for rescuing my grand-daughter that day in the woods. It was quite a shock for both of you. I'm so glad you were able to reach Bill and get help. I shudder to think what might have happened to her had you not been there." She beamed at him.

She could match Rick Davis any day when it came to charm.

Rick turned to me. "Are you sure you're related to Abby? She's charming and friendly."

Yeah, you think she's charming. You just wait, buster, she's steel in a velvet glove. Instead of voicing my opinion, I raised my eyebrows and smiled sweetly at him. After all this man had put me through, I felt no sympathy for what was about to happen to him. Abby handed me the basket. Ah, here it comes.

"Well, I really must go." She leaned forward around the huge arrangement and gave me a peck on the cheek. When she turned to Rick, she extended her hand. The fool took it.

"Rick, it was so nice to meet you." Abby placed her other hand on top of their joined hands and stared at him purposefully.

Rick's eyes grew wide and his pupils dilated. I knew the energy from Abby's hands was traveling up his arm, warming his skin and invading his mind. It only lasted a couple of seconds, then Abby dropped his hand. He swayed slightly when she released him. Shaking his head, he gazed at her, then at me, his eyes a little unfocused.

"Yeah, yeah. I'd—I'd better go, too. Nice to meet you."

Abby and I watched Rick totter off, wobbling a little when he went out the door.

"He'll be okay in a few minutes. My, I hate doing that. It seems like such an invasion of a person's privacy, but we had to know."

"Well?"

"He's not the one you seek this time, but he isn't who he says he is. He, too, wears a mask, but there is no evil behind it. Maybe a little overconfidence, and a lot of determination." Abby smiled. "But inside he's a good man."

What did she mean by "this time"? I let the comment pass. He wasn't the bad guy, so I could put my earlier thoughts to rest. I was amazed at my relief. Ever since I'd met him, I had tried to convince Rick, and myself, that I didn't like him. Why should I be relieved he wasn't the bad guy? And what did he mean by "You don't know what you're dealing with"?

"What else did you see?"

"You know how it is, jumbled thoughts, feelings. But should we be talking about this here? Why don't we go to your office?"

I walked to the counter and handed the arrangement to Darci.

"Don't ask," I said to her as she took the basket. "Abby and I are going downstairs if you need anything."

"I'll be okay. I don't think we'll be very busy today. Everyone seems pretty subdued," she said, picking at the side of the basket.

I lightly touched her hand. "Did you go by the Jones house last night?"

"Yeah, I took over some food. Beth was resting, but I talked to Mike."

"Do they know what happened?"

"Not for sure, but they've accepted the fact Doug was probably high on meth. They knew something was wrong. His grades were falling and he'd quit basketball. He had also been losing weight. They thought it was over some girl." Her voice sounded thick, and she cleared her throat. "Doug was such a good kid, and he had such a bright future."

"Any idea where he got it?"

"No. Everyone in town knows who the users are, but no one thinks they live next door to a meth lab. They think it's all coming out of Des Moines, since it's the largest city close to Summerset."

I nodded. "Just like they don't think they live next door to a murderer."

"Exactly. All I know is this town has some real problems, and unless we want more dead kids, people need to quit burying their heads in the sand and take some action." She paused. "By the way, I saw Rick leave. He looked funny. What was wrong with him?"

"Abby read him. It always scrambles their brain a little when that happens."

"What did she find out?"

"She didn't tell me everything yet, but she did say he wasn't one of the bad guys."

"Well, you must be relieved. It would have been hard on you, falling for a guy and then finding out he's a criminal."

"I'm not *falling* for anyone. We don't even like each other," I said emphatically.

"Right." She picked up the returned books. "Isn't Abby waiting for you?"

"Yeah. We'll talk later, and I'll fill you in."

When I entered my office, Abby was at the desk, in front of the computer, playing with the mouse.

Her face wore a big smile while she used the mouse to swirl the cursor around the screen. "Ophelia, you must teach me how to use one of these. This is fascinating."

I laughed. "You're right. Maybe I should. You'd love the Internet. But you have to promise me if I do teach you, you won't become a computer junkie."

Abby continued staring at the monitor and the cursor as it darted back and forth.

"So what did you learn from Rick?"

She sat back, reluctantly letting go of the mouse, and folded her hands in her lap. "Like I said, he's a good man, a little overconfident maybe. His driving force seems to be curiosity. He's not from a small town."

"No kidding, I knew that without touching him. What else?" I asked, sitting on the corner of the desk.

"He's known success—one of the reasons for his confidence—but more is to come. He's as involved as you are in what will happen and he shares your danger. I thought about warning him, but when the time comes, you'll be together. You must trust him and protect each other."

"Hmm, he was warning me," I said, stroking my chin.

"What did you say?" Abby asked.

"Nothing, nothing," I said, returning my focus to her. "Did you see this danger?"

"No, but it's drawing closer, like a circle getting smaller and smaller. You and he are in the center of the circle."

Great, that was reassuring.

"Now what about you? Did you learn anything last night when you sought your answers?"

"How did you know?"

"You have the look. I know you don't like this, but you have to accept what you are. Once you do, you'll find the peace you've been looking for."

"Abby, where's the peace in knowing the pain waiting for others? You knew about Doug before Claire told us, didn't you?"

"I knew part of it. I felt the tragedy coming, but I didn't know where it would strike."

"What a burden for you," I said, reaching over and touching her shoulder.

"Yes, sometimes it is a burden, but it can be a great joy, too. Someday you'll see the joy," she said, patting my hand. "What did you see last night?"

"Could we talk about it later? So much has happened the past few days, and I'm so far behind in paperwork. In fact, I'm staying late tonight to work on it."

"Do you think that's wise? Staying here alone?"

"I'll be as safe here as at home. I promise I'll call right before I leave, so you know I'm on my way home, okay?"

"Whatever you think, dear. Well, I must go."

We both stood and Abby gave me a tight hug.

"Don't forget to call, all right?" she said, taking a step back while she tucked a strand of hair behind my ear.

"Don't worry," I said, and kissed her cheek. "I won't forget." Sitting down at my desk, I grabbed a pile of papers. "Oh, and Abby?" I remembered one last thing. "No salt."

She smiled mysteriously and glided out the door.

The rest of the day flew by. I'd made a sizable dent in the pile on my desk and was surprised when Darci stood at the door.

"Time to close, Ophelia."

"I know, but I'm just about finished with all of this. I'm going to stay till I am. I don't want to deal with it tomorrow."

"Will you be okay?"

"Yeah, don't worry. Tomorrow's Friday, and since we don't open until after lunch, maybe we can get together in the morning and compare notes."

"If you're sure?"

"Go. I'll be fine."

Two hours later I finished. I grabbed my backpack and headed up the stairs. Darci had thoughtfully left the lights on, so I wouldn't have to feel my way across the library. I shut them off as I went.

When I locked the door, I thought I heard something. I stopped and listened closely. Nothing, I thought while I shot the lock home. It was just my imagination, stimulated by Darci's and Abby's concern. Then I heard it again. A rustling followed by a groan. Do I investigate or call 911?

The groan came again, followed by, "Ophelia."

I turned, trying to see what stood at the bottom of the steps. In the dim light of the streetlamp, I made out a shadow to the left of the steps. While I watched, it moved forward, into the light. It was Rick, and even from where I stood, I could see the blood dripping down his face.

# Twenty-one

"What happened?" I said, running over to him. Pulling a handkerchief from my pocket, I shoved it in his hand.

"Thanks," he said, holding the cloth to his head. "Somebody was waiting for me when I got back to my room. I don't know, must have been behind the door and swung at me when I came through. I saw stars and that was it."

"Come on, we need to get you to a doctor," I said, grabbing his arm.

"No, no doctor," he replied, jerking his arm away from my grasp.

I reached out to steady him as he staggered. "Why? You might have a concussion."

"No," he said, his mouth set in a stubborn line. "Too many questions."

Okay, then. I watched the blood continue to leak past the handkerchief and down Rick's face. We could stand here arguing while he bled all over the sidewalk, or I could take him to someone who could at least stop the bleeding.

"Get in the car," I said, and tugged on his sleeve.

"No doctor?" he asked, looking at me suspiciously.

"Nope, no doctor," I replied while leading him to my car. After he slid into the passenger side, I got in, started the car and pulled away.

"Where are you taking me?"

"Abby's. She knows a lot about first aid, but if she says you need a doctor, you're going." I peeked at Rick from the corner of my eye.

He sat with his head drooping. And his skin, lighted by the dim glow of dash lights, looked pale.

I nudged his arm. "Hey, don't go to sleep on me. I do know you can't do that with a head injury. Insult me or something, will you?"

He lifted his head and smiled weakly. "Sorry, I seem to be fresh out at the moment. Don't worry, I won't go to sleep. My head hurts like a sonofabitch."

"Why didn't you call for Georgia? She would've helped you. Why drive, bleeding, to the library?" I asked.

"I couldn't get the bleeding to stop, and you're the only one I could think of who'd help me without blabbing about it all over town." He leaned his head back. "Georgia would've called 911, and then her boyfriend, Alan, the deputy. Too much attention, too much suspicion, I don't need that right now," he said, and his eyelids drifted down.

I poked him again. "No sleeping, remember?"

He snapped his head forward. "Ouch. That hurt." He dabbed at his scalp. "Remind me not to move my head so much, will you?"

"Are you going to tell me why you don't want too much attention?"

"Not right now." He held the cloth out and looked at it. "You can grill me later, okay?"

I tapped my finger on the steering wheel as I drove.

Ha, me grill Rick? What a switch. Usually it was the other way around. Could be fun. I looked at him from the corner of my eye. His face was too pale. I tightened my grip on the wheel and pushed the gas pedal down a little farther. If he passed out, I couldn't question him. I needed to get him to Abby. She'd know how to deal with his injury.

She opened the door before I could even knock. Her thick braid lay over the shoulder of her plaid flannel robe. And the tiny buttons of her nightgown peeked out from the vee of her robe. I watched her brow knit together while she assessed Rick's condition.

"Back this way," she said, taking his arm.

I clasped Rick's other arm and we guided him toward the kitchen. I didn't know if she heard the car come up the drive or was waiting. Should I ask her in front of Rick? From behind his back I gave Abby a questioning look, but she shook her head, telling me, *"Not now."* And I clamped my mouth shut.

When we reached the kitchen, my question was answered. A fire burned in the wood stove, and the steam from a large pot of water filled the air. On the counter, next to the stove, a pile of clean white rags were stacked and waiting. Assembled on the worn top of the butcher-block table, along with her mortar and pestle, were various herbs. She knew.

After seating Rick at her kitchen table, Abby settled into the chair beside him.

"Ophelia? Will you put the kettle on and make some tea for yourself? The fire's already stoked. I'll check Rick out," Abby said while she gently parted Rick's hair and looked at the wound. It had stopped bleeding freely, but the cut was still oozing.

"Well, you have quite a bump, young man, but it

doesn't seem to be serious. You must have a hard head." She looked in Rick's eyes. "Your pupils aren't dilated; that's a good sign. It means you don't have a concussion. Looks like the cut's the worst of it."

"He's bled a lot, Abby."

"Not really, it just looks that way. Cuts on the head or face always seem to bleed a lot. I'll get him cleaned up, and other than a headache, he'll be as right as rain."

"Are you a nurse or something?" Rick asked.

"No, my mother was a healer in the mountains of Appalachia. When I was a girl, I would help her tend our neighbors," she said, rising and crossing to the butcher-block table.

Taking her mortar and pestle, she ground dried leaves to a fine powder, then sprinkled it in the boiling water. The kitchen filled with the aroma of wood sorrel.

"Ophelia, I need an infusion of rosemary for Rick. The rosemary is on the table. The infusion should help the headache."

She took the hot water from the stove. Using one of the rags from the counter, she cleaned Rick's scalp.

"What's that stuff you sprinkled in the water?"

"Wood sorrel. It'll clean the wound and help it heal. Ophelia, the tea ball is in the left-hand cupboard."

I put some leaves and dried flowers in the ball and poured hot water over it. It needed to steep for about five minutes before he could drink it.

Rick smiled. "This is a side of you I've never seen. Are you sure you know what you're doing? You aren't going to put any surprise ingredients in that cup, are you?"

"Don't tempt me, Davis. You must be feeling better— you're insulting me now. Do you feel like telling us what happened?"

"Like I told you, someone was in my room. I'd been playing pool at Stumpy's and had dinner at Joe's. The house was locked when I got there. I knew Georgia wouldn't be there because she told me she had a date with Alan tonight. There was nothing to tip me off. I didn't see any sign of a break-in. Maybe they came in through a window; I don't know."

"No, that wouldn't have been necessary," I said. "Everybody in town knows Georgia keeps a key to the back door under the flower pot on the stoop."

He shook his head. "Georgia has some security issues, doesn't she? By the way, how many room keys does she have floating around?"

I flushed when I handed him the tea. "Okay, I'm not going to lie, but how did you know it was me?"

"You didn't get my boxers put back the right way." Rick winked at Abby. "But we'll talk about my boxers when your grandmother isn't around."

"That told you someone had been there, but how did you know it was me?"

"When Darci showed up at the door with that load of crap about the mouse in the basement. She saved you, you know. I'd already checked in the drawer and found the matchbook gone. I was about to check the closet when she knocked. You were hiding there, weren't you? It's where I found Georgia's gloves."

"Drink your tea," I said, my face turning a deeper shade of red.

"Wow, that's hot. What did you say it is?"

"An infusion of rosemary, to help the headache," Abby said.

I picked up the bowl of water and carried it to the sink. "All right, so now you know the truth about me—"

"I doubt that, but I'll let it pass for now."

I frowned. "Let's get to the point. I think it's safe to say I know you're not a chemical salesman, so you can quit feeding me that line. Tell me, Davis, just who the hell are you?"

"It's not Davis, it's Delaney. I'm Rick Delaney, a reporter with the *Minneapolis Sun*."

Damn, a journalist.

Abby caught my eye and nodded slightly. Unspoken words passed between us. Rick was telling the truth this time. Next question: Why would a journalist from Minneapolis be in Summerset, Iowa?

Before I could ask, Abby picked up the rest of the supplies, set them on the counter, and turned to leave.

"I'm going to bed now. You don't need me to hash this all out—Ophelia can tell me about it tomorrow. Are you going back to Georgia's, Rick, or would you like to stay here? Ophelia can show you to a spare bedroom."

I groaned.

"Thanks, Abby, but I'd better go back. I want to clean up the room before Georgia sees it." Rick looked around the kitchen at Abby's hanging herbs, candles, and crystals. "I didn't know anyone in Summerset would be into all this New Age stuff."

From the doorway, she laughed. "It's not New Age, Rick. It's old age—very old age. Good night."

I pulled out a chair and sat at the table across from Rick.

"What's a journalist from Minnesota doing in Summerset?"

"Following a lead on a drug ring," Rick said, sipping his tea.

"Oh, come on. Summerset doesn't have any drug ring. We're a small town. We've got our users, but that stuff is coming in from one of the big cities."

"I don't think so. I'm pretty sure it's right here. Next, you're going to tell me small towns don't have dead bodies lying in the woods?"

Looking down at my cup of tea, I thought about it. He had a point; we weren't supposed to have those either.

"Look, I want to ask you something before you start grilling me. How did you know about the matchbook?"

Thinking fast, I shrugged. "I could tell it was something important—you had it in a Ziploc—so I took it. You're really not a very convincing chemical salesman, Rick. And I thought the matches might help me figure out who you were and why you were here."

"You know I found them on the dead man, don't you?"

"Yeah, that's obvious when you open the Ziploc. How could you stand to touch them?"

"Why do you think I put them in a bag?"

"Let's get back to why you're here. What makes you think we have a drug ring?"

"Not just a drug ring, a major drug ring. That's why I tried warning you today at the library. If you go blundering around and they get the idea you know something—"

"Okay," I said, stopping him. "I get it. A major drug ring. Why here?"

"Two months ago a guy was busted in Minneapolis running meth. His trunk was full of it. I knew something big was going down when the police put a lid on the whole case. I couldn't even get my source in the department to tell me anything. And forget about an interview. So I went to the street to check with my snitch, Weasel—"

I laughed. "You have a snitch named Weasel? Isn't that—I don't know—kind of Sam Spade?"

"Look, I can't help it if the guy reads too many detective novels, okay? Now, do you want to hear this or not?"

"Go ahead."

"Anyway, Weasel said—"

The snort came out before I could stop it. "Sorry."

"Hey, I'm not too crazy about the name *'Bubba,'* but you don't hear me snorting every time somebody says it. Are you going to listen or not?"

"Yes, and no more snorts, I promise," I said, crossing my heart.

"My snitch said there was a lot more to it than the police were telling. And even on the street, people got real quiet when he started asking questions. All he could find out is there's big money behind it, and it's coming out of Iowa. So I checked the Internet for all recent stories about chemical thefts. Summerset was the name that popped up."

"But that doesn't mean the drug ring's here. They could be stealing the anhydrous here and making the drugs somewhere else, couldn't they?"

"Yes, of course, that's what I'm trying to find out. But then I get here and there's another theft and we find a dead body."

"It could be a coincidence."

"I don't think so. Do you know how much money meth brings on the street? For less than twenty-five dollars' worth of chemicals, a dealer can make twenty grams of meth. He turns around and sells the twenty grams on the street for about four hundred dollars. A large lab can produce a pound a day—so we're talking over nine thousand dollars a *day*. That's a lot of money—more than enough to kill for."

"What about the matches? Do you really think that

ties the dead guy to Summerset? He could have picked them up anywhere."

"That's true, but don't you think it's odd that the same weekend of the murder, Ned's pictures of the Korn Karnival were destroyed? Except for the mess, the pictures were the only thing torched."

"You think the dead man was tied to the drug ring, had been here in Summerset—probably meeting with his killer—and that Ned might have managed to photograph the two of them together?"

"Yeah."

"Do Bill and Alan know who you are and what you're doing here?"

"Well, they know who I am now. I had to tell them after we found the dead body. But I lied about why I was here."

"Did they tell you anything?"

"No. Bill told me to keep my nose out of it and let them handle it. It's the reason I didn't want Georgia to call Alan tonight. If Bill found out about the break-in, he'd think I was stirring up trouble, and would probably make a strong suggestion that I go back to Minneapolis." Rick paused and swirled his tea in his cup. "I'm not ready to leave yet."

"What if whoever searched your room comes back?" I clenched my cup tighter. I didn't like thinking about what might happen to Rick if they did.

From the look on his face, the idea of facing his burglars again didn't bother him. He ignored my question, sipped his tea, then set his cup on the table.

"I was hoping I could get chummy with Ned and find out what he knows, but that won't happen now."

"Why not?"

Rick smiled. "In case you haven't noticed, Ned doesn't like me. I think he sees me as competition."

I blushed. "Oh, don't be ridiculous. Ned and I are friends." I had an awful thought then that maybe he meant Darci, not me. I turned a deeper red. "Ahh, you did mean because of me, didn't you?"

"Yes, Ophelia, I meant because of you."

Rick crossed his arms and placed them on the table. I leaned back, away from him.

"You're not very comfortable with that, are you?"

I scooted my chair away from the table. "We're not talking about me, we're talking about you and what you're doing here."

"You really are very good at evasion." He changed the subject when he saw my glare. "Okay, okay, I won't say anything more about your personal life. But you've known Ned since you moved here, right?"

"Right. Why?"

"Do you trust him?"

"I guess. You don't think he's involved?"

"I don't know; he didn't like me asking questions about the Korn Karnival. He seemed to be hedging." Rick rubbed his forehead. "I don't know who to trust—except you, that is. For all I know, even Bill and Alan could be involved. This kind of money can corrupt people."

"What do you do now?"

"I've been trying to get on the inside with some users in town, find out who supplies them, but they're not the most trusting souls, either."

"What are you going to do?"

"My idea's still good. Rule number one, always follow the money. But I need help."

"So who's going to help you? You said you don't trust anyone except—"

What a dumb question. I knew what his next words would be.

"You. You and Darci. I want you both to help me."

# Twenty-two

The dreams continued to trouble my sleep. They came unbidden now, and I never knew when they would happen. Every night new scenes would be added. The scenes would fly by in my mind faster and faster. Sometimes she would be standing with the soldier next to a red convertible, outside of the bar. Sometimes they would be driving down the road in the red car. Sometimes she would be making out with him in her car. But the rage I'd felt from someone, or something, never returned. Thank God.

And the song from those dreams haunted my waking hours. Abby could make no sense of it, and neither could I.

The community was still reeling from the tragedy of Doug Jones's death. Rumors and innuendos circulated endlessly. Several people blamed Bill and Alan for not being more aggressive. Talk of a new police force ran rampant. If Adam Hoffman chose that as a running platform, the job of mayor would be his.

I tried to function normally, but my nerves were stretched and ready to snap. Rick and Darci's big plan didn't help. At least, the plan didn't involve burglary.

So here I was, in Darci's car, looking at myself in the mirror.

"Darci, I've lived here four years, and I've never been in this bar. What will Mrs. Abernathy say if she hears I'm hanging out at Stumpy's Bar and Billiards?"

It was time to launch the plan—Darci and I were meeting Rick at Stumpy's. It was stupid, and I shouldn't have let her and Rick talk me into it.

Darci tossed her head. "Oh, who cares about Mrs. Abernathy? She gossips about everyone. Believe me, nobody listens to her."

She found the idea of helping Rick with his investigation thrilling. I think she fancied herself a midwestern Mata Hari. Certainly, she dressed the part in black leather pants, black turtleneck, and black boots. All she needed was a trench coat and a fedora and she would have looked the perfect spy. She tried to convince me to dress in a similar fashion, but I drew the line at the leather pants. I felt exotic enough after Darci finished with me. I allowed her to *do* my face. Darci said I looked great. I thought I looked like a hooker. But it was too late now to wipe it off, so I followed Darci when she sailed in the door.

The first thing I noticed was the number of people in the bar. Even though it was Monday night, the place was full, the air thick from smoke. Several men in the back were playing pool. I heard the crack when the balls struck. Darci found us a table in back and ordered two beers. I fought the desire to clean the tabletop with a napkin. It appeared to be moist, almost sweaty. I tried to find a place to put my hands but finally gave up and stuck them in my coat pockets. A TV, with the sound turned down and a pro football game playing, hung on the wall to the right of the bar. The bar itself was scarred and scratched from too many beers sliding across its surface. The decor was completed by several pairs of antlers positioned around the aged mirror behind the bar. I had never really understood the term "joint" when referring to a drinking establishment, but now I did. There certainly wasn't anything upscale about this place. And where was Rick? He was supposed to meet us there.

Darci busied herself noticing men noticing her. I prayed none of them would decide to make our acquaintance. However, Darci already knew most of them; her dating record was phenomenal. My prayer went unanswered when Jake Jenkins swaggered over. He spun an empty chair around so the back was facing the table and sat down.

It was apparent Jake wasn't on the subscription list of *GQ*. He wore boots and jeans with a work shirt, as did most of the patrons, but Jake's was unbuttoned halfway down his chest, revealing a thick mat of hair. Nestled in the hair was a gold chain. It was not a good look for Jake.

He eyed us both thoughtfully while he sipped his beer, holding the bottle with thumb and forefinger.

"Darci, how's it going?" he asked, resting his arms on the back of the chair.

"Okay." Darci leaned back in her chair.

Jake, having apparently exhausted his supply of snappy dialogue, was silent for a moment. He smiled, with what I'm sure he considered great charm, but a sneer would have been a better description. "You know, you really should go out with me, Darci. I could show a girl like you a real good time, if you know what I mean."

I knew what he meant, and so did Darci.

"Sorry, Jake. I already told you I'm not interested."

"What, you too good for me?" Jake's sneer became ugly.

The tension between Jake and Darci shot up a notch. She dropped her head. It was obvious she wasn't going to respond to him. The desire to defend Darci became overwhelming. I had to put my two cents in.

"Jake, Darci has already said no. Not meaning to sound trite, but what part of that don't you understand?"

Jake, tight-lipped, turned to me. "You got a thing for her or what?"

"I beg your pardon?"

"Everyone in town knows you don't date, so you must be queer," he said, leering at me.

My temper flared. And I fought the desire to pick up the beer bottle and bop him on the head.

Ignoring the sweaty tabletop and whatever else might be lying on the filmy surface, I placed both hands on the table and gave him an icy stare. "Tell me, Jake, does it take practice to be that stupid?"

He leaned toward me from across the table. "Listen, sister, what you need is a real man to straighten you out."

"Gee, Jake," I said sweetly, sitting back and crossing my arms, "know where I can find one?"

He looked quickly to his right to see if the next table heard my insult to his manhood. They did, and were snickering. A red flush spread up his thick neck to his face. He drained his beer and jerked to his feet, slamming the bottle down. He didn't exactly slink away, but he wasn't swaggering, either.

Darci watched him leave. "I appreciate you defending me, but you shouldn't have said that to Jake."

"You're right," I said with a quick nod. "Instead, I

should have told him extreme homophobia sometimes indicates closet homosexuality in males. But I imagine those words are too long for him to understand."

Darci paled at the thought of me insinuating to Jake that he was gay.

"Jake is a bully. People who insult him always pay some kind of price. You remember Matt Wilson? He got into a disagreement with Jake and later his dog was found dead. Poisoned. Matt never did prove it was Jake, but . . ."

I got her point, but I wasn't going to let Jake Jenkins bully me.

When Rick finally walked in, every woman in the place went on point. He was that good-looking. A calculating look flickered across several of their faces, but he didn't seem to notice. His first stop was at the bar to pick up a beer. While he made his way through the crowded room with an easy grace, I noticed several of the men spoke to him. He certainly had made himself at home in Summerset, and he appeared to fit right in with the good ol' boy set. He would've made a good actor.

"So, how long have you been here?" Rick said when he slid onto the chair next to me. No spinning the chair around and sitting in it backward for him.

"Long enough for Darci to get hit on by a creep. Where were you? I thought you were going be here at seven." I have a low tolerance for people being late.

"Sorry, I was held up. Who hit on you, Darci?"

"Oh, Jake Jenkins, but Ophelia took care of him."

I wasn't paying attention to their conversation. I was still thinking about the *"Sorry, I was held up."* In my opinion, it was not a legitimate explanation. I looked at Rick and saw him staring at me.

"Hmm?" I was caught wool gathering.

"Ophelia, I said, 'How did you take care of him?'" Rick asked.

"Oh, I just cast aspersions on his masculinity and he left." I shrugged.

Rick sputtered his beer. "That'll do it. Most men tend to be rather sensitive about that."

Darci rushed to my defense. "He told Ophelia she needed a real man. Of course, that was after she called him ignorant and he called her—"

I smiled and held up my hand, interrupting her. "That's okay, Darci, I think Rick gets the picture."

I didn't want to have that conversation again, especially with Rick. A conversation that included what I might or might not need from a man.

"Who's that guy over there by the pool table?" Rick asked abruptly. "The stringy one, with the ponytail?"

Rick was talking about Larry Durbin, and he was right. Everything about Larry was stringy. His hair, worn in a long, thin ponytail, and his body, resplendent with tattoos. And there was a whiteness about him, like he never spent time in the sun. It was amazing that the same small town produced both a Larry Durbin and a Jake Jenkins. They were opposites on the human spectrum.

"Oh, that's Larry Durbin, a friend of Darci's."

Darci frowned. "Larry's not so bad. Maybe if his parents hadn't pushed him so hard, if they hadn't sheltered him so much, maybe he wouldn't have gone so wild in college. He sure made up for lost time. There wasn't anything he didn't try. He got sucked into drugs and kicked out of college his freshman year. After that he bounced around from school to school, burning up his parents' money. When it ran out, he drifted around the country. Three years ago he came home to Sum-merset. He lives in a run-down trailer outside of town. It's a regular stop for Bill and Alan."

"Hey, aren't we here for a purpose?" I asked.

Rick twirled his beer bottle. "Yeah, you're right."

I leaned over and whispered, "Well, you're the ex-pert, Mr. Investigative Reporter. What do we do?"

"Let's go play pool."

"Pool."

"Yeah, pool. Come on, Darci."

I failed to see how playing pool was going to help bust a drug ring, but what do I know? I'm just a librar-ian. The three of us walked to the back, picking up more beer on the way. The pool tables were all in use, so we waited until a table opened. After the balls were racked, we started to play.

Rick and Darci both knew their way around a pool cue, unlike me. Rick gave me pointers, which I found most annoying. After the fourth such helpful tip, I glanced up at him as I was lining up my shot. "If this is where you say, 'See the ball, be the ball,' I'm going to use this cue on you."

Rick laughed. "I wouldn't think of it, Ophelia."

I took my shot, and the ball almost made it in the pocket. I was very pleased with myself.

It was Rick's turn. He ran the table, game over. His shots earned the attention of the guys milling around.

"Hey man, you're pretty good." The praise came from Larry Durbin. He looked at Rick with anticipa-tion. "Wanna play some eight ball? Five bucks a piece, winner take all?"

"Sure. Rack 'em up."

Personally, I thought Larry had made a sucker's bet. Rick had just finished running the table. He would have been better off challenging me. Maybe this was some guy thing I didn't understand.

Darci and I leaned against the wall and watched the contest. Rick sank the first ball, a solid color, so I assumed his job was to hit all of those in. Larry got the striped ones. Darci, being the expert, gave me a play-by-play report. They seemed fairly well matched to me. First Rick would hit a few in, then miss. Larry would do the same. Eventually it was down to one of the little striped ones, the eight ball, and the cue ball. It was Rick's turn. Darci said he had to hit the black one with the white one and call which pocket it was going in.

"Eight ball in the corner pocket," Rick said, and lined up the cue stick.

By this time everyone was standing around, engrossed in the game. The black ball went in the corner pocket, followed by the white ball. I thought he won and we could leave. But everyone groaned, and Larry scooped up the money. I didn't understand, so I turned to question Darci.

"Rick scratched," she said before I could ask.

Scratched? What's scratched? Darci very patiently explained that it wasn't a good thing if the white ball goes in, too. Oh well, we'd still get to leave. Wrong.

"Wanna try again?" Larry said smugly. "Double or nothing?"

"Okay."

Now I groaned. One hour and four games later, Rick was several dollars poorer, and I had decided investigating drug rings wasn't all it was cracked up to be. Rick and Larry seemed best buds. I was relieved when Rick suggested to Darci and me that we leave. Finally. I couldn't conceive why Rick was so pleased with himself while he walked Darci and me to the car.

"So, what did you accomplish? Other than you have a new friend named Larry?"

"I may not be the smartest person in the world, Ophelia," Darci said, "but even I know a setup when I see one. Didn't you figure that out?"

"What?"

"Yeah." Rick smiled. "Not only do I have a new friend, but I've got one who's in on the drug scene in Summerset."

# Twenty-three

"Do you think Larry's going to tell you anything?"

"Yeah, I do."

The night was cold. I lifted my chin and took a deep breath. The smell of snow was in the air. It was refreshing after so many hours in the crowded, smoky bar.

Darci looked at Rick. "I told Georgia I'd stop by tonight, and I know Ophelia doesn't want to go. Would you mind giving her a ride home?"

This request was accompanied by a dazzling smile, not leaving him much room to say no.

"Sure, no problem."

"Really, Rick, it isn't necessary," I said. "I can go with Darci to Georgia's." I elbowed Darci in the side.

"Now, Ophelia, don't you remember saying how tired you were?" Darci said. "I don't want to keep you out any longer, but I did promise Georgia." She opened her car door and slipped inside.

Rick shut the door for her and looked at me. "I guess you're stuck with me."

Lowering my eyes and walking a couple of steps behind Rick, I thought about what he'd said. There were worse things than being stuck with Rick Delaney. And plenty of women would love to have been in my size seven shoes right then.

I raised my eyes to the sky and tried to see the stars beyond the streetlamps. But those women weren't me. They didn't have strange dreams at night, they didn't shrink from human touch, and they couldn't see the future. The night sky blurred for a moment, but I shook the tears away. *Quit feeling sorry for yourself, Jensen,* said a voice inside my head. *You are who you are and you can't change it.*

Rick gave me a puzzled look as he opened the passenger door for me, but I responded with a slight shake of my head and slid in the car. Within seconds we were on our way.

"You really think Larry's going to confide in you?" I asked.

"Yup, most people trust me."

"Must be the Boy Scout in you."

"How did you know?"

I looked over at him, surprised. "You really were a Boy Scout?"

"Yes." Rick's glance met mine. "You find that hard to believe?"

"Oh, I don't know. I'm tired and I'm not making much sense. This whole thing gives me the creeps," I said, rolling my shoulders.

Rick started to reach for my hand but stopped and put his hand back on the steering wheel.

"What do you know about Larry Durbin?"

"Just what Darci told you tonight. She doesn't think he's a bad person, just misguided," I said while I stared out the windshield. "It's too bad when someone gets into drugs like that. Larry had potential and he blew it. I feel sorry for him."

"I don't. Larry made his choices. His life doesn't have to be this way."

"Really? That's kind of cold, isn't it?"

"No, I don't think so. Sooner or later everyone has to take responsibility for themselves. You can only blame society, parents, or even fate, for your misfortune for so long."

I thought for a moment. "Do you believe in fate, or do you believe people have choices?"

"Hmm, I don't know. I suppose I believe they have choices. Most everyone chooses their own destiny."

"You don't believe you were meant to be a journalist?"

Rick smiled. "No, *that* I believe. I can't imagine doing anything else."

"Then you do believe in destiny."

"I don't know. I don't believe there's some big plan for all of us. I probably could have been happy doing something else, but I like my job so much, it's hard to imagine it. Does that make sense?"

"Yeah."

"What about you, do you believe in fate and destiny?"

"I think I'm starting to. I have it on the best authority some things are meant to be."

"I don't believe this." Rick slapped the steering wheel.

"Believe what? What's wrong?" I sat forward in the seat.

We were almost at my house. Was there something up ahead?

"We've actually had a real conversation and haven't insulted each other for, oh, at least five minutes. That's got to be a record for us." Rick smiled while he pulled into my driveway.

I grinned. "Jeez, I hate to let you down, Rick, but I

can't seem to think of anything insulting to say to you right now."

Rick turned and put his arm across the back of the seat.

"You know, I do like you, Ophelia. I always have, from that first day, when you caught me staring at you. You're an interesting woman, and you make me laugh." Rick leaned forward. "I hope, after this is all over, we can—"

He suddenly turned his head and looked down the street.

"Is that truck always parked there?"

I looked out the rear window. "No. And I don't recognize it. Is someone in it?"

"I think so. Put your seat belt back on. I'm going to double back and come up behind him."

Before Rick reached the truck, it lit out, tires spinning and rubber smoking. His hands gripped the steering wheel while he followed.

"Can you see the license plate?" Rick asked.

"No. Be careful, there's a sharp curve coming up."

The speedometer registered seventy. We lost sight of the taillights when Rick negotiated the curve. We saw them again about a mile ahead of us. Rick pushed on the gas pedal and I grasped the door. The truck made a quick turn onto a gravel road. Rick followed, but the car's tires skidded when they hit the gravel. The next thing I knew we were cruising sideways down the road with the ditch getting closer and closer. Rick's hands clung to the wheel while he tried to steer the car out of the spin. I saw the tall weeds fly by my window while the car continued to slide.

I closed my eyes and prayed.

\* \* \*

The car skidded to a halt, the left front tire almost over the edge of the ditch. We were now headed in the opposite direction, facing the corner we'd turned. The truck was long gone.

Rick slowly backed up the car until we were once again on the road. He shifted to park and turned in his seat to look at me.

"Are you okay?"

"You mean other than I think my heart's stopped?"

Rick reached out—he didn't hesitate this time. He took my shaking hand and brought it to his lips. Turning it over, he placed a soft kiss on the inside of my wrist. Well, at least I now knew my heart hadn't stopped—it was thumping in my chest.

Then it was over. Rick had both hands on the wheel and was staring straight ahead.

"You're something else, Ophelia Jensen. No hysterics for you. I'm sorry. That was stupid, and I could've gotten us killed."

This time I was the one who touched him. I laid my hand gently on his arm. It must have shocked him; his eyes widened. I removed my hand quickly. If it lingered, I might see things I didn't want to see.

"It's okay, Rick. We made it. You did a good job keeping the car out of the ditch, but I think we'd better get back to town."

"Yeah. When we get to your house, I want you to pack. I'm taking you to Abby's. You're not staying alone tonight."

I resented his tone. "Now wait a second. You can't tell me what to do."

He stared at me. "You have two choices—either spend the night with Abby or with me. Pick."

"Abby's," I said, and turned my head toward the side window.

At my house, Rick followed me like a bodyguard from room to room while I gathered my things. He even followed me up the stairs. I held up my hand and stopped him at the door to my bedroom.

"Oh, no you don't. You're not coming in here."

"Why? Afraid I'll search your drawers like you searched mine? Remember handling my boxers?"

"Trust me, Rick, it wasn't that big a thrill," I said with a wink and pointed to the floor. "Stay out here."

"What if someone's in there?"

"I'll scream, then you can come rushing in and save me."

"You're no fun. Did I happen to mention you look very nice tonight, Ophelia?" he asked, tilting his head and putting a shoulder against the wall.

"What is it with you?" I stared at him in exasperation. "You get near a woman and a bedroom and the charm clicks on like a lightbulb?"

He winked at me.

"Oh, knock it off," I said, rolling my eyes. "You can stand in the doorway, but don't you dare come in."

I grabbed my backpack and stuffed a clean nightgown and clothes in. Rick leaned against the door frame, watching me.

"Any idea who was in the truck?" he asked.

"Probably the same guy who sent me the note." I crossed to the bathroom for the rest of my stuff.

"What note?"

I jumped when I looked up and saw Rick's reflection staring at me in the mirror.

"You were supposed to stay in the doorway."

"To hell with that. I asked you, what note?"

"No need to lose your temper." I quickly tossed my toothbrush and toothpaste in the bag. "Ummm. Didn't I mention the note?" I said giving him a stealthy look.

His arms were crossed over his chest and his eyes were narrowed. "No, you *did not* mention the note. Why don't you tell me about it?"

"I can't even remember what day it was now." I hesitated, tapping my finger on my chin. "Wait. It was the day after I searched your room. That afternoon I found a note on my desk at the library. Do you want to see it?"

"Yes, I want to see it," Rick said, his voice tight.

I unzipped the side of the pack, removed the note and handed it to him. His jaw clenched while he read it.

"Nice. Did you tell Bill or Alan?" he asked when he handed it back to me.

"No, what would I tell them? I don't know who did this. At first I suspected you. It could be a prank, but after what I found in Abby's woods, probably not."

"What did you find in *Abby's woods*?" Rick was beginning to sound mad again.

"I don't know what it was, some kind of trip wire. When I caught my ankle on it, it set off this smoke thing."

"Was the smoke colored?"

"Yes, yellow."

"Smoke grenade."

"What's a smoke grenade?"

"I'll explain later. Did you find anything else?"

"Just some kind of brass casings. I found them when I fell."

"Do you still have them?"

"Yes. I suppose you want to see those, too."

"Uh-huh. I sure do."

I reached back in the bag and handed those to him. He rolled them carefully around in his palm.

"Mind if I keep these?"

"No, do you know what they are?" I asked.

"Not for sure, but I know someone who will. You have any other surprises in that bag of yours?"

"No, just the matches. Do you want those?"

"No, keep them. I imagine your bag is probably the safest place for them. And speaking of surprises, is there anything else? Anything at all you haven't told me?"

"Why, no," I said, and bent to rummage in my bag. If I met Rick's stare, he would know I was lying.

It didn't work. He knew anyway. He yanked on my arm and spun me around.

"Ophelia, if there is anything else, you'd better tell me. These guys are not fooling around. Keeping a secret this time could get you killed."

"I'm not keeping a secret," I said, pulling back. "If you're done lecturing me now, could we go? I don't want to keep Abby up all night."

Rick followed me silently down the stairs. I loaded Queenie in the cat carrier and Rick put Lady in the backseat. If it wasn't safe for me—it wasn't safe for them. In spite of Rick's protests, I refused to leave them.

I knew he was angry. His face was rigid and he clenched and unclenched his jaw. All the way to Abby's. The tension between us was almost solid. When we pulled in the drive, I saw every light on in Abby's house. She stood on the front porch, a shawl wrapped tightly around her.

She ran down the steps as soon as Rick stopped the car. The door was jerked open, and in an instant Abby held my hands firmly in hers. I felt the power in the hands that gripped mine. Her strength flowed into me.

Rick stood behind us. I didn't have to see his face to know that the strange scene puzzled him, but I knew Abby didn't care. She put her arm around me and guided me to the house, leaving Rick to deal with the dog, the cat, and my bag.

We were in the kitchen when he walked in. His face was still a rigid mask.

"What was that all about outside?"

Abby was near the stove, pouring the tea. "Never mind. Here's a cup of tea. It will help."

"That's Abby's remedy for everything. Tea."

She joined us at the table. "The truck was stolen, you know."

"By who?" I asked, and blew on my tea.

"I don't know." She wrapped her shawl tighter around her shoulders. "I couldn't see a face."

I gave a long sigh and scowled. "You know, Abby, it would be helpful if for once you could see a face."

Rick's eyes moved first to Abby, then to me, and back to Abby. He reminded me of someone watching a tennis match.

"Excuse me if I interrupt, but what are you two talking about? She saw the truck? How could she see the truck?"

Rick's eyebrows drew together while he thought about it. He surveyed the kitchen, taking in the drying herbs, the crystals glowing in the light of the burning candles. I saw the dawn of realization light his eyes.

# *Twenty-four*

"Well, I'll be damned. She's a witch, isn't she?" he said, his eyes wide while he scanned the kitchen.

"How do you know about witches?" I asked, suddenly wary.

"A friend of mine did a story for the paper about New Age stuff." Rick looked at Abby. "Wiccan?"

"No, I follow the path of my mother and her mother before her."

Rick looked pointedly at me.

"Oh no, don't look at me," I said, waving my hands. "I don't believe in this stuff. This is Abby's thing, not mine."

Rick watched Abby while she sat at the table. "If it's not Wiccan, what is it?"

"It's hard to explain. Some might call it sympathetic or white magick, but I think that's too simplistic. It's a seeing in your mind, looking beyond the physical. It's an understanding of nature and the world around you. Every thing, every place, has energy, a power—some more than others. I'm just a conduit for that power, to pull it inside me and send it back out. The power isn't me. It's there with or without me."

"Are you clairvoyant, too?"

Abby smiled and nodded. "I suppose that doesn't shock you?"

"No, I know a couple psychics in Minneapolis. The police force uses them some of the time. They deny it, of course."

I didn't think it was the best conversation for Abby to be having with a journalist.

"I suppose now you're going to do a big exposé and tell a secret that Abby's kept all of her life?" The bitterness in my voice sounded harsh, even to me.

"Why would I do that?"

"Think of the papers it would sell. That's your job, isn't it, selling papers?"

"No. It's not. I like to think my job is to find the truth. And I think we have more pressing matters than me blowing Abby's secret wide open. Like what's going on around here, and what you know that has someone scared."

"But I don't know anything," I protested.

I stopped and tried to convince myself I was telling the truth. I didn't know anything. I knew about dreams, evil circles, men wearing masks, but I couldn't tell Rick about them without sounding crazy. So I had to lie. Looking at Abby, I pleaded silently for her help.

Her look said, *"You're on your own."*

Thanks, Abby.

I shifted my attention back to Rick. "Really. I've told you everything," I said with fake sincerity.

"Maybe the answer is in the woods?" Rick said, more to himself than me. And I could almost see the wheels turning while he processed the information he had. "There has to be something you're missing. Think, Ophelia—"

At last Abby intervened. "I don't think anyone will solve anything tonight. I suggest both of you go to bed. Rick, you're welcome to stay here if you want. I have plenty of room. Tomorrow Ophelia can show you what she found in the woods."

The next morning, the smell of fresh coffee and frying bacon tickled my senses. I glanced at the window and saw the pale November sun hanging just above the horizon. Wrapping the quilt around me, I went to the window. The sky was heavy with low hanging clouds. In the distance I could see the woods, standing dark against the gray sky.

I dressed quickly and hurried down the stairs, hoping to talk to Abby before Rick made an appearance. The voices coming from the kitchen told me I was too late.

Rick sat at the table with Queenie curled in a tight ball in his lap, as if he belonged there. Abby was at the stove, turning the bacon. What a homey scene. It irritated me. Rick Davis—Delaney, I reminded myself—seemed to be infiltrating my life. The whole idea made me uncomfortable.

"Good morning, Ophelia. Did you sleep well?" she asked while she flipped the bacon onto a plate.

"Yes, I did," I replied, and put a hand on my hip. "What was in the tea, Abby?"

"Oh, just a little chamomile. I thought after all the excitement, you and Rick could both use a good night's sleep."

Rick's eyes slid to mine and he smiled. "Abby has been telling me about her childhood in Appalachia. And I managed to wrangle an invitation for Thanksgiving dinner from her."

I didn't return the smile. He didn't need to hear stories of my grandmother's childhood. And he didn't need to spend Thanksgiving with us. Rick Delaney, with his easy charm and his warm brown eyes, was getting close, too close, to breaking down my defenses. When this was all over, he would go back to his world and I would stay in mine. All connection between us would be broken, but I didn't want my heart to be broken with it.

I crossed to the coffeepot and poured a cup. Leaning against the counter, I eyed Rick. "Don't you think we should get started? I do have to go to work today. It's okay if I'm a little late, but I can't spend all day tromping around the woods with you."

"What's your problem this morning?"

"Hmmm, let's see—someone is watching my house, your room was searched and you were knocked unconscious, we found a dead body lying on the riverbank, someone is stealing anhydrous and probably running a meth lab around here somewhere. And something weird is going on in the woods. Other than that, Rick, I guess I don't have one."

"Boy, are you always this cross in the morning?"

"Oh, shut up. Could we just please get this over with?"

Rick shoved his chair back from the table. "Okay, let's go, then. Abby, thank you for your hospitality."

He jerked his jacket off the back of the chair and stomped out the door. Queenie, deprived of her resting place, gave me an injured look. The look on Abby's face matched the cat's. Shaking my head at both of them, I followed Rick outside.

He was at the edge of the woods by the time I caught up with him.

"There's no need to run, you know," I said, trying to catch my breath.

"I thought you were in a hurry," he replied, not looking at me.

"Look, I'm sorry if I made you mad, but—"

Rick stopped and turned on me. "You know, you amaze me. Whenever I think we're finally developing some sort of a friendship, you suddenly treat me like one of the bad guys. Don't you ever get tired of being so cold?"

The sudden tears I felt surprised me. I was not cold. I just didn't want him worming his way into my life any more than he already had. I lowered my head so Rick wouldn't see the tears. I didn't need to bother; when I raised it, he was already entering the woods.

I don't know if it was Rick's silence while we walked or something else, but today the woods felt ominous. Not friendly and welcoming at all. The air felt charged with an angry force. A damp cold breeze seemed to snake around our legs as we trudged over the leaves and fallen branches. The only sound was our footsteps, and the chill cut through my jacket. I shivered and hunched my shoulders, trying to block it.

At the pace Rick set, we reached the spot where I had found the trip wire quickly.

"There," I said, pointing to the tree.

He studied the spot. "I don't see anything. Are you sure you've got the right tree? There's a lot of them around here."

"Ha ha. No, I'm sure that's the right tree. I spent most of my childhood roaming around these woods. I know where I am."

He knelt to examine the base of the tree.

"I don't see any wire. The bark looks fine . . . no, wait a second—you said the smoke was yellow?"

"Yes."

"Here, right here—the bark's got a spot on it. And it's yellow." He rubbed at the tree.

We both heard it at the same time—the loud snap of a branch breaking.

"You two are out kind of early, aren't you?" a familiar voice said.

Great, the sheriff had joined us.

"Bill. You startled me. What are you doing out here?"

"Abby asked me to keep an eye on the woods, said she thought she had trespassers."

"She never told me she planned on talking to you."

"Your grandmother's an independent woman. Bet she does a lot of things she doesn't tell you about."

Bill was right about that, but I found it hard to believe she would have talked to him without telling me about it.

Rick crossed to where Bill and I stood.

"Bill, I've been trying to call you," he said, "but you never seem to be there. If I didn't know better, I'd think you're dodging me."

"We're conducting a murder investigation, Rick. I don't have time to answer a lot of questions," he replied, his tone serious.

"I know. Just one. And it won't take much time. Any idea yet who the dead man is?"

"Nope, still waiting."

"How much longer will it be before you find out?"

"You sure do like to ask questions, don't you?" Bill said, and looked down at his boots. "To answer you— don't know. And once we do find out, I can't tell you till we track down the guy's family. You ought to know that." He raised his eyes and met Rick's straight on. "But you didn't answer my question. What are you doing here this time of day?"

"Just out for a morning walk," Rick replied, his voice casual.

"I see. Like I said, kind of early, isn't it?" Bill asked, his eyes never leaving Rick's face.

"Ophelia has to go to work and wanted to take a hike before she left. She's been complaining about not getting enough exercise."

I would just as soon that Rick had kept me out of his bullshit session. They were both lying through their teeth to each other. And they both knew it.

"Spent the night at Abby's last night, did you?"

Rick smiled. "Yes we did. We went to the bar and stopped by here after. Abby didn't want us on the road after we'd been drinking, so we crashed here."

I could see by the look on Bill's face that he wasn't buying it. But unless he called Rick a liar to his face, he'd have to swallow it.

"I take it Ophelia knows who you really are now?"

"Yeah, can't keep a secret from her. She's too smart."

One of Abby's favorite expressions came to mind with that remark. *"Roll up your pant legs, 'cause it's too late to save your boots."* I had to put an end to this.

"I already knew you were at the bar. Heard you were playing pool with Larry Durbin last night."

"Yeah. That's not illegal, is it?"

"No, but what Larry did after was. Went over to the Clancy place and tried to steal a tank of anhydrous with his pickup. The fool got it stuck in the field, so he tried stealing a tractor. Guess he thought he'd use the tractor to pull his truck out." Bill spit on the ground.

"Cecil heard the racket. Came out with his shotgun and held Larry at gunpoint till we got there and arrested him."

"Oh." Rick sounded like he didn't care about Larry's fate and was only making polite conversation. "Did he confess to the other thefts?"

"He's not saying anything, says it was all a misunderstanding. He say anything to you last night?"

"About stealing? No, even Larry isn't that stupid."

"Oh gee! Look at the time," I said, glancing at my watch. "I'm going to be late, Rick, if we don't hurry."

"One last thing before you two take off. I want to remind you, we are conducting a murder investigation, and I wouldn't take kindly to any interference from a reporter and a librarian. One who'd be safer doing what this town pays her for."

"We wouldn't dream of interfering, would we, Rick?" I pulled on his arm.

He was as easy to move as a block of stone. His eyes never left Bill's face. I pulled again, this time harder.

"No, I've always had a lot of respect for law enforcement," Rick said. "I wouldn't want to do anything that might let a murderer get away."

"That's good to know, Delaney. 'Cause sometimes innocent bystanders can get caught in the crossfire by being at the wrong place at the wrong time. And I don't need any more dead bodies turning up."

Bill turned sharply on his heel and hiked off in the opposite direction.

Rick stood and watched him leave. When Bill was out of sight, he kicked at the ground. "Damn, Bill's not going to let me get within ten feet of Larry's jail cell. There goes *that* plan. We're back to square one."

We started walking back to the house.

"Obviously, anybody stupid enough to get their truck stuck during a theft isn't smart enough to run what you said was a major drug ring," I said.

"I never thought Larry was the brains behind this operation, but I thought he might have heard something I could use."

"What are you going to do now?"

"I don't have much choice. I'm going back to Minneapolis."

"You're quitting?" For some reason, my heart took a little dip at the thought.

"No, I never give up on a story. I'm going back and talk to a friend who's with the crime bureau. Maybe I can get some information from him, or get him to call Bill."

"Would he do that for you?"

"Yeah, he owes me. I gave him a tip that cracked a big case for him."

I thought for a moment. "Could you tell anything by the mark on the tree?"

Rick shook his head. "Could've been a smoke grenade, hard to tell now, but I didn't see any wires or shells."

Pausing, I stared off into the distance and faced the truth. It was too late to stop Rick from worming his way into my life; he was already there. And I'd miss him when he left.

"How long will you be gone?" I asked, keeping my voice even.

"A few days maybe. I don't know if I can reach him over the weekend. I'll call you when I get back."

"Sure. What do you want Darci and me to do while you're gone?"

Rick frowned. "Nothing. Just try and stay out of trouble, will you?"

* * *

I thought about Rick's warning while I drove home after work. I'd stay out of trouble, all right. I hadn't wanted anything to do with this in the first place. It would take me about ten minutes to get more clothes, and I intended to stay at Abby's.

I felt the disruption in the air when I opened the door, a faint energy that didn't belong there. Going from room to room, my eyes scanned each one while I tried to find anything missing. There wasn't. My needlepoint was the only thing out of place.

The energy grew stronger as I walked up the stairs. I eased the door to my bedroom open. Anger, frustration, whirled around me like a mist. I blinked at the impact. Whoever had been in my house had been very angry by the time they reached this room.

I ran my hands over the dresser and across the bed but could sense nothing. Standing in the middle of the room, I closed my eyes and willed the images to come, but nothing. Nothing except a song—the same song from my dream.

## *Twenty-five*

The rain drummed on the roof while I lay in my child-hood bed at Abby's. Familiar things looked down at me from the shelves. My favorite doll from when I was six, the rock that looked like a toad, which I'd found in the stream that ran through Abby's woods, a drawing of a tree I'd done for Grandpa when I was nine. They represented security, safety, and I was in desperate need of them. I was exhausted, worn-out by all the stress of the past week.

I rolled over in the bed and listened to the rhythm of the rain, looked at my old toys, and thought about the peace I always felt at Abby's. I shut my eyes and prayed for a good night's sleep. But sometime during the night the vision began to unfold in my mind.

The neon sign was burning out. The T in MOTEL flashed above the parking lot with annoying regularity. On the bungalows, paint peeled from the weathered boards, and the once dark green shutters were now a chalky green.

The red convertible whipped into the motel's gravel parking lot and the soldier got out. While he was gone, the girl sat behind the steering wheel, at first drumming her hands on the wheel, then studying her face in the car mirror. She made a little pout while she applied more lipstick. She fluffed her long blond hair with her hands and then tossed her head, sending the curls tumbling around her pretty face. When she saw the soldier come out of the manager's office, dangling a key in his hand, she gave him a big smile and jumped out of the car.

He threw an arm around the girl's shoulders. And together they staggered across the parking lot, while the hot wind blew dust around their feet.

When they reached the bungalow door, the soldier fumbled fitting the key into the lock. Balancing his body against the door frame, he tried again. Suddenly the door swung open, and he tripped across the threshold.

The girl made a move to follow, but she hesitated at the door and allowed her eyes to travel the sad little room.

Covering the bed was a olive green and gold bedspread, its colors shadows of what they once had been. In a cheap frame above the bed hung a painting that looked like it had been made from a "paint by the numbers" kit. The curtains hanging on the painted window were stained and crooked. And the musty air circulated by the noisy air conditioner seemed to reach out and grab her. She took a half step forward and rubbed a sandaled foot across the matted and dirty shag carpet, frowning in disgust.

After turning on the light in the bathroom, the soldier crossed to the window, grabbed the wand hanging from the curtain rod and pulled sideways. But the curtains moved only halfway to the center, leaving a gap that let the blinking light from the neon sign illuminate the room. With a shrug and a smile, he took the girl's hand and pulled her into the room, shutting the door with a kick. He walked her to the bed and drew out a bottle from a deep shirt pocket. Unscrewing the cap, he handed it to the girl.

Old bedsprings groaned when the girl, with the bottle in her hand, sat down. She gave the soldier a teasing look and took a swig. In an instant she sputtered and coughed as the booze burned her throat.

Leaning close, the soldier took the bottle from her hand, and as he did, pushed her back on the bed. The girl looked startled at first, but her look turned to a smile when the soldier stroked her face with his finger. He scooted closer until his body covered hers. Running his hands up her body, he grasped both of her wrists and held her hands tightly over her head. He bent his head and pressed his mouth to her neck. The girl murmured in response.

And then, to the rhythm of the flashing neon light, the age-old dance between male and female, man and woman, began.

I didn't want to watch. The vision I was witnessing in my mind made me feel like a voyeur, and I fought to free myself. *Wake up, wake up,* my brain screamed. I tried shutting my eyes, but it seemed like tiny clamps held them open. I tried turning my head away from the scene on the bed, but it felt like a vise held my head in place. My arms hung at my sides and I didn't have the strength to lift them and shield my face. Helplessly, I stood, in my mind, invisible to the couple on the bed, and watched the young girl play grown-up games.

When it was over, the soldier rolled over on his back and grabbed his pants, drawing out a pack of cigarettes from the pocket. After lighting one, he took a deep drag and settled back on the pillows. He stared at the ceiling while he blew lazy smoke rings.

The girl lay on her side, curled in a tight ball. And I felt her anger. Tonight she had expected to be petted and pampered, as she had been before, but the drunken soldier had thought only of his own pleasure. When he touched her shoulder, offering her his cigarette, her rage exploded. Knocking the cigarette from his fingers, she surged out of the bed and stood glowering at him.

The soldier, too busy hunting for the cigarette, didn't notice her. He found the cigarette smoldering on the ancient bedspread and grabbed it. Stubbing it out in the ashtray on the nightstand, he turned, with a smirk, and for the first time looked at the girl.

Her face wasn't smirking. It was full of fury, and I saw her mouth moving. But the sounds were indistinct, muffled, as though my ears were stuffed with cotton.

I watched the smirk slide from the soldier's face while she derided him. His skin became mottled with angry, red spots and a vein on his forehead stood out.

The girl, so wrapped up in her indignation, failed to see the warning signs on the soldier's face and continued her tirade.

The vein on his forehead began to throb, slowly at first but faster while the girl ranted on. Finally, with a roar, he threw off the sheet and loomed in front of her. Surprised, she drew back her hand and slapped him with enough force that his head snapped to his right. He slowly turned to face her. Now the angry, red spots had fused together, turning his skin almost purple. Grabbing her by the shoulders, he shook her till her head bobbled up and down like a toy dog with its head on a spring.

She grasped his wrists, trying to wrench them from

her shoulders, but the soldier's grip was too strong. She pummeled his chest with her fists, but he didn't move. Finally, she kicked him with her foot, putting all the force and strength she had as a dancer behind it.

The soldier hollered when her foot connected with his shin. He grabbed her upper arms and slung her away from him.

Time slowed. And the girl seemed to float toward the bed. For an instant it was as if she hung suspended above its surface. Suddenly, time sped up, and she crashed onto the mattress. Her body landed on the bed, but her head and neck hit the sharp edge of the night-stand with a crack that echoed on and on in the dingy room.

The girl exhaled a long, slow breath. And I could see it. The breath came out in a stream of pale white light that gathered over her body. After lingering above her an instant, the light began to drift away.

While I watched the light grow fainter, I heard the song again. The melody the girl had danced to with vibrancy flowed through the room. And on the last, final note the light flickered and died.

Oh my God—he'd killed her.

The next morning my eyes felt gritty and it seemed like I'd run a marathon. And I couldn't shake the vision I'd had the night before. Dragging myself out of bed, I dressed and went in search of Abby. Maybe she could make some sense out of the dream. Not finding her in the house, I wandered to the greenhouse.

The last of the season's mums sat clustered by the door. Purple, deep yellow, dark burgundy, and white— their colors looked too bright to my tired eyes. Thanks-giving cactus were next to the mums, their buds ready to burst into blooms of coral and pink. Around the pots of flowers, Abby had placed small pumpkins and squash. Near them were bushel baskets full of green, gold, and orange striped gourds. Nailed to the posts by the baskets were bundles of Indian corn. The earth had given Abby a rich harvest this year. Food to fill the body and beauty to fill the soul, and for some reason it made me sad.

I took a deep breath of the warm, moist air, and the smell of fertile soil filled my senses. The scent held a promise, a promise of next year's harvest. But for the young girl in my dream there would be no harvest. She would never experience the changing of the seasons, never see the earth's cycle of life. Her life was cut too short.

"Dark thoughts for so early in the morning, isn't it?"

Abby's voice startled me out of my brooding. She paused in the doorway to the back of the greenhouse, her watering can held loosely in one hand, before she crossed over and laid her hand on my shoulder.

"She's dead, Abby," I said, my voice bleak.

"The girl you've been dreaming about?" she asked, and squeezed my shoulder softly.

"Yes." I wandered over to where her ancient cash register sat on the counter. Pulling out a stool, I sat and watched while she plucked the spent blooms from the mums.

"I figured as much," she said, her attention on the flowers.

"Why? Why did you think that?"

Abby sighed deeply. "It's the way things work. The bad catches our attention more than the good."

"That sucks," I said with a scowl.

She brushed my remark aside with a shrug. "Everyone has the habit of focusing on the negative. Do people gossip about positive things? No. They usually gossip about their neighbors' misfortune."

"I suppose."

"But it doesn't have to be that way." She straightened and crumpled the dead blossoms. "By sensing the good around us, we can send its positive energy back out into the world to fight the negative. That's the secret of our gift, the secret of magick."

"I don't see it," I scoffed. "How can there be anything 'good' about a young girl's death in a run-down motel? How do I turn something so tragic into something good?"

"You were given the dream for a reason," she said, walking to the trash can behind me. "Figure out the reason." She tossed the blooms inside the can and slammed the lid.

"I can't," I said, my voice rising in frustration.

"Yes, you can," Abby said with certainty. "Make the connection between the dream and what's happening now. And you'll have your answer."

"What connection? I don't know who she is. And I don't know where or when the girl died. All I know is she died after having sex with a soldier in a wretched, little motel."

"Did you recognize the motel?"

"No. I've never had much experience with seedy motels," I said sarcastically.

Abby chuckled. "Well, I'm glad to hear it."

"Sorry," I muttered, studying my hands. "I didn't mean it the way it came out."

She patted my arm. "Don't worry. I know what you meant. Let me rephrase my question. Have you ever *driven by* the motel you saw in your dream?"

"No. I don't think it's in Iowa. The weather didn't seem right," I said with a frown. "It was hot, but not like it is here."

"Drier?"

"Yeah." I nodded, trying to remember the dream. "And dusty. Like a desert."

Images floated in my head—hot, dry wind blowing dust over the girl's shoes. Did I see vegetation, like a cactus or tumbleweeds? No, in the vision it was too dark.

"Arizona?" Abby asked.

I shook my head, baffled. "I don't know. Maybe."

"What branch of the service was the soldier in?"

His uniform? What color was it? Closing my eyes, I tried to summon the vision from the corners of my brain, concentrating on what the soldier looked like.

"Umm, dark green pants and shirt, shirt has stuff on it—"

"What kind of 'stuff'?" she asked, her voice sounding far away as I sank deeper into my mind.

"A— A kind of a triangle, gold on a black circle, on his sleeve. A rectangle above the circle, gold and red wavy lines." My eyes popped open. "His pocket has a name—"

"What's the name?" Abby butted in.

"*Smith.*" I rolled my eyes in disgust. "How many Smiths do you suppose there are in the service?"

"Several, I would imagine."

"Right." I pushed off the stool and jammed my hands in my pockets. "Several thousands, you mean. And how in the devil am I supposed to narrow it down to one?"

"Dark green clothes, that's the Army isn't it?"

"I think so."

"And the patches—wouldn't they represent what unit the soldier belonged to?"

"Maybe," I answered, confused. "I don't know anything about the military, Abby."

"But you can find out on that computer of yours, can't you?"

I jerked my hands out of my pockets and snapped my fingers. "That's right. I can look up Army patches on the Internet, find out what the rectangle with the wavy lines means. If it's his unit insignia, I'll know where he was stationed," I said, almost skipping to the door. "Then I can search for news reports of the girl's death. It might take a few days, but I bet I can find something."

Abby's voice stopped me. "Ophelia, the circle grows smaller—you don't have a few days."

# Twenty-six

I don't know if it was my imagination or if what Abby said about the circle was true. But I felt it shrinking around me while I worked at the computer in my office on Monday. Typing in *Army patches,* I got a listing of over 133,000 Web sites. One site alone had over one hundred pages.

Discouraged, I picked up a pen and rolled it around in my hands. Okay. No patch. What about military bases? Tossing the pen down, I typed *Army bases* in the search field. Oh good, only 249,000 listings.

I was losing my focus. My mind kept churning over everything that happened since the day Rick Delaney showed up at the library. The song from the dream began to play in my mind along with Rick's words about staying out of trouble. How was I supposed to stay out of trouble when the trouble was looking for me?

Giving up on the Internet, I stared at the phone on my desk, willing it to ring.

Yeah, yeah, it was only Monday, and he said he'd be gone a few days. But he could at least call me from Minneapolis and tell me what he'd learned.

"A watched pot never boils," said a voice from the doorway.

"Rick," I said, startled to see him. "You're back."

He moved a stack of books and sat down. He studied me a moment before he answered.

"Just got back and I came straight here." He gazed at his hands. "Ophelia, I want you to stay out of this. There's more going on than we thought."

"Did you find out who the dead man was?"

He looked up, his face grim. "Yes, my friend pulled some strings with the Justice Department. Seems they've been looking for the dead man, too. They were notified he'd been murdered when the lab ID'd him through dental records. He was a former Army sergeant, Raymond 'Butch' Fisher."

A soldier? I tuned Rick out. The man in my dream was a soldier. Could it be the same man?

"Ophelia—"

"What? I'm listening," I said carefully.

"No, you weren't. Is there something you want to tell me?" he asked.

I shook my head. "No. Go ahead with your story."

With a doubtful look, Rick continued, "He lost his stripes five years ago for getting in a fight with a local police officer when he was stationed in Texas. Shortly after that he went AWOL. The Army's been looking for him ever since."

"I understand why the Army wanted to find him, but why the Justice Department?"

"After going AWOL, Fisher found a new home with a militia group operating in Montana. The department suspected he's been using connections he made while in the Army to supply the militia with illegal weapons.

And they *really* wanted to talk to him. They're not happy he's dead."

"That still doesn't answer why he was in Summerset."

"Well, the logical assumption would be there's a militia cell here."

"That's ridiculous."

"No, it's not, these people draw recruits from all over the country. It's possible one of their cells operates here. It would also explain what you found in the woods. My guess—they were using Abby's woods to play a few war games."

Boy, oh boy, Abby wasn't going to like that one.

"Didn't you say hardly anyone goes into those woods? Local gossip says they're haunted? It would be a perfect place for them. They could play army without worrying about anyone seeing them."

"Yes, but war games? Come on," I said, picking up a pen and fiddling with it.

"Those casings you found? I checked with a ballistics expert. He said they could have come from an AR-15, looks like an Army M-16. Perfect for the militia."

"But how does that figure into the drugs? I thought those right-wing extremists didn't like druggies."

"You're right, they don't. We have two separate things happening."

"Are you sure about all of this?" I asked while I drew tiny little question marks across a piece of paper.

"Yes, my friend at the bureau talked with the agent in charge of searching for Fisher."

"How did you manage to get him to do that?"

"I told my friend I had some information that might help with the drug bust they made in Minnesota but that I wouldn't tell him unless he promised to share what he learned. After threatening me a few times with aiding and abetting, he agreed and called the Justice Department. Then he called Bill, and Bill confirmed the information about Fisher. But they decided the two—the drugs and the possible militia cell—weren't connected."

"Did Bill tell your friend anything about Larry? Has he talked?" I asked.

"No," Rick replied.

"Georgia told Darci that Alan and Bill searched Larry's place. He has been making meth, but on a small scale. Not enough to sell out of state."

"Damn. Now we're really back where we started. Any ideas? How about Abby? She's psychic. Does she see anything?"

"You believe in psychics?" I asked, tapping the pencil on my drawings and not looking at him.

"Hey, anything's possible," Rick said, his voice non-committal. "As I told you, the police in Minneapolis sometimes use them, and it's not like we're learning a lot from 'normal' sources. So why not try a psychic?"

"Well," I said drawing X's through the question marks. "She has received vague images. A man hiding behind a mask, the danger growing—that kind of stupid stuff."

"You don't have a very high opinion of Abby's gift, do you?"

"What gift?" I pouted and threw the pencil down. "It seems more like a curse to me. She always has a premonition something's going to happen, but can never seem to change the outcome." I shook my head. "But back to the sergeant and the drugs, I don't know if I agree with your friend and Bill. A favorite saying of Abby's, 'There's no such thing as a coincidence.' What if she's right, what if the two are connected but we can't see it right now?"

"If we only had Ned's pictures of the Korn Karnival, maybe we could find the sergeant in them."

I suddenly remembered Darci's remark about Agnes McPhearson. "Do you know what he looked like?"

"No, but I can have my friend fax me a picture. Why?"

"You need to talk to Agnes McPhearson." I smiled, thinking of all the fun Rick would have spending the afternoon with her.

"Who's she?" Rick cocked an eyebrow.

"Oh, you're in for such a treat. Agnes is this small, rather plain woman—reminds me of a partridge—who sees herself as the town's historian. And she loves taking pictures. At every event, there's Agnes with her camera. I bet she's got a ton of pictures from the Korn Karnival. All you have to do is talk her into showing them to you."

"Will that be hard?"

"Not for you, Slick, just turn on the charm."

"Okay." Rick grinned. "I'll call my friend and have him fax me a picture, then I'll contact Agnes and ask to see her photographs."

"Oh, Rick," I said, stopping him, "you're not allergic to cats are you?"

"No, why?"

"Well, in addition to her love of photography, Agnes also loves cats. In fact, she has about fifteen of them—all in the house. So don't wear black, okay?"

Rick groaned. "Thanks, thanks a lot. I'll be back after I talk to Agnes."

I turned back to the computer, but my concentration had gone from bad to worse. I couldn't get our conversation out of my mind. Blaming Abby for my conviction that somehow the drugs and the dead sergeant were tied together was a dodge. I knew they were tied together, and somewhere in this convoluted mess, the girl from my dream was involved. It was the key, the beginning. Even after talking to Rick, the song still played in my mind, still evaded recognition.

Rick said Sergeant Fisher had been stationed in Texas. Parts of Texas were hot and dry, weren't they? I typed in *Army bases and Texas.* Wow, 54,000 Web sites. Well, at least the field was narrowing. I selected the first one, Fort Arnold.

I tapped my fingers on my desk while I waited for the site to download. A photograph appearing in the center of the screen caught my attention. It flashed off and another photo took its place. Dang, I recalled the first one, tapping my fingers faster, waiting for it to appear again.

There on the left side of the Fort Arnold sign—did I see a rectangle with gold and red wavy lines? I quickly scrolled down to *Units and Organizations.* Opening that page, I counted fourteen listed. I got lucky on the fourth one.

Pictured on the screen was the same patch worn by the soldier in my dream. It was the insignia of the Fifteenth Artillery Brigade. The soldier had been stationed in Texas, just like Sergeant Fisher. The connection Abby talked about? Was the soldier from my dream Fisher? But what about the girl?

The base was located near Riley a small Texas town. The soldier would've been charged, maybe not with first degree murder, but at least with manslaughter. I tried searching for a story about a trial in Riley. Nothing. Maybe they would have moved the trial location to a bigger city. I tried El Paso. Nothing. Houston, Dallas,

San Antonio. Nothing, not a word about a young girl dying at the hands of a soldier.

Frustrated, I shut off the computer. I needed to talk to Darci.

I found her putting jackets on our new book order.

"Darci, do you know if anyone from Summerset ever lived in Texas. Or if someone has family in Texas?"

"I don't know." She thought for a moment. "Mr. Carroll has a daughter who lives in Texas."

Mr. Carroll, drugs, and the militia? It didn't compute.

"Does, or did, he have a granddaughter there?" I asked.

"No. Grandsons. Why?"

"The girl from my dream. She lived in Texas."

Darci looked confused. "How do you know?"

"Long story—but I dreamed about her last night. And in the dream, she was killed after having sex with a soldier—"

"Oh my gosh," Darci exclaimed.

"Yes." I shuddered. "What I saw was terrible. But I think her death was an accident. And I've found where the soldier was stationed. Fort Arnold. It's near Riley, Texas. So I thought maybe if someone around here had a connection to Texas . . ."

"The connection would be the reason you're dreaming about her," Darci finished for me. "No. And I think if anyone around here was connected to a tragedy like that, we'd all know about it. But I could ask Georgia, she might know something."

"Okay, but don't tell her why."

"Don't worry, I won't, I'll make something up. What did Rick have to say?"

I watched Darci's jaw drop farther and farther while I related what Rick had learned in Minneapolis.

"Sergeant Fisher was stationed in Texas? Same place as the guy from your dream?"

"Rick didn't know where Fisher lived while he was in Texas."

"But maybe Fisher is the soldier in your dream."

"No. The soldier in the dream's name is Smith. I saw it on his pocket."

"And a militia cell." Darci looked dumbfounded. "That can't be. I know we have a lot of people around here who lean to the right, but none of them lean *that* far."

"I don't know, Rick is convinced there's a cell operating here and that they're using Abby's woods to practice."

"You're not going to tell her, are you?" Darci asked, her eyes full of concern.

"Are you kidding? She'd go marching out there and try and hex them or something. No, I need to find out who that girl is."

Darci thought for a moment. "You know, there are a lot of guys running around with guns, but I always figured it was just a guy thing. But Rick's information makes me wonder."

"What do you mean?"

"Well, I know for a fact that Alan's brother, Ted, has three guns in his truck. A handgun under the seat, one above the visor, and a shotgun in the gun rack."

"You're kidding. What does he think he's going to shoot with all those guns?"

"I guess he believes in being prepared. Oh, he's a John Wayne wannabe, anyway. He tried to get into law enforcement, but they wouldn't take him. He reminds me of Jake that way. Jake tried to enlist in the Marines, but they wouldn't take him, either. And talk about John

Wayne wannabes, ha. Have you ever noticed the way Jake tries to imitate that walk John Wayne had?"

"Darci." I cringed at the thought of Jake walking like John Wayne. "I try not to notice Jake any more than I have to."

When I glanced over at Darci, she was waving her hands frantically.

"What?" I jumped when Benny spoke from behind me.

"Sorry, Miss Ophelia, but where did you say you wanted them empty boxes put?"

How much had Benny heard? I knew he'd run right to Jake and tell him.

"Ahh, in the basement, Benny. We'll put them in the recycle bin later."

After Benny left, I spun around to Darci.

"How much did he hear?" I asked, grasping her arm.

"Just what you said about Jake. I saw him coming and tried to warn you. You know, for a psychic, you can be kind of dense sometimes, Ophelia."

"I *really* hope that was all he heard. I don't need any more trouble."

The rest of the day seemed spent in futile pursuits. I searched the Internet, looking again in news archives for any mention of a girl dying in or around Riley, Texas, but found nothing. A dead end. Darci had called Georgia and learned nothing. Another dead end. At the end of the day we were no closer to the truth, and I felt as though I'd been in a fog all day.

When Rick and Darci showed up at closing time, they found me sitting at the computer, staring blankly at the screen. I looked at Rick and the fog lifted a little.

"Well, did you have a good time with Agnes and her

cats? They didn't use your leg for a scratching post, did they?" I asked, leaning back and smiling.

Rick grinned. "Sorry to disappoint you. I know you were looking forward to me spending the afternoon with Agnes and her cats, but she wasn't home. I did get my fax from Minneapolis, though," he said, handing me a picture. "Do you recognize him?"

I looked at the photograph. Staring at me from the grainy surface of the fax was a grim, bald man. His nose was slightly off center, as if it had been broken one too many times. And a thick neck was visible above the collar of his shirt. He reminded me of a bulldog. It gave me the chills to think this was the body we found by the river.

"Definitely not him. He's old enough to be her father," I murmured.

"What?" Rick looked puzzled.

"Nothing," I said, handing the picture to Darci. "I don't remember him, do you, Darci?"

"No, but I think I would if I'd ever seen him. He looks nasty." Darci wrinkled her nose.

"He was," Rick said. "My friend checked up on him. His military record was full of reprimands for fighting, and his former commanding officer said he was a real loose cannon. It didn't surprise him the guy was found murdered."

"Where was Fisher stationed?" I asked.

"Fort Arnold, Texas," Rick answered.

Darci's eyebrows shot up and she opened her mouth to say something. But when her eyes met mine, her jaw clamped shut.

"What's next?" I asked, turning back to Rick.

"First, you leave your car here and I'll take you

home. You're spending the night again at Abby's. Tomorrow, I run the elusive Agnes down and look at the
photographs from the Korn Karnival. Darci, I want you
to stay with Georgia tonight. We're not taking any
chances. You both have been asking too many questions, and as of today you're both staying out of this.
I'm going to Bill and telling him everything I know.
We're in over our heads."

"But Rick, I planned to stay at my house tonight.
Abby took Lady and Queenie back there this morning.
And what about my car? I can't leave it here all night."

"I don't care what you planned. Darci can come
back with Georgia and pick up the car."

The look on his face told me it would be pointless to
argue.

"But what about the girl?" Darci asked, still studying
the picture.

"Shh, Darci," I said, shaking my head frantically.

"What girl?" Rick asked.

"The dead girl Ophelia keeps seeing in her dreams.
She's sure this all started with her."

I stifled a groan.

Rick pulled his hand through his hair, "Great, well,
that explains a lot. You're clairvoyant, too."

"Let me explain—"

"Later, first I want to get you to Abby's. Darci,
promise me you'll stay with Georgia."

"Okay," Darci piped up.

Once in the car, Rick turned to me. "Does anyone
else in town know about you and Abby?"

"No. We've always been very careful. This talent
isn't exactly one a person advertises. Especially not in
a small town."

"Good," he said, pulling away from the curb. "We

don't need anyone coming after you because they think you *see* something."

"Rick, I hate to tell you, but I think they're already after me. I didn't want to tell you this earlier, but someone has been in my house."

The tires squealed when Rick hit the brakes. I grabbed the dash to stop myself from hitting the windshield.

"Jeez, Rick."

"How do you know someone was in your house? Did you tell Bill?"

"I felt it, okay? I walked in the door and there it was—someone else's energy, and hate, and anger. It was strongest in the bedroom, but nothing was taken. And no, I didn't tell Bill. It would've been kind of hard to explain, now wouldn't it?"

"I don't suppose you picked up who it might have been?"

"No, of course not. The powers don't want to make it too easy for people like me. Most of the time it's like looking at something through a cloudy mirror. The shapes and the feelings are there, but obscured. I hate it."

I stared out the window as Rick drove down the street. The bare trees were swaying in the wind, and the clouds were drifting in. It looked like the snow Abby predicted would be here before tomorrow night.

I don't remember Rick pulling in the driveway. I don't remember screaming. But I do remember stumbling and falling and fighting him as he tried to stop me from reaching the porch.

*Those bastards killed Lady.*

# Twenty-seven

The ground was cold and hard beneath my knees. My sobbing shook my shoulders, and I covered my face with my hands. I was lifted to my feet and arms were wrapped around me, but I was so lost in my misery, no sensation other than warmth registered. Soothing words began to penetrate the misery, sounding jumbled and strained at first. They became clearer.

"Ophelia, it isn't Lady. It's a coyote. Ophelia, do you understand?"

I stepped back from the embrace and looked up at Rick's face. "Coyote?"

"Yes, but don't look. Give me the keys to your house, okay? I want you to go sit in the car, and don't look at the porch."

I handed Rick the keys from my pocket and allowed him to guide me to the car. I tried to do what he said, but my eyes were drawn to the carcass swinging on my porch. I watched while he stepped carefully around the poor animal and unlocked my front door. He came back a few minutes later and cut the rope. The animal flopped when it hit the porch floor. Rick turned and walked slowly back to the car. He opened the door and slid in beside me.

"You watched, didn't you?"

I wiped the cold tears from my face. "Yeah. I'm sorry, I couldn't help it." I grabbed his arm. "Is Lady okay?"

"Yeah, they were both upstairs and came running down when I stepped inside."

A sigh of relief escaped. "Rick, who would do such a sick thing?"

"Somebody who wants you out of this. And wants it bad enough to do something like this in broad daylight. I called Bill. They'll be right over." Rick paused. "They're getting desperate. I want you to leave town till this is over."

"I can't."

"Why not?"

I shook my head. "I don't think you'll understand, but I have to stay. It's part of my destiny."

He smacked the steering wheel. "You're right, I don't understand."

Ever since my grandfather's death I'd fought my so-called heritage, but now I knew it might be the only thing that would save me.

"Look, that first night you were here in Summerset, Abby called me—"

"But the phones were dead that night. I remember, I tried calling the paper."

"Abby made sure she called before they went down. She told me that night, I think, as she put it, the evil was growing and it would be up to me to stop it. You and I are in the center of the circle and will face danger. I tried leaving town once and Abby said I had to stay. I know that sounds crazy, but believe me, Abby *knows*. I've seen this happen too many times to discount what she says."

"Therefore, it's your destiny. You're right, it is crazy. You're going to risk your life because your grandmother has some kind of vision?" Rick shook his head.

"It's not just what Abby thinks, I feel it, too. I have to stay and see it through."

"How do you know you haven't already done what you were supposed to? You said the visions were vague, maybe you're misinterpreting them?"

"Rick, I appreciate your concern, I really do, but I *know* I have to stay. I don't have any choice."

"Lord, you're stubborn." Rick studied me and frowned. "All right, you're staying in Summerset, but I don't think you should stay at Abby's. What if they decided to come after you there? You sure as hell can't stay here by yourself. So Ophelia, I hope you like having a roommate, 'cause I'm moving in till this is over."

"You can't. Everybody in town will have a fit. We'd be the favorite topic at Joe's."

"You know something, I don't give a rat's ass what people around here say. And the Irish can be just as stubborn as the Danes, so give it up. I'm staying. I'll go get my things while Bill's here."

A tap on the window drew our attention. Bill and Alan stood by the car, their faces grim. They motioned toward the house. We got out of the car and followed Bill to the porch. I watched while he turned the coyote over.

"Ophelia, why don't you go inside?" Rick said.

I opened my mouth to argue. This habit of ordering me about was getting old. But after one look at Bill and Rick, I decided it would be a good idea for me to go inside.

Lady rushed to my side when I walked in the door. Her whole body wriggled with excitement. She stayed at my heels while I walked to the living room. When I sat down in the wing chair, she curled up and laid her head on my feet. Bill found us sitting there several minutes later.

"Don't suppose you know who might have done this?"

"No."

"Then do you want to tell me why you didn't tell me about the letter or the smoke grenade or the fact someone was in your house snooping?"

I sat silently staring at Lady. I didn't have the courage to look at Bill.

"I didn't think so. Delaney will be right back; I hear he's spending the night. I seriously thought about making you both guests of the county for impeding an ongoing investigation, until this is solved, but he talked me out of it. He assured me I wouldn't be stumbling over the two of you anymore. You let us do our job." Bill removed his hat and polished his bald head. "One more thing—we'll be sending a car by Abby's every so often."

My head snapped up. Abby. I made a move to stand, but Bill waved me down.

"Sit still. Alan's already talked to her, and he told her to stay put where we can find her. I don't need a seventy-three-year-old woman out, running around the countryside, chasing bad guys, either."

My eyes shifted away from Bill and I saw Rick standing at the edge of the living room.

"Thanks for leaving me to face Bill by myself," I told him.

"She must be feeling better." Bill chuckled, glancing at Rick. Looking back at me, he said, "Don't worry, Delaney got his on the porch. I'll be sending a patrol car around at intervals."

"Thanks, Bill," Rick said, shaking Bill's hand.

Bill paused at the door. "Oh, and, Delaney, try to keep her out of trouble."

"Sure thing, Bill," Rick said, looking at me with determination.

"You two act like I'm the one who's guilty of something," I said after Bill left.

"Well, definitely guilty of lacking common sense. You really should leave town."

"Look, I explained that already. Do you want something to eat?" I said, standing.

"Already taken care of—courtesy of Georgia. She's bringing dinner over in a little bit."

"Oh, that's just great. Georgia knows you're staying here? Why don't I put a sign in the front yard—'Rick Delaney Slept Here.' "

Rick laughed. "Don't worry about it. I *want* everyone to know I'm staying here. Then maybe you won't have any unexpected visitors."

I flounced into the kitchen to pout. Resentment over my life being controlled by two men ran through me. I opened a cupboard, and not seeing what I wanted, slammed the door shut. I opened another cupboard and slammed it shut, too. Leaning against the counter, I took a deep breath.

"My mom does the same thing when she's mad at my dad," Rick said from the doorway.

"What?" I turned and glared at him.

"Slams the doors shut, paces the room, that kind of thing. Eventually, she tells Dad what's bothering her and they talk about it. Do you want to talk?"

I passed a hand over my tired eyes. "Not really."

"Okay. I'll leave you alone, then. Would you mind if I started a fire?"

"No, go ahead." I hesitated, chewing on my lip. "I need some time to think."

"I'll be in there if you change your mind."

I splashed water on my face. What was I missing? What did I know that had someone worried? How did all this tie together? And what about the girl? Who was she? If I could just remember the name of that damned song, it might help. The haunting melody played over and over again in my mind.

I was concentrating so hard on the song, I didn't hear the door open and close when Georgia brought the food. Rick found me still standing at the counter, thinking.

"Dinner's served. Want to eat in front of the fire? It's a perfect night for it."

Rick had the living room arranged for dinner. The coffee table was cleared of all my knickknacks, and a big round candle burned in the center. The fire cast a warm glow around the room. The whole scene, under other circumstances, would have been very romantic.

"Sit down, I'll get plates and silverware. You don't have any wine, do you?"

"Beer."

"Beer works for me. I'll get you one, too."

The aroma of Georgia's cooking made my stomach growl. I inhaled deeply—lasagna. Georgia might have had her faults, but cooking wasn't one of them.

During dinner Rick talked nonstop. Lady's and Queenie's eyes watched his plate. They followed each bite from the plate to his mouth. When he thought I wouldn't notice, he'd sneak them food.

He told me about his life in Minneapolis, his family—youngest of six, baby of the family. Most of all he talked about his work. The passion he felt for it lit up his face. I smiled watching him.

"I know what you're trying to do."

"Yeah, what?" he asked, trying to look blameless.

"You're trying to distract me by giving me a running commentary on your life."

"That obvious, huh? Let's don't talk about drugs, militia, or dead sergeants tonight, okay? It will all still be there in the morning. And I did promise Bill we'd stay out of it."

"But—"

"No, don't say it. Here, give me that." Rick took my plate. "Do you want another beer?"

"No, but you have one if you want."

When Rick returned, I had moved to the couch and was curled under my afghan. Rick sat on the floor next to me and stared at the fire. He seemed lost in his thoughts while he drank his beer.

While he stared at the fire, I stared at his profile. Golden shadows danced across his face, and I noticed how his dark hair gleamed in the soft light. I fought the urge to reach out and touch him. My skin felt flush, like all my blood had suddenly pooled near the surface.

He frowned. "I've got a question. Is being a psychic why you don't like to be touched?"

"Let's say I've had some very bad experiences along those lines," I said, forcing my eyes away from him.

Rick turned and knelt by the couch, his face level with mine.

"Can you read minds all the time?"

"What do you mean?" I raised my head.

"Well, can you read my mind right now?"

Staring into Rick's warm brown eyes robbed me of speech. I shook my head.

"No? Good."

He cupped my face with one hand while his other slowly, seductively, brushed a strand of hair away from my face. The touch was hypnotic. I was unable to look away, unable to see anything but him. My eyelids drifted shut.

The touch was light at first, a brief brush of his lips across mine, but it crowded my senses. When the pressure increased, I felt the loneliness, the isolation, of the past four years melt away. The warmth grew and filled my heart. I wanted this. Maybe Rick would stay and I could have this warmth forever. All I had to do was let the wall I'd built around myself fall away, brick by lonely brick. But I couldn't. Not now, maybe not ever.

Even though the kiss lasted only a moment, it was long enough for me to know this wasn't our time or our place. It wasn't part of my destiny, or Rick's. Like Abby had said, he wasn't the one I sought. The warmth was replaced by a great sadness.

Rick drew back and his eyes searched my face.

"Wow," he said softly while his thumb stroked my cheek. "Do all psychics kiss like that, or just you?"

I shook my head and smiled. He saw something in my eyes and leaned farther back. The moment was gone.

"I think I'd better get to bed," I said, standing. "The

spare room is down that hall to the left. Towels are in the linen closet next to the bath. Is there anything else you need?"

"No, I'm fine, but if you don't mind, I think I'll have another beer and watch the fire for a while."

"That's fine. Good night."

Rick gazed up at me. "Good night, Ophelia. I'll see you in the morning."

At the foot of the stairs I glanced back. "You know, Rick, you're not too bad yourself."

The sound of his laughter followed me up the stairs.

# *Twenty-eight*

My head felt thick and fuzzy the next morning. Sleep, when it finally came, had been restless. The girl and the song wouldn't leave me alone. I'd see her dancing with power and strength in the empty studio, then driving the red convertible with the top down, her blond hair whipping around her face, and finally, falling across the bed and striking her head on the nightstand. The scenes were an endless loop that ran through my mind all night.

Abby said the light I saw above her body was her spirit leaving. And each time in my vision, when the light flickered out, I was filled with such regret and sadness.

But the rage that struck me with so much force the first time I saw the girl dancing was absent. Did it mean something? I didn't know, and the frustration ground at me.

"You look tired," Rick said when I entered the kitchen. He handed me a cup of coffee and pulled out a chair for me. "Do you want something to eat?"

"No, coffee's fine. I'm not really hungry."

"Are you going to work today?"

"Yes."

"Do you think you should? Wouldn't it be better if you stayed home? I don't know if you've looked outside yet, but it's starting to snow. A good day to stay here, curled up under your afghan, don't you think?"

I smiled faintly. "Rick, I can't hide in the house until Bill catches the bad guys. Work will be good for me. And as far as the snow, it won't storm till late this afternoon."

"But the weatherman said—"

I lifted an eyebrow.

"Okay, you can do that, too, huh?"

"Abby's better. Her accuracy is amazing, far better than mine," I said, and rubbed my temples.

"Do you have a headache?"

"No, not really. I didn't sleep well. Darci told you, I keep dreaming about this girl—a young girl, a dancer. One minute she's dancing, full of life, but the next she's dying."

I told Rick about the dream, the girl, and the soldier.

"Do you recognize the girl?" he asked when I'd finished.

"No, but the soldier with her in the dream was stationed at Fort Arnold."

"You're kidding. Fort Arnold? Same as Fisher?" Rick looked shocked.

"Yup, Fort Arnold. I remembered the patch on his sleeve and looked it up on the Internet. Darci tried to find out if anyone around here has some tie to Texas, but the answer was no. I know this girl is the key. If I only knew who she was; it's driving me crazy."

"Maybe work would be the best for you. It might take your mind off it."

"Yeah, I'm ready to go anytime you are. Since

Agnes wasn't home yesterday, are you going back over there today?"

"Yeah, I've already called her. I'm going to her house after I drop you off at the library."

"Well, watch out for her cats. And you might want to pass if Agnes offers you food."

"Why?" Rick asked slowly.

"Cat hair," I said, and wrinkled my nose. "Gets in the food."

"Ugh." Rick's face turned pale.

I guess he did have a weak stomach. Grinning, I snatched my backpack from the table and headed for the door.

While slipping on my coat, I noticed the bottom of the door was covered with deep scratches. Dang it, I'd have to hire Benny to fix them.

When I walked into the library, Darci stood behind the counter. Nearby, Benny, screwdriver in hand, worked on a defective light switch. While he worked, he cast shy looks in Darci's direction.

Darci rushed over when she saw me. "I didn't think you'd be in today. Are you all right?"

"Yeah. I suppose it's all over town about the coyote?"

"Naturally, and Rick spending the night at your house. People saw his car in your driveway. Mrs. Carroll is shocked, by the way. More about Rick staying the night than the coyote, I think."

I frowned. "I'm not going to be lambasted by Mrs. Carroll or anyone else. I'll spend the whole day in my office if I have to."

"Well, if you want to avoid them, Nina Hoffman called. I told her the books she ordered are in, but Adam doesn't want her to drive in the snow. She asked if anyone could please bring them to her. You could do it. It would get you out of here for a while."

"I don't have my car; Rick drove me."

"You can take mine if you want."

"You've got a deal," I said, catching the keys Darci threw to me.

The drive took about five minutes. The Hoffmans lived at the opposite end of town. And their house reflected Adam's position in the community. A huge one-story glass and brick located on a yard the size of a postage stamp. Its numerous windows were covered with heavy blinds, always drawn tight, like eyes always shut. Everyone in town speculated what it looked like inside, but no one had ever been invited to visit. That would change if Adam followed through with his plan to run for mayor. Entertaining voters would be required.

Nina answered the door before the doorbell had stopped chiming. Still in her robe, she looked fragile and wan as ever. I expected her to take the books and close the door, but instead she held it open.

"Come in, Ophelia. Thank you so much for bringing the books to me, especially on a day like today," she said, and closed the door behind me.

"Really, Nina, no problem. It's not snowing that much yet. The streets are fine." I handed her the books.

She set them down on a small table in the entry. "Would you like a cup of coffee? I don't get many visitors. Adam says the strain isn't good for me."

The last thing I wanted was Nina Hoffman entertaining me, dressed in her robe, and plying me with coffee. She looked so lonely, though, that I agreed.

I followed her through the living room into the kitchen. Everything in the house was white and in pristine condition. No homey touches, no clutter. It looked empty, uninhabited. In fact, the house was devoid of all personality. It said nothing of the couple who lived there. I tried to imagine Adam Hoffman kicking his shoes off and watching a football game, but the image eluded me. I felt a chill from the cold, sterile environment.

Nina chattered while she poured the coffee, mostly about the latest self-help book she had read. I tuned most of it out. While she talked, I thought reading a few books on decorating wouldn't hurt her, either.

I drank my coffee as quickly as possible and refused Nina's repeated efforts to give me more. The all-white room was making me jumpy. I wanted out of there. When I stood to leave, Nina stood, too.

"Would you like to see the rest of the house?" she asked eagerly.

I searched for an excuse, but my mind blanked. Unless I wanted to appear rude, I had to agree. The house was big, but maybe I could hurry her along.

We went from one white room to the next, each as clean and clutter-free as the living room and kitchen. I made all the appropriate comments and praised her choices. When she opened the door to the last room, I blinked, and blinked again. The room was full of riotous color. It hit me in the face like a bucket of paint.

"My goodness, Nina," I said, at a loss for words.

Nina's eyes fluttered around the room as if she were searching for something lost long ago. "Do you like it?"

"Well, yes. It's certainly different than the rest of your house."

"I know, this is where I keep Ashley's things."

"Ashley?" Did I miss something here?

"Yes, Ashley, my daughter," Nina said while she

walked around the room and traced her fingers lovingly over the dust-free surface furniture.

"I'm sorry, I didn't realize you and Adam had children."

"We don't, not now." A tear crept down Nina's cheek when she picked up a photograph and handed it to me. "This is Ashley; isn't she lovely? She died. And Adam says I haven't been right since."

I was about ready to agree with Adam until I looked at the picture. It was the girl from my dream. She wore a pink dance costume with a long flowing skirt. On her head was a cap with a short veil, a Juliet cap. That was it—the song—the theme from *Romeo and Juliet*.

"Yes, yes, she's lovely," I stuttered. "She looks like Juliet."

"Exactly. 'Romeo and Juliet' was her favorite song. She selected it for her last dance recital," Nina said, gently taking the picture from my numb fingers. "This photograph was taken then. She wanted to be a ballerina desperately. Her plan was to graduate early, leave Texas, and move to New York to study ballet."

"You lived in Texas? I didn't know that." My eyes flared in surprise.

"Yes, Adam was career Army and stationed there. Fort Arnold. But we don't talk about it." She hesitated for a moment. "Adam left the Army after Ashley's death. Five years ago. She was raped and murdered, you know," she said in a whisper.

I scowled, looking around the room at the rest of the pictures. Rape and murder? It didn't fit what I saw in the dream. A picture sitting on the desk caught my attention. It was of Ashley standing beside a bright red convertible.

"This is of Ashley, too?"

":Yes, Adam insisted on buying her the car for her sixteenth birthday." Nina picked up the picture and stroked the smooth surface of the glass. "She loved that car. We couldn't bear to sell it after her death. No one has driven it since she died. He spent a small fortune having it transported to the farm."

"The farm? The one Benny rents?"

"Yes, Adam has it stored in the machine shed. Benny doesn't mind."

I resisted the urge to smack myself on the forehead. Abby had said find the connection and I'd have my answers. Well, this was the connection, the red convertible. Except for the first dream, the car had been in every one. But I'd been so focused on finding the soldier that I hadn't paid attention to the convertible. Ashley was in the car the night she died, and now the car was here. A physical link between what happened in Texas and what was happening in Summerset. I didn't understand how they were linked, but I knew I *had* to see that car. Only problem—how could I get away from Nina gracefully?

My dilemma was solved when Adam's car pulled in the driveway.

"Oh my, Adam's home." Nina wrung her hands.

I didn't think I wanted Adam to find me standing in this particular room. The whole thing was so strange—a shrine to a dead girl, a car no one would ever drive again.

"Nina, I need to get back. Thanks for the coffee," I said, exiting the strange room. I looked over my shoulder and saw Nina following me, still wringing her hands. We were in the entry when Adam came in through the kitchen.

"Nina," Adam said, his eyes drilling right into her. "I didn't realize you invited Ophelia to stop by."

"Oh, oh, I—I didn't invite her over exactly." Nina's eyes flicked back and forth from the ceiling to the floor, never once meeting Adam's stare. "She dropped off the books I ordered from the library and had coffee with me."

"That was kind of her but unnecessary, I would have picked them up for you, dear. You had only to ask," Adam said, his smile tight and forced.

Nina's eyes continued their rapid movement. "But Adam, you're so busy at the bank, I hated to bother you."

I watched the whole scene in disbelief. Nina's fear blipped across my radar. It came in short pulses. What was she frightened of? Adam? He never struck me as the abusive type. Or was she afraid he would find out that I'd seen the room? Whatever the reason, the fear was contagious, and I felt a surge of adrenaline. Fight or flight. Flight won.

"Adam, Nina, I really must be going. Nina, enjoy the books," I said, struggling into my coat.

While I walked to my car, I could feel Adam's eyes on my back. My steps faltered but I finally reached the car. I tugged at the door. Damn, I'd locked it. Stupid, stupid, why did I lock it? I fumbled in my pocket for the keys. The first one didn't work. Wrong key. Meanwhile, Adam watched from the window. Finally, I used the right one. The door opened and I got the hell out of there.

Several blocks away I pulled over. The cold sterility of the Hoffmans' house had penetrated my very soul. I rested my head on the steering wheel and let the trembling I'd been fighting take over.

# Twenty-nine

The cold pinched at my nose while I tromped through the somber woods. The snow fell faster now. It drifted down in gossamer flakes from steel gray clouds that seemed to hang just above the treetops. My steps were muffled while I waded through the deep snow. My muscles began to tire from the effort, but I had to keep going. I knew the answer was in the red convertible.

My duplicity troubled me slightly. I had called Darci from my cell phone and made a lame excuse for not returning to the library. If I had told her my real reason, she would have insisted on coming, too. I also felt I was inadvertently lying to Bill. I hadn't forgotten my promise to stay out of this and let him do his job, but it would've been pointless to call him. What could I tell him? *"You need to check out a dead girl's red convertible. It has the clue you need."* No, I'd look at the car first, then go to Bill.

Rick was another matter. I could only imagine his anger when he learned I'd gone to the farm by myself, but I couldn't wait. He would be spending the entire day with Agnes and her cats, and I had to go now, when

I knew where Benny was. I didn't want Benny to come home and find me snooping around the property.

Finally, I reached the barbwire fence separating Abby's woods from Adam's farm. In the gray light, I could see the farm buildings through the curtain of snow. It seemed to be falling harder on the plowed field that lay between the buildings and me. Walking would be treacherous across the uneven ground. I grasped the barbwire fence with my gloved hand and carefully climbed over.

The wind picked up as I crossed the field, and the once gentle flakes pelted my face. I pulled my hat down and my collar up to protect it from the stinging little crystals. With this much wind, the blowing snow would drift across the roads, blocking them. I'd be stranded. One more reason to hurry.

I walked past the feed lots, but I could barely see the cattle huddled together in a tight group, their heads hung low and their backs covered with a frosting of snow. The only sound was the clank of metal against metal as the pigs in the next lot lifted and dropped the lids of their feeders. The sound rumbled in the white stillness.

The machine shed suddenly loomed in front of me. The old boards were covered with chips of rusty paint that clung tenaciously to the rough surface. My gloves caught on them while I edged my way to the window. I grasped the window ledge and pulled myself up to peer inside. Thirty years of grime made it difficult to see. I could barely make out the car covered with a tarp.

A hand clamped across my mouth and an arm thrown around my shoulders pulled me down and backward into a hard body. My heart jackhammered in my chest.

"What in the hell are you doing here?" a man whispered, the warm breath tickling the side of my face.

My body slumped with relief, but the relief was followed by acute irritation. I brought the heel of my boot down hard on top of his foot. The hand and arm quickly released me.

"Ouch. Why did you do that?" Rick asked.

"How dare you scare me like that?"

Rick's eyebrows gathered in a frown. "You deserve to be scared. What were you thinking of, coming out here by yourself? You were supposed to stay out of trouble, remember?"

"Long story—I told you in the note."

"What note?"

"The note I left with Georgia, telling you where I was going and what I found out. Didn't you get it?"

"No, I've spent the entire afternoon with Agnes. I found a great picture of our friend, the sergeant, locked in deep conversation with Jake Jenkins."

"Jake? Jake's the bad guy?" I shook my head. "I can't see Jake as a murderer."

"Maybe not, but Jake's involved in this somehow. I tried to reach Bill, but he's covering an accident on 925. I decided to come out here myself. Now, why are you here?"

"I know who the girl in my dream was—Ashley Hoffman. She died five years ago in Texas, when Adam was stationed at Fort Arnold. Adam stores her car here. The car from the dream."

"Did you say Fort Arnold?" he asked.

"Yeah."

"Wow." Rick sounded surprised. "No one mentioned Adam had been in the Army or that they had a daughter."

"No one knew. The Hoffmans don't talk about it. Strange, don't you think?"

"Not only strange, but a pretty big coincidence that Adam was stationed at the same base as Fisher." Rick stopped and looked me over. "I don't suppose I can persuade you to leave and let me go in by myself?"

"Nope, I've got to see that car."

"Didn't think so. Come on," Rick said, taking my arm. "We're not accomplishing anything standing here talking. Let's check out the inside."

We walked around to the front of the building. The rickety wooden door faced away from the feed lot.

Rick rattled the door's handle. "It's not locked. Either whatever's in there isn't important or they're not worried about visitors."

I peered over Rick's shoulder into the gloomy building. "Oh, it's important, all right. Come on." I pushed past him into the shed.

"How do you know it's important?" Rick thought for a moment. "Never mind, dumb question."

I stopped a few feet inside the door and looked around.

"I don't suppose you have a flashlight?"

"No, but here's a lantern."

In the faint light of the lantern, the machinery cast huge shadows around the building. Cobwebs drifted from the rafters. They danced in the cold drafts that seeped through cracks in the old structure. The drafts seemed to circle around me and goose bumps prickled my skin. My ears began to ring with a faint buzzing. It grew louder, louder—

"Ophelia."

I jumped. "Huh?"

"What's wrong with you? Didn't you hear me?"

"No." I looked at Rick. He was holding the corner of a tarp in one hand. The rest of the tarp lay in a crumpled pile at his feet.

"I said, is this what you're looking for?"

It sat gleaming in the lantern light—a cherry red convertible. Not a speck of dust could be seen on its shiny surface. Someone had to wash and wax this once a week for it to be this clean. Was it one of the jobs Benny did for Adam?

"Do you need the light, or can I take it?" he asked. "We need to see what else is in here."

"No, I don't need a light," I said, still staring at the car.

I wouldn't need light for what I was going to do.

I got in the car and rubbed my hands lightly over the white leather steering wheel. I emptied my mind of all thought, but the resistance I had built over the past four years acted like a shield. It wasn't working. I rotated my head to loosen the stiff muscles in my neck. Focus, I needed to focus. I stared out the windshield. What little light there had been was failing, and all I could see was the front end of the car. Everything else hung in deepening shadows. I closed my eyes and thought of the picture of Ashley.

It came gently at first, soft and indistinct. I strained to hear, and as I did, the melody became louder. I could once again see Ashley dancing with such power and grace. My thoughts reached out, drawing the girl closer and closer. In some part of my brain, my increasing grip on the steering wheel registered. Finally, my thoughts touched the image of Ashley. I felt what she felt. A smile curled at my mouth while the song picked me up and carried me with her.

I felt wild joy while I experienced the dance with her. I was lost in the music just like Ashley. My heart raced with hers in exhilaration as she moved through the complicated leaps and turns. Her desire for perfection tugged at me.

It ended with a final leap, and while she knelt on the floor, I felt her nagging disappointment. *The last arabesque was a half beat off. Never get into ballet school with that kind of performance. It must be perfect, perfect.*

The scene in my mind shifted, and we were driving down the gray ribbon of highway with the top down. I felt the wind tossing my hair, and Aerosmith played at a deafening level on the radio. *This is so cool—my own car. Daddy is the best. I have to take it with me when I go to New York to study. Mom won't want me to, but I'll talk Daddy into it.*

A slow smile spread across Ashley's face. *I wonder if Blake could get transferred to New York. Daddy could pull a few strings.* She laughed. *No, Daddy would kill Blake if he found out. We've been careful, so careful.*

Excitement seemed to coil within her and I knew. She was on her way to pick up the soldier, to pick up Blake. And tonight was the last night of her life.

The knowing made me sick to my soul. I couldn't stop what would happen to her—her death was five years in the past—but it still made me sick. I couldn't bear to see her in my mind and know her life was about to be snuffed out. Turning away from Ashley, I watched the telephone poles rush by. Faster and faster, until they became a blur.

Darkness began to shadow the vision, until I saw nothing. I felt a deep, quiet grief tight in my heart. Was the grief mine, or did it belong to someone else? I didn't know. My hand rhythmically stroked the smooth leather of the seat next to me while the tears built inside of me. They slipped silently down my face. The weight of the grief pressed down on me till I felt like I was crumbling. I had to open my eyes or be smothered by the awful grief.

I forced my eyes open and found myself looking in the rearview mirror, only it wasn't my face I saw. It was a face contorted with anger and hate. No gentle grief there. The eyes were wide and the pupils dilated. The mouth was fixed in a snarl, and his white, even teeth looked predatory. It was a face I had seen many times, but always smiling, never like this. Now it was misshapen into a mask of vengeance. How could Abby have missed this?

The terror I felt threatened to crush me. I had to break the connection. I pushed my body back against the seat and searched desperately for the door handle. My fingers curled around the cold metal and I pushed with all my strength. It opened and the next instant I was lying facedown on the dirt floor. Fine, gritty dust rose around my mouth and nose while I lay there panting. I had to leave, now.

From a great distance I heard Rick calling me. The instincts for self-preservation tightened my throat, making sound impossible. I staggered to my feet and stumbled toward the faint light in the back of the shed.

Rick stood by a workbench. Its top was covered with paraphernalia. The light flickered off a dozen mason jars and glass gallon jugs, the kind apple cider is sold in. A thick coil of plastic tubing lay beside them. Boxes of over-the-counter cold medicine were scattered everywhere. Several cans of drain cleaner stood in a straight row behind them.

The floor under the bench had boxes stacked two

high. In the faint light I could read the words "starter fluid." Next to them were several bright red plastic gas cans.

"Looks like we've found the meth lab." He turned and looked at me.

In the dim light, I knew he couldn't read the fear on my face. How could I get him out of there?

"Benny?" I croaked, my throat still tight.

"Looks like. The brothers have been busy boys—one is hooked up with the militia and the other is cooking meth. We'd better get out of here."

Rick walked past me carrying the lantern, but I couldn't seem to move. I felt frozen to the spot, still looking at all the equipment in the room.

"Come—"

Before I could turn, another hand clamped over my mouth and nose. A rough cloth held tightly to my face, the smell of ether . . .

# Thirty

When I opened my eyes, dizziness and nausea made my head spin. I took deep breaths to clear the awful smell of ether from my brain. I looked around. It took a moment or two, but I finally got my bearings. We were in a different part of the old shed, away from the meth lab.

The interior was lit with an old kerosene lantern. The three of us sat in its faint pool of light. It had a smell of old grease, gasoline, and dust. Pigeons cooed faintly in the rafters. I sat on the rough dirt floor with my hands behind my back, tied to the center pole. The coarse timber rubbed against the sensitive skin on the inside of my wrist. Rick was behind me on the other side, tied the same way. He was slumped over, unconscious. Benny sat a few feet away with a rifle trained on us.

Was this the way my life would end? In a dirty old shed, dispatched by the town's joke? Everything in me rebelled at the thought.

Rick moaned softly, and I suddenly felt his hand clutch my arm. The images the touch conveyed began to overwhelm me. I couldn't afford to lose myself in visions right now. I had to think of a way out of this for us both. My life would not end without a fight. We would get loose somehow. It was too much to hope Rick had a knife. Even if he did, there would be no way to get to it with our hands bound.

Benny's eyes never wavered. He reminded me of a cat watching a mouse hole, just waiting to pounce at the first movement. I watched him watching us. What if I appealed to his sense of mercy? I knew Benny was only his brother's dupe, and there was an undercurrent of anxiety emanating from him.

"Benny, you really don't want to hurt us. This is all your brother's idea. Bad things are going to happen if you don't let us go."

"No, they won't. Jake said everything would be fine. We're going to make lots of money on these drugs and give it to the cause. They'll be so grateful, and Jake and me are going to be important. Jake said so."

"Don't you care that these drugs are going to hurt people?"

"Jake said they're all a bunch of losers anyway and they deserve what happens to them."

I let my mind reach out to his. Regardless of what he said, his uncertainty was palpable. However, I sensed it was overridden by his enduring loyalty to his brother.

"Benny, I'm telling you, bad things are going to happen if you don't stop this now."

"You don't know what you're talking about. You're just trying to scare me."

"No, I'm not, Benny. I know things. I have the sight," I said, trying to sound confident.

"You're lying. You're just a woman, and the librarian to boot. You don't have no powers."

Benny sounded sure of himself, but his eyes wouldn't meet mine.

"If I don't have the sight, how do I know about the time Jake found you out behind the barn with those dirty books?"

Benny blanched. "Just shut up."

I concentrated on Benny, searching for something else to convince him. Suddenly, my mind became aware of something more, deep within the earth. It was power—the power I had always scoffed at—Abby's power. The power of magick.

It was one of those places Abby had told Rick about the night he discovered she was a witch. This shed had been built over a place of energy, and I could feel it moving like electricity beneath me, just like Abby said it did.

What had she always told me about the preparation, before you call on the forces? Damn, I couldn't remember. Why hadn't I paid attention? But this was our only chance, and I knew it.

I sent a silent, humble apology and asked for help. Closing my eyes, I let my breath come deep from the diaphragm as Abby had tried to teach me. While I did, I emptied my mind of all except the power. At first it came like a warm flush engulfing my body, but it gained in intensity. From outside the shed the wind seemed to blow in harmony with the energy flowing around and through me. The pigeons responded by rustling their feathers. I heard the night sounds out there with amazing clarity.

I opened my eyes and let my gaze drill Benny. His eyes flew wide in surprise.

"Benny, you must let us go."

Benny shook his head in disbelief at my demand. I tried again.

"Benny, not only do I have the sight, but I'm a witch. Can't you feel my power?" I focused on him. "The spirits are angry that you're holding us. Do you want the spirits angry?"

I felt the energy dancing in the space between us; so did Benny. It was written on his face. The pigeons were becoming agitated and left their perches, flapping their wings and circling overhead. The very air crackled. The wind outside surged; a coyote howled in the distance.

It was the howl that really spooked Benny. He stumbled to his feet, looking recklessly around and clutching his gun to his chest. His eyes bugged out and he looked terrified.

"*Benny,* let us go."

At the sound of my voice, his gun thudded to the floor. Running over, he began to untie the knots. I sent a heartfelt thank-you to the power.

"Benny, what in the hell are you doing?" said a voice from the doorway.

The power stopped as abruptly as if someone had thrown a light switch. The wind ceased and the pigeons scattered. Benny's fingers froze on the knots. We both twisted simultaneously to see Jake and Adam Hoffman silhouetted in the open doorway.

Benny cowered at my side when he heard his brother's voice. Jake rushed over to where we sat, trussed like turkeys. He grabbed Benny by his collar and flung him away from us. Adam Hoffman stood in the doorway, watching and holding a very deadly looking little gun in his hand.

"You fool. You were going to turn them loose, weren't you?" Jake towered over his cringing brother.

"Jake, she's spooky. She's a witch, and she was going to hex me if I didn't."

"You're an idiot, Benny. She's a stupid woman. What have I always told you about women?"

"That you have to watch them, that they're always trying to trick you." Benny's eyes glistened with tears. "I'm sorry, Jake. She was scaring me."

"What kind of a man are you? Do you think the cause wants a man who's such a sissy that he lets some librarian scare him?"

Benny hung his head in shame. Since Jake had made his point, his anger evaporated like rain on hot cement. He bent over and pulled Benny to his feet.

He threw an arm around Benny's shoulder. "It's okay, Benny. You're not going to do anything else stupid, are you?"

Benny shook his head, his face shining with admiration for his brother, and my hope vanished as quickly as the magick.

All this time, Rick had remained silent. I thought maybe he had slipped back into unconsciousness, but I felt a tug on my ropes and a slight squeeze on my arm. The unspoken message was clear. Rick was awake and working the knots Benny had loosened.

With Rick behind me, he was out of the vision of the three men. We needed a distraction so they wouldn't notice what Rick was doing. The effort I had made summoning the magick left me drained, and I didn't have the strength to try it again.

"Mr. Hoffman, so you're involved in this, too," I said to draw their attention to me and not Rick.

"You don't seem surprised, Ophelia."

I needed something to spook Benny again.

"No, I'm not." I shrugged, trying to bluff my way through. "When I ran into you at your house, I saw your aura as gray. I sensed a dark side and that you were hiding something."

My statement had the desired effect on Benny. His face lost its color and he turned to his brother.

"See, I told you, Jake, she's a witch."

"Shut up, Benny."

I felt Jake's anger spark.

Adam was unfazed and he laughed. "Really, Ophelia, that mumbo jumbo might work on poor Benny, but not me. If you are a witch, what are you doing here? Where were your powers when Jake caught you?"

He had a point. I wished Rick would hurry up with those knots.

"I have a couple of questions for you, Adam," I said. "Was Ashley's death the reason you left the Army? And did Fisher recruit you for the militia?"

A direct hit. Adam quit smiling.

"You know about Fisher. I wondered how long it would take the authorities to discover his identity." Adam looked petulant. "It's all your fault. If you hadn't been stupid enough to find Fisher's body, none of this would've happened. I could've finished my work here and left town. But now you've forced me to kill you."

His last remark seemed like a big leap in logic to me, but since Adam held the gun, not me, I knew that arguing with him might not be such a good idea.

"You didn't answer my question about Ashley."

"Nina showed you Ashley's room. I thought so," Adam said, more to himself than me. "That woman talks too much. I'll have to make sure she's more isolated."

"You're dodging the question, Adam. What about Ashley?" I persisted.

His eyes shifted from me to Benny and Jake, and then back again. "Ashley is no concern of yours."

"Was Ashley's accidental death—"

His eyes flew wide and he took a step closer. The gun trembled in his hand.

Adam exploded. "It wasn't an accident!" he raged, waving the gun. "She was raped and murdered! At the trial, that soldier, that Blake Smith, lied! Ashley would never have done the things he said."

Spit formed at the corners of his mouth, and as he shouted, it sprayed toward me. I shifted to avoid getting hit.

"She didn't deserve to die." His voice thundered through the machine shed.

"You're right, Adam. She didn't," I said quietly.

Adam's hand, holding the gun, dropped and his body seemed to droop, his grief overcoming his rage. "Ashley was the light of my life. A beautiful, beautiful girl. An innocent girl. But the court believed Smith's lies. They found him guilty of manslaughter. He'll be released in two more years," he said, his eyes flat and lifeless. "And when he's out, I will hunt him down and kill him."

"But in the meantime you're planning on overthrowing the government?"

"The government," Adam scoffed. "The government is supposed to protect young girls. But they are so inept that they let murderers run free. Ashley's death was the turning point for me. What kind of a country do we live in? It couldn't even protect my daughter from scum. That's when Fisher talked to me about the militia movement. And the difference was obvious. They'll return our country to what it was meant to be. They are the true patriots."

His eyes were no longer flat and lifeless. They glowed with the light of fanaticism. And he slowly raised his gun.

I winced, expecting a bullet at any moment. We had to get loose; this guy was crazy. In desperation, I tugged at my ropes, but Rick's hand squeezed my wrist, stopping me. *Keep him talking* was the unspoken message. Thoughts tumbled through my mind while I scrambled to think of something to say.

"Ahh, so life will be better if the militia were in charge?"

I groaned. My comment sounded so lame, but Adam didn't notice. He lowered the gun and rocked back and forth on his heels, like a teacher about to give a lecture.

"Of course life will be better. If the militia were in control, they wouldn't allow young, innocent girls to be raped and murdered. And if anyone tried, the militia's justice would be swift and sure," he said with a smug smile.

On cue, like puppets in the hands of a master puppeteer, Jake and Benny nodded their heads in agreement.

"But what about the young girls who will die from the stuff you're selling. Aren't you concerned about them?"

"Yes. However, the cause needs money; weapons are expensive. There's an obscene amount of money in drugs. If they knew, some of the leaders might not approve of my methods, but they have yet to refuse my donations. Young girls dying? Unfortunately, every revolution must have its martyrs." He smiled again. He actually smiled.

His fanaticism and complacent attitude made me angry. I thought of poor Doug Jones and his family. How could Adam Hoffman be willing to subject other families to the pain of losing a child, the same pain he had experienced? And all in the name of a cause. For the first time in my life I wanted to work Abby's magick against someone.

"What about you, Mr. Delaney? I know you're awake." He shifted his position and waved the gun at Rick. "Do you have any questions before we kill you?"

Rick's shoulders tensed. "A few—did you kill Sergeant Fisher or did Jake?"

"I did. The man was becoming a problem. He wanted to try his hand at some environmental terrorism, but I couldn't allow it. He even had the audacity to show up in Summerset during the Korn Karnival. Ned, unfortunately, took his picture while he was chatting with Jake. In light of Fisher's fate, I needed those pictures destroyed. Jake and Benny took care of it for me."

"Who trashed my room?"

"Jake, with help from Benny."

"Figures. You'd have your stooges do a job like that."

Jake made a move forward. Adam held his arm out, stopping him.

"Who was stalking Ophelia? You or Jake?"

"Oh, that was a joint operation. I left the warning on her desk, but she was too dumb to pay attention to it. Benny had seen her, you know, that day she set off the smoke grenade. Jake wasn't pleased that Ophelia ruined our training exercises."

"The dead coyote?"

"That was me," Jake said, smirking. "That damn dog of hers almost ruined it, though. Heard me on the porch and went wild. Thought she was going to tear the door down. Think after we're done with you, I'll go back and shoot her. Never could stand that dog."

If my hands were free, I'd have thrown them up in the air. Of course, the scratches on the front door. Lady had made them, trying to get at Jake.

Rick ignored Jake. "Well, Adam, I'd say that covers it. I am rather disappointed in myself that we weren't on to you sooner. I should have known Jake and Benny weren't in charge of this. Neither one of them could find their ass in the dark, let alone run an operation like this."

From his position by Benny, Jake glowered at Rick.

"Never mind," Adam said, turning to Jake. "Mr. Delaney won't be able to insult you much longer. Luckily it's stopped snowing. It will be easier to get rid of the bodies. After we do, I want to dismantle everything and shut down for a while. I plan on taking a little vacation with my wife. I've made arrangements for you and Benny to go to the training camp in Montana. I want you to stay there until I'm sure there are no more loose ends."

"Did you hear that, Jake?" Benny looked like he had won the lottery. "Me and you get to go to Montana. I ain't never been out of Iowa."

I wondered if Jake and Benny would actually make it to Montana. I was sure Adam considered Jake and Benny two of his loose ends. We were running out of time. A sense of foreboding trembled through me.

From deep inside my soul came a call for help; I didn't want to die. My sense of awareness sharpened, once again I felt the stirrings of the power. With one short burst of energy, I sent the vibrations out and away from me.

All became quiet—more than quiet, it was a total

absence of sound. It hung in the air, heavy and oppressive around us. Benny's face flared with fear. Jake spun this way and that, brandishing his gun. Adam Hoffman's eyes narrowed and bore into me.

My senses sharpened, and I felt the rhythm of my heart. First beat, second beat—the knots broke and the shed exploded in a conflagration of sound. Harsh, discordant sound. The pigeons took flight in a mad flurry of flapping wings. The wind raged against the building, making the rafters groan. Out of the darkness came the rats scurrying, squeaking, rushing the three men. In the pandemonium, I lost sight of Adam.

Benny fell to his knees, his chest heaving. Jake fired wildly at the rats. One of the bullets struck the pole above me. Rick jumped to his feet, pulling me with him.

"Run!" he yelled above the din.

Clutching his hand, I was propelled forward through the door into the night while the sound of gunshots echoed around us.

# *Thirty-one*

We ran, heedless of where we were going, while the wind spun the snow around us. In the cloud of snow, I had no sense of direction. We could have been running in circles for all I knew, but it did seem the sound of the gunshots grew fainter and fainter. Were we headed toward the woods or away from them? Were they following us? I fought the urge to look.

I tried to ask Rick, but I didn't have enough air in my lungs to speak. My legs felt as heavy as tree stumps, wading through the deep snow. Sweat at the exertion ran down my back under my heavy coat. I clung tightly to Rick's hand. It seemed the only reality in the all-white world. All-white world—just like the Hoffman's house. A hysterical giggle bubbled inside of me.

While we ran, the wind seemed to slowly diminish till finally it was only a whisper. The air became clear, no longer full of spinning snow. The storm had passed, and the full moon lit the glistening landscape. I still didn't know where we were. A gate appeared in front of us. Rick pulled me toward it. From behind me came the sound of labored breathing. *They're following us* registered right before the pop of a gun sent a dusting of snow into the air to my right. Rick must have heard it, too. He let go of my hand and flung the gate open. Grabbing my arm, he pulled me through the open gate.

A sense of déjà vu hit me. I knew where we were now—the old cemetery from my dream. The headstones from the dream were now covered with snow. Great white lumps sparkling in the moonlight.

I tugged on Rick's hand. "Wait—"

"We can't. They're right behind us."

"I can't run anymore, Rick."

Another pop sent chips of stone flying.

"Come on." Rick shoved me forward.

We ran deeper into the old cemetery. Wind began to gust again, sending the light snow swirling into the air. Thick clouds of it obscured the light from the moon. Another pop from the gun broke the silence, and an owl hooted in the distance.

First, I felt a burning in my side as if someone had stabbed me with a hot poker. Then the pain came, waves and waves of agonizing pain. It drove all the fear from me, until nothing was left except the pain. My legs buckled and I fell, pulling Rick down with me.

"Ophelia, Ophelia. Answer me."

The wind suddenly died and I could see the ground where I lay on my side.

"Look, Rick, the snow's red."

Another shot muffled his answer and a dark shape loomed a few feet from us. Adam Hoffman. With a yell, Rick launched himself at Adam. They both went down. The gun Adam held flew from his hand when Rick tackled him. It sank in the soft snow. Too far away for me to reach.

I struggled to prop myself up against a headstone, but the effort was too much. The pain in my side was fierce, and I felt a wetness seep through my coat. I didn't know if it was melting snow or—blood.

Adam and Rick rolled in the snow a few feet away. Rick was the first to his feet. Adam soon followed. I heard the dull thuds of fists striking flesh. From where I sat, I could see Adam's face. His lips were pulled back from his teeth in a feral snarl. Rage and hate seethed around him. One blow knocked Rick to the ground, and Adam kicked him repeatedly. Rick grabbed Adam's ankle and jerked, sending Adam toppling backward. Rick was on him in an instant. He pinned Adam to the ground and hit Adam's exposed face again and again.

While I lay there, the pain receded, replaced by a numbness that slowly crept up my body. In the distance I saw lights bobbing up and down in the night, closer and closer, but I couldn't focus on them.

"There they are," said one of the bobbing lights.

The cold snow felt so good against my face. Maybe if I just closed my eyes—

# Thirty-two

"I think she's awake."

I opened one eye and Rick's face swam into focus. I felt his hand brush the strands of hair back from my forehead.

"Did the good guys win?" I asked. My voice cracked and my throat felt scratchy.

Rick laughed. "Yes, the good guys won. How do you feel?"

"Like I've been shot. That is what happened, isn't it?"

"Yeah." He stroked my cheek. "You were hit in the side. It may not seem like this to you right now, but you were lucky. The snow stopped you from bleeding to death."

"Right, lucky. It hurts like hell, and my head feels like it's wrapped in cotton."

"It's the drugs. They have you doped up on pain meds."

Must have been some pretty good stuff. Rick's face faded away as my eyes closed.

The next time my eyes opened, my vision was clear. Sunlight came through the open blinds. Rick stood near the window, looking out. He still wore the same clothes and a dark shadow of a beard covered his lower face. His hair was rumpled, as if he had repeatedly combed his fingers through it. Had he been here all night?

Abby sat in the chair near the window, crocheting. Her face wore a half smile while her hook flashed in the sunlight. She was an island of calm, just as she had been all my life. The tears gathered in my eyes while I watched her. She lifted her head and smiled at me. After she put down her crocheting, she crossed the room to my bed. She leaned over and kissed my forehead.

"Good morning. Or afternoon, I should say. How are you feeling?"

"Not too bad, I guess, all things considered."

"Do you feel well enough to talk to Bill? He can always come back later."

"No, I'll talk to him."

"I'll go get him," Rick said, and headed for the door.

"No, you stay here. I'll get Bill," Abby said.

Rick walked to the bedside. "Are you sure you feel up to this?"

"Yeah, might as well get the lecture over with."

"Don't worry, he'll be nice to you. Me—he threatened to arrest about a hundred times. Seems we blundered into a DEA investigation," Rick said, running his hands back and forth across the bed railing.

"You sure as hell did," Bill said as he walked into the room. "You're lucky they were watching the farm and moved in when they heard gunshots. Too bad Hoffman got away from them and shot Ophelia. He's not going anywhere now, though. We've got all three of them locked up tighter than ticks."

"What about Nina?" I asked.

Bill stood by my bed twirling his hat. "Her sister from Fairfield came and took her home with her. Had a real interesting conversation with her. Seems Adam went off the deep end when their daughter died. He started acting weird and shut himself in the girl's room for hours and wouldn't talk to anyone. Became obsessed with her car." Bill paused, frowning as if Adam's obsession didn't make sense to him. He gave a slight shrug and continued. "Finally, Adam seemed to snap out of it. Quit the Army and they moved back to Fairfield. Her family didn't know about Adam's involvement in the militia, but they were asking Nina a lot of questions. Too many to suit Adam, so he packed up Nina and came here. Wouldn't let her have any contact with her family. They've been worried about her but didn't know what to do about it."

"Will Nina be okay?"

"Yeah, I think so," Bill said, and leaned closer to the bed. "So, how are you feeling?"

"I don't know." I winced as I scooted my hip over. "Rick told me I was lucky. I guess I am."

"Yes, you are, young lady. I hope you've learned your lesson and in the future won't be getting mixed up in things that don't concern you. I guess I really don't have any questions for you. Main reason I stopped was to see how you were doing. Delaney here has told me everything, haven't you, Delaney?"

"Of course, Sheriff."

Rick wouldn't meet Bill's eyes. Instead he seemed fascinated with the IV pole.

"Only question I've got is how you got loose. Nobody's explained that one. Adam's refusing to talk, Jake's blaming everything on Adam, and Benny—well, poor Benny's a blubbering mass of flesh. Keeps mumbling about hexes and the sight," Bill said, scratching his head. "Can't make heads or tails out of it."

I glanced at Rick. Now he was staring at the blinds.

"Umm, ahh. Benny loosened the ropes before Adam and Jake got there," I said. "He was going to let us go, but Jake stopped him. Rick managed to finish the job Benny started."

Bill settled his hat on his head. "Okay, that's what I'll put in the report. Sure sounds more reasonable than Benny's explanation. I'll come back later to check on you, Ophelia. I would say it was nice meeting you, Delaney, but you caused me a lot of trouble." He smiled and shook Rick's hand. "I hope if you ever visit Summerset again, it's not on business."

"Don't worry, Bill, I think I've learned my lesson, too." Rick smiled.

Rick and I watched Bill leave. Silent minutes stretched while I plucked at the blanket. I was the first to break it.

"What did you tell him?"

"Pretty much everything—except for the part about you being a witch."

"I'm—"

"It's okay, Ophelia, your secret's safe with me. I don't know exactly what you did out there, but whatever it was, it saved our lives. I'm just sorry you got hurt."

Rick picked up my hand and brought it up to his mouth. He turned it over and kissed the inside of my wrist, like the night in the car. I felt the regret in his touch.

"You're leaving, aren't you?" I said, not looking at him.

"Yeah, the DEA was pretty upset with us, too. They

called my editor to complain, but he managed to talk them into me going to Montana with them. They're going after the group Hoffman sent the money. He worked out a deal with them that if they take me and give the paper an exclusive, then he'll put a lid on the story till the investigation is over. He also pointed out it would be in their best interest to know where I was."

"He must be even more persuasive than you are."

Rick grinned. "That's why he's the editor. Don't worry about you and Abby—you won't be part of the story. I figure I owe you at least that much."

"Thanks."

"You know, Ophelia Jensen, you're okay."

"Even if I'm prissy and tight-lipped." I lifted an eyebrow.

"I wondered if you overheard that." Rick laughed. "Yeah, for a prickly librarian, you're all right. I'm really glad I met you."

"You're not so bad yourself, Delaney."

"For an arrogant, self-absorbed jerk?"

"Right. But you forgot the thick-headed part."

"Listen, can I call you sometime, you know, just to talk?" A hot blush covered Rick's face.

What's this, Rick Delaney shy? I couldn't believe it.

"Sure, I'd like that."

Our eyes locked and my lips parted in anticipation as Rick leaned closer to the bed. A knock at the door suddenly yanked him back. A nurse stuck her head in the room.

"Mr. Delaney, Bill called the desk and said they're leaving now."

"Okay, thanks. I'll be there in a minute," Rick said over his shoulder to the nurse, his eyes never leaving my face.

"Well, you'd better get going—"

Rick cut off my words with a kiss. Everything was in that kiss—sadness, regret at what might have been. Warm tears gathered beneath my closed eyelids. Would our paths ever cross again?

"I want out, and I want out now." I sat on the bed, dressed and ready to leave, but the damn doctor hadn't signed the release orders yet.

Darci and Abby exchanged looks.

"As soon as the doctor comes and releases you. Being impatient won't make him come any sooner."

"Honestly, Ophelia, you have to be the worst patient in the world. I bet the nurses will be glad to see the last of you," Darci said, fussing with the flowers. "You know, I might have been able to help you at the farm. I'm still mad you didn't take me with you."

"Why? So you could have been shot, too?"

Darci smiled at Abby. "She must be feeling better, she's getting sarcastic. Say, these are lovely flowers Ned sent you. He's been here several times, hasn't he?"

"Yeah," I said, trying to look noncommittal. "He wants to take me out to dinner when I'm feeling better."

"That's great. You know, if we cut about two inches off your hair and plucked your eyebrows a little, it would give you a whole different look," she said as she scrutinized my face.

I groaned. "You can keep your scissors and your tweezers to yourself, Darci. I've already been a victim of one of your makeovers. And if Ned doesn't like the way I look—tough."

My words had no effect—Darci still looked at me with a speculative gleam in her eye.

"Darci, would you mind checking with the nurse to

see if they have the release orders yet? I would like to talk to Ophelia."

"Sure thing, Abby," Darci said, and left.

Abby watched her leave and then turned to me. "You're fighting a losing battle, you know. She won't give up. I imagine she'll make you buy clothes for the occasion, too."

I winced at the thought of what Darci would consider the right outfit for a date with Ned. "I know."

Abby took my hand. "Did he break your heart?"

"No, just cracked it a little." I smiled. "I knew it wasn't meant to be. Our paths are in different directions, but . . ."

Abby didn't say anything, but stroked my hand. I could feel the healing power flow from her touch.

"I've had a lot of time to think about things, lying here. Grief made Adam what he was—"

"Well, I think the sickness was already there, but the grief pushed it out."

"My grief over Brian pushed me, too, didn't it? Pushed me inside myself."

"Yes," she said, and squeezed my hand lightly.

"I don't want to be inside myself anymore, retreat inside my wall. I think I'd miss Darci." I cringed. "God, never thought I'd say that one."

Abby laughed.

"Anyway, I've thought a lot about what happened that night in the machine shed. I'm sorry I've scoffed at your magick all these years."

"It's not *my* magick. The world is full of magick, whether we see it or not. You are one of the chosen. You have been given the gift to see the magick if you want."

"Could you show me how?"

A slow smile crossed Abby's face.

"Yes, dear, I can show you how."

"Abby, there is one thing that still bothers me." I fiddled with the blanket. "Do you remember when this all started—the night I dreamt about the cemetery?"

Abby nodded.

"Well, at the beginning of the dream, I drank a glass of water at the kitchen sink and I placed the glass on the counter. The next morning the glass was there. How could that be? If it was a dream? Was I sleepwalking?"

"I don't know, maybe. Or it could be you have talents we don't know about yet."

"Yeah, like what?"

She shrugged. "My mother always said Great-aunt Mary was an expert at astral projection. You might have inherited that talent, too."

My mouth dropped open. Great. Being a psychic wasn't enough?

"Oh, don't worry, Ophelia. We'll figure it out." She paused. "You've made a wise choice. There are circles in your life that must be closed. It will be up to you to close them. You will need all your talents to do so, but we have time."

My hackles stood up and my skin tingled. She couldn't possibly mean . . .

Oh no, here we go again.

**Sign up for the FREE HarperCollins monthly mystery newsletter,**

# The Scene of the Crime,

**and get to know your favorite authors, win free books, and be the first to learn about the best new mysteries going on sale.**

To register, simply go to www.HarperCollins.com, visit our mystery channel page, and at the bottom of the page, enter your email address where it states "Sign up for our mystery newsletter." Then you can tap into monthly Hot Reads, check out our award nominees, sneak a peek at upcoming titles, and discover the best whodunits each and every month.

*Get to know the magnificent mystery authors of HarperCollins and sign up today!*